I0614608

Genuine Fake

by

Susan Vaughan

Devlin Security Force, Protecting Priceless Treasures

Genuine Fake

Cover Art by *Kim Mendoza*

The Wild Rose Press, Inc.
PO Box 708
Adams Basin, NY 14410-0708
Visit us at www.thewildrosepress.com

Publishing History
First Edition, 2023
Trade Paperback ISBN 978-1-5092-5116-2
Digital ISBN 978-1-5092-5117-9

Devlin Security Force, Protecting Priceless Treasures
Published in the United States of America
Previously Published 2021 by Gullwood Press

Gemma's heart fluttered against her ribs. Could it be Boyd? There'd been so much noise on his end of his call—voices talking over each other, laughter—she wasn't sure what he'd said after she gave him the address.

The door swung inward and Boyd Kirby filled the space. His steel-gray gaze mapped the room before landing on her. He swept her head to toe, then nodded, apparently satisfied she was all in one piece.

And oh my, the man did fill out a tuxedo. The jacket molded the muscularity of his wide shoulders. The ends of a bow tie stuck out of his breast pocket, and the blinding-white dress shirt hung open partway, displaying smooth, solid muscle dusted with bronze hairs.

"Gemma, you okay?"

She was, now that he'd arrived, and that he came right away, tonight. Her whole being felt lighter as warmth bloomed in her chest, but apparently her brain had left the building. Finally she managed to say, "Yes, yes, I'm good. As you see."

She took two steps toward him before she forced herself to halt. She'd promised herself to keep it all business. But damn, she wanted nothing more but to feel his strong arms around her.

Praise for Susan Vaughan

Dedication

To my car and construction guy, my wonderful husband; and to Chuck Jones for further engineering info about the railing; and to author Bruce Robert Coffin for answers to my policing questions; and finally, to Margaret McGovern, loyal reader and reviewer extraordinaire!

Chapter One

GEMMA GUIDED THE paint pen across the rayon fabric, her lips compressed in concentration, her other hand steadying the stretcher frame. No slips allowed. The image must be perfectly outlined to create the three-dimensional illusion of ribs. One rib. Then the next and the next.

She stepped back and capped the pen. A perfect scallop shell. The other shell was a whelk, more difficult for coloring, but she'd already drawn the image on the tunic. She could add tiny periwinkles as accents. Use of the dauber to create the sand around the shells would be the finishing touch. The design was *so* Virginia seashore. Her sister would love her birthday gift.

Smiling, Gemma flung her arms over her head and twirled around the table. And came up against the project she ought to be working on.

The anchor. Her serious art. Worthy or not, it might as well be her albatross. Still, she'd almost completed the painting. If only he were here, her grandfather would tell her to focus on it, not on the fabric painting. He would've guided her. She pressed the heels of her hands to her eyes. She missed him so much.

She'd disappointed him bigtime once and could still picture the sorrow in his eyes. *Guilty, guilty*, whispered inside her head. She drew two deep breaths against ever present ball of tension in her chest. Why had her grandfather then trusted her with his legacy? She'd never know. Maybe she should've taken Tina up on her offer to share the responsibilities… No, she had to prove to him and to herself she could do this.

"I'm trying, Silvio. I'll make you proud one day."

Shaking away her maudlin reverie, she set the stretcher frame back on the table. Maybe she should leave aside the tunic for now. She had plenty of time before Tina's birthday.

She tilted her head at the anchor painting. She was close. Something about the color of the anchor's rust was—

Van Halen's screaming guitar erupted from her cell phone.

Gemma's heartbeat clattered. *Troy!* She dashed to her phone, which she'd foolishly left out of reach on the far table. "What took you so long? You left town without a word. Are you o—"

"Gemma, slow down. I'm good. No prob."

"Where did you go? Why didn't you call me? Dammit, it's been two weeks. *Two* weeks. I've been worried sick." Except for when she didn't want to bonk him over the head for not calling.

"I couldn't call. Don't ask why."

Her friend's voice pitched higher than normal, taut as stretched wire. He wasn't okay, but she'd find out more later.

"Where are you? Do you need help? What's wrong?"

"I called to warn you, Gemma. Watch your back. Be careful." The phone went dead.

Warn her? Watch her back? Why the warning? Tears welled. Was he hurt? Mixed up in— No, she wouldn't think it, not that the idea hadn't reared its Medusa head many times since his disappearance. Those snakes could bite in more than one direction.

She hit speed dial. The screen read *user is temporarily unavailable*. She stared at the words. Crap, he turned off his phone.

Five minutes later, painting gear swapped out for the sundress and flats she'd worn earlier, she tossed her tote onto the passenger seat of the car and punched the garage door remote.

Was he in his apartment? Maybe he returned to get clean clothes or his mail. Where could he have been? She'd even phoned his folks, but they hadn't heard from him in a month.

The temp had to be ninety in her garage and in this clunker. Finally the air conditioning kicked in, and she rolled out into the June night's cool-down. She left the condo development and headed south to Linley Harbor.

Her phone jangled with "Get the Party Started." She set the phone on speaker and laid it on the other seat. "Hey, Pia. What's up?"

"You at Galerie Flora?"

"Nope. I changed my day from Friday to Tuesday." She and a few other local artists worked there because Flora was such an art supporter. Besides, having the artists there brought in more shoppers. As it was, Gemma barely had enough time to organize exhibits and shipments of Silvio's works or to complete her own projects.

She reached Linley Harbor and turned right. The street rose gently up a hill across side streets. The neighborhood stretched away from the town docks on the Potomac.

"Well, then, girlfriend, you can meet Ritchie and me at The River House for drinks."

"I'll bet he has a buddy you want to introduce to me." Pia was always fixing her up with guys. Sometimes they hit it off, but she kept things light, well short of relationship. "No time tonight, sorry."

"Hmm, Pia the All-Seeing knows. I hear street sounds, a car horn. You're going to Troy's place again."

For some reason, telling Pia about Troy's phone call didn't feel right. "I have to do *something*. This time I'll find a clue, something the police missed. Maybe in Fairfax and Alexandria, they go to whatever detective school Virginia has. Not in this burg south of the Beltway."

The local cops had told her his missing laptop and duffel meant Troy had left on a trip and not to worry. But his call… the warning. How could she not worry? She prayed he was in the apartment.

"I know when to give up. You're a loyal friend," Pia said, her voice softening. "You have your car back?"

She pulled over and parked in front of Troy's small redbrick building.

"Still have this older loaner with no technology. Ugh, and the seat cushions smell of stale beer. The body shop had to order parts for mine."

"Brakes shouldn't just fail like that."

"This time they did."

"You're lucky you weren't killed."

"It wasn't that bad. When I veered off the highway, I went into a ditch is all." And just missed hitting a boulder. A shudder worked through her as she remembered the horror of having no braking power. Her chest clamped tight. Again. She forced in a deep breath.

4

"Hey, I'm fine, and I'll have my hybrid back soon. Gotta go now. I'm at Troy's place. Bye."

She lifted her tote and exited. Lights glimmered in curtained windows on two of the building's three stories.

And blazed from the bare third-floor dormer windows.

Yes, he's there!

Gemma's pulse kicked up. But if he's there, why did he shut off his phone? Her elation fizzled. Her shoulders slumped and her lips thinned as she entered the foyer. Was he in some sort of trouble? And that cryptic warning?

By the time she reached the third-floor landing, she'd imagined all sorts of dire scenarios. Shoot, the ceiling light was out too. In the gloom, she glared at the door. From inside came the sounds of a dish shattering and a clunk as something fell on the floor.

She rapped sharply on the wood. The door creaked partway inward, spilling light onto the landing. "Troy?"

Footsteps clomped toward the door. A large man filled the opening. He swatted her aside like a mosquito.

She slammed onto the floor. Reeling, she pitched forward toward the steep stairs. She grabbed the newel post and collapsed next to it.

He stepped around her and hit the stairs. A second man hustled through the door behind him. As he passed, his heavy shoe struck her hip. She yelped at the pain.

She could hear them stomping on downward. Farther below, a cell phone rang the universal default tune. The front door banged. They were gone.

No tenants on the lower floors came out to investigate. Gemma was on her own.

What had those guys been doing in Troy's

apartment? She didn't get much of a look at either one. On the first one, only an impression of dark clothing and a hat pulled low.

She hauled in a deep breath. Her tote…where? Did those men take it? She turned her head, searched in the gloom. The triangle of light from the doorway revealed the bag in a corner. She managed to scoot over and snag it.

Another deep breath, and she assessed. She ached, was probably bruised. She'd be stiff tomorrow, but nothing seemed broken. Trembling all over, she clutched the wooden railing as she climbed to her feet.

"Troy?" No reply. No sound at all from inside. Was he in there, hurt?

She took one step inside the apartment, then another. Her throat tightened.

The futon mattress lay flat on the floor, slashed open and bleeding stuffing. Pots and pans, broken dishes, utensils, papers littered the floor. His art portfolios dumped and trampled. Stale odors, the dust that layered everything including the old air conditioning unit.

But no Troy.

Lightheaded, she sank to the floor. Police. She needed to call the police. She fumbled her phone from her bag and tapped 911. When the dispatcher answered, she managed, "A burglary, they… they broke in." To the next question, "No, my friend's place. He… he's not here." One more question. "Two men. Gone. The apartment is trashed." Finally she rasped out the address.

Her gaze fell to the sketches scattered on the floor. Pointed ears and an equine face caught her eye. She probably shouldn't touch anything. Leave it to the police. But… that image, the angle of the head. She nudged aside the paper atop the horse. And inhaled, recoiling as if it were a snake poised to strike. *No*, it couldn't be.

Troy was definitely in trouble. Why hadn't she seen it sooner? She couldn't help feeling responsible. He wasn't strong. Sometimes, well, most of the time, he resented her hovering. Now what? Tears burned and she blinked them away.

Police or not, she pushed to her feet. She had to study the sketch, make certain. It went into her tote, between the pages of her drawing pad.

She couldn't bear to look at the mess. Feeling marginally better, she went to sit on the top step. Why'd she bother to call the Linley Harbor police? But it *was* a crime. And the jerks had trashed Troy's stuff. She didn't trust the local guys to do much. Her dad or Uncle James maybe. But no, they thought Troy was a bad influence. They'd tell her to mind her own business.

She needed someone who'd *do* something.

The image of a rugged face and pewter-gray eyes popped into her mind. What about Boyd?

When she'd needed to move Silvio's unsold sketches and paintings from a crowded unit to a larger secure art storage facility, she'd contracted with Devlin Security Force. A perfect choice, because the company's mission was protecting and retrieving art and artifacts. Boyd Kirby managed the process with complete competence. She fretted about the whole venture, but Boyd kept her reassured.

He was quietly intense, with sword-sharp intelligence. He radiated heat and strength. She sensed something solid about him, and an air of command. And yet he had a wry sense of humor.

At dinner after all was finished, he'd told her a little

about his time in Afghanistan, about what his team did to help the villagers. But nothing about the danger she was certain he and his men had faced daily.

When he walked her to her car, she stood on tiptoes, intending a quick buss of thanks. But the press of Boyd's firm lips gave her heart a jumpstart, the zing of desire blotting out her ugly past. She pressed against him as he deepened the kiss. He pulled her closer, lifted her onto the car hood, and brought his mouth back to hers. Wanting more, she wrapped her legs around his slim hips and hung on for the ride. She must've moaned or something because he ended what had been until that moment an endless embrace and lowered his forehead to hers. He'd apologized. She'd mumbled something about no need and two consenting adults.

At the memory, a flutter skipped around in her belly. She touched her lips, trying in vain to conjure the sensation of his mouth on hers. Or maybe their embrace hadn't been as hot as memory made it out to be.

Even if it had, getting too involved with any man was risky.

Boyd was a security operative. He'd know how to solve this mystery and what to do to find Troy. But calling him would be awkward. They'd had that one sort-of date, and the award-winning kiss, but he'd never followed up. Maybe her chatter about art bored him, and kissing her was compensation. She should've known not to trust he'd want to see her again.

So if she called, he might refuse. Maybe he'd tell her to hire Devlin Security the official way. Or… She stared at her phone, clutched in both hands.

The wail of sirens growing louder forced her decision.

Chapter Two

BOYD KIRBY WISHED his fancy cut-crystal rocks glass contained something stronger than water. Posh events like this made him long to be back in his Army Ranger uniform and with his team, not in a tuxedo pretending he belonged among the D.C. movers and shakers. Nix to the grousing. He needed to be alert. This evening would put to the test Devlin Security's investment in his college studies. The company covered what the GI Bill didn't.

His boss's aunt led the way through the glitterati and across the ballroom's polished hardwood. A couple of Sikorsky Black Hawks would fit inside this one room of the Potomac mansion.

"A tossup which sparkles more," Thomas Devlin's aunt Velma muttered to him, "the chandeliers overhead or the diamonds and gold weighing down the guests."

"A heavy hitter crowd," Boyd said.

A string trio and a grand piano provided a musical backdrop, barely audible above the voices trading stock tips, political dirt, and gossip. Aromas of roast beef from the buffet teased his nose. A contrast to the cloying perfume some guests had poured on.

According to Thomas Devlin, his aunt had come to him with suspicions about a painting she'd seen after having tea with their host's mother. The women had been friends since their now-deceased husbands were U.S. senators.

"Our target is at the end of the gallery." The older woman nodded in that direction, toward a room separate from the ballroom.

At Velma's word choice, Boyd grinned. He took her elbow to guide her around a knot of people chatting. When she stopped to greet an acquaintance, he observed their host deep in conversation with three men who seemed to hang on his every word.

Aubrey Nicholl was the founder of one of the largest hedge funds in the country. What hair he had left was in retreat, and his round glasses made him look more like a college professor than a billionaire. But no professor could afford that tuxedo, or even the polished shoes.

As Boyd stared, the man's face morphed into different features, a younger man with a jagged scar on his cheek. *Hawk*. His eyes speared an accusation at Boyd. And then he and the others exploded into body parts.

Boyd's mouth dried to sand. He closed his eyes against the carnage. When he opened them again, he focused on Velma's silk sleeve beneath his fingers to return him to the present. The face across the room again belonged to Nicholl. Ghosts banished until the next time. She apparently hadn't noticed his lapse. They moved on.

In the wide hallway that served as a gallery, they paused at exhibits in the collection. Dark oils that could be Old Masters, realistic portraits, abstracts, sculptures of nudes and swooping shapes. Nicholl must've bought out the national supply of gold frames and marble pedestals.

"Obscene." Velma's lips turned down. "Aubrey's

mother agrees with me, but concedes he earned his money, so he can do what he likes with it." She leaned closer. "Between us, Boyd, I think it's his new wife who's the gaudy one."

"And possibly the greedy one?"

"That's what I suggested to Thomas, but it may be only because I dislike the woman, so put it down to that and don't let it color your judgment." Velma halted so abruptly he nearly knocked her over. "Here we are."

They'd reached her "target," the painting that might be the Mickalene Golden she'd viewed several years ago at the Museum of Modern Art. Afterward, Velma had set a gallery on watch for the sale or auction of any Golden works. This one had never appeared for public sale. She insisted to Boyd MOMA wouldn't have sold one of this premier twentieth century artist's signature pieces.

Her spotting this painting couldn't have come at a better time. FBI Art Crime had brought Devlin Security in on stopping a spate of forged art in parts of the East. Private sales of older paintings by well-known deceased artists had garnered the crooks a million bucks. And those were the ones they knew about.

Being seen photographing any of the art would be frowned on at the least and at the most get him ejected—along with Velma. He snapped three quick shots with the miniature camera concealed as one of his buttons. He had some art background, and a company researcher had armed him with technical shit about this painting, *Cousin Louise*. He'd memorized the details. The size looked about the twenty-five inches vertical by thirty-five horizontal. He studied the brush strokes, the colors, the use of light, the woman's intense stare. Something about the painting seemed... off.

"When Marty and I lived in New York, I was a member at the museum," Velma whispered, "I remember that special exhibit and this painting, the way the artist portrayed this regal woman's intense emotion. Is it real?"

"Now, Velma, you know I'm only an operative. DSF will consult art authentication experts." And FBI Art Crime. "Be patient."

Again the mischievous grin. "And discreet."

They continued their tour of the gallery. As Velma stopped to greet an acquaintance, Boyd's cell vibrated in his breast pocket. Could be Devlin or Rivera about this assignment. Not a call, but a text. When he saw who'd sent it, his heart knocked against his sternum.

I need help. I don't know who else to ask. Oh sorry it's Gemma Bellini. Remember me from a couple years ago?

Remember her? He remembered everything about Gemma. A slender pixie with luminous skin beneath a mop of glossy dark curls. Her sea-green eyes and sweet smile. Her gentle nature. Their one kiss, their one *long* kiss. Like tasting sunshine. He'd been so hot for her he'd nearly taken her on a car hood. So much for his vaunted self-control.

Some irresistible quality in her drew him. Just hearing her diamond bright voice cheered him. She was unlike any other woman. And unattainable. Wealthy, connected. A woman way out of his league.

He was too fucked up anyway.

He'd be a damn idiot if he if he let himself think he deserved even that one kiss. But just remembering sent fire through his veins.

And now she wanted his help. What kind of help?

Something bugged him about her contacting him at

the same time as the rash of forged paintings. Including the one tonight. Maybe. But it couldn't be a coincidence that the granddaughter of another premier twentieth century artist just asked him for help.

He stepped out the patio door with his phone.

****

Gemma lingered beside the ruined futon, deep in thought while the police officers—a man and a woman—poked and searched. She twisted a curl beside her ear. The window air unit hummed beneath the sounds of their murmurings.

The siren and the officers' dash up the stairs had brought out some of the lower floor tenants, but after Gemma assured them there was no danger, they went back to bed.

The studio apartment wasn't much more than a garret and it looked worse now. The breakfast bar divided the tiny kitchen from the rest, the whole place no more than about twenty by twenty. A futon and two deck chairs with faded green canvas seats Troy found at the Salvation Army, brushes on a table by the empty easel. The faint smells of brush cleaner and acrylic paint hanging in the air. Black fingerprint powder smudged hard surfaces.

"All we can do for now, ma'am."

Gemma started, blinking away her worry. "Oh, yes. Thank you—" she slid a glance to the brass bar on the woman's blue uniform shirt "—Sergeant Long. "I wish I could tell if anything is missing."

"Like y'all said, he didn't have much. What I see so far is a break-in and an assault. We'll look into this." The sergeant was square-shouldered, with grave dark eyes. She seemed capable, more so than the officer who came when Gemma reported Troy missing.

"I understand." But what could they do? She hadn't been able to give them much of a description of the burglars. She offered a smile, but feared it was a sad imitation of one. "Can you tell me anything about where Troy is or what his strange warning might mean?"

Long's mocha-brown features softened. "I know y'all are worried about your friend. I'll touch base with the other officer about Dupree being missing. Feel free to call in a few days." She handed Gemma her card.

The sound of footsteps pounding up the stairs turned everyone toward the half-open door. Long placed a hand on the butt of the pistol at her side.

Gemma's heart fluttered against her ribs. Could it be? There'd been so much noise on Boyd's end of his call—voices talking over each other, laughter—she wasn't sure what he'd said after she gave him Troy's address.

The door swung inward and Boyd Kirby filled the space. His steel-gray gaze mapped the room before landing on her. He swept her head to toe, then nodded, apparently satisfied she was all in one piece.

And oh my, the man did fill out a tuxedo. The jacket molded the muscularity of his wide shoulders. The ends of a bow tie stuck out of his breast pocket, and the blinding-white dress shirt hung open partway, displaying smooth, solid muscle dusted with bronze hairs.

"Gemma, you okay?"

She was, now that he'd arrived, and that he came right away, tonight. Her whole being felt lighter as warmth bloomed in her chest, but apparently her brain had left the building. Finally she managed to say, "Yes, yes, I'm good. As you see."

She took two steps toward him before she forced herself to halt. She'd promised herself to keep it all business. But damn, she wanted nothing more but to feel his strong arms around her.

"Who is this?" Long asked, in a tone of feminine appreciation that pulled Gemma's focus from Boyd.

"Oh, it's—" she began.

"Boyd Kirby, Sergeant. A friend. Gemma called me." He strode to Gemma's side and shot her a warning glance. About what? He stared unsmiling at the two officers. "You figure out what happened here?"

Back in cop mode, Long picked up her kit and headed to the door, her partner at her heels. "Hard to say so far." She turned to Gemma with a small smile. "Y'all are in good hands then, ma'am."

After that bit of good will, they left. Their wide leather equipment belts creaked as they hit the stairs.

Chapter Three

"THANKS FOR COMING, Boyd, but you didn't have to leave a party. You could've waited until tomorrow morning." She couldn't help it, she had to touch him, to feel his solid presence. She gripped his forearm. Even through the jacket, his tensile strength and heat reassured her.

He shook his head. "Better I look this over tonight, so I can see things the way the ass— burglars left them."

She huffed as she swept an arm to encompass the mess. "The way they left this place all cattywampus, assholes perfectly describes them."

At her easy use of the word, a rascal's crooked grin deepened sexy laugh lines framing his mouth and eyes. Heat flashed low in her body.

"Assholes it is then." He tilted his head and placed his big hands on her shoulders. "No bruises, nothing broken? You said on the phone they nearly knocked you down the stairs."

His warmth seeped into her, further easing the tightness. She might have black and blue on her hip. And a nightmare or two. But she firmed her jaw and her stance. She refused to be the weepy damsel in distress, especially if he'd left a date to come to her rescue.

"Nothing. Really."

"I'd have been here sooner, but I couldn't leave the

shindig Devlin sent me to. And first I had to take home the client. Nearly midnight but traffic on the Beltway was like rush hour."

Client, so no date then. Not that she was interested.

"Nice tux. Looks made for you."

"Yeah, thanks. Actually feels comfortable, not like a vise. For security details among the rich and famous, I used to rent, but Mr. Devlin said I needed a suit tailored for my ape shoulders. Well, he didn't exactly put it that way, but my mom would."

She wouldn't call him ape shouldered, but hunk came to mind. And buff. Laughing, she said, "Mr. Devlin was right." She wobbled a little as he lifted his hands.

"Hey, you're exhausted." He righted one of the overturned deck chairs and brushed fingerprint powder off the wooden arm. "Sit before you fall over."

"Yes, Dad." But she sat. Gratefully, smiling at his Boston no-R ending on *over*. Oh my, it was good to hear his voice again. "Why didn't you want me to introduce you?"

He dragged the other chair over next to her and curved an arm along her chair back. She leaned closer, but short of snuggling against him.

"Wanted to keep Devlin Security under the radar. Less complicated that way. Now let's figure out what's going on. The assholes did a number on the door. Tell me about them."

"I can tell you what I told the police. I didn't get enough of a look to describe them except for size. About as tall as you. Hefty, both of them. One wore a hat, maybe a ball cap. And I don't know if they wore gloves. I wish I…" She slumped.

"Honey, they didn't give you a chance to see much.

17

What did the cops say about this?" He swept an arm at the room's disarray.

"Only what you heard. 'Hard to say.'"

"Following police procedure. If they find a clue or a lead, they might share it."

"I called the landlord," she said, "He wasn't too happy to be disturbed. But he said he'd take care of replacing the door and the lock."

"That's good. Now tell me about Troy. How do you know this guy?"

"We were both art majors in the Corcoran School of the Arts & Design at GW—George Washington U. We buddied up, helped each other, supported each other." Even during the darkest time.

"So you're still close. You live in the same town."

"I came here to be near Silvio. He lived an hour or so south of here. Plus, Linley Harbor's a growing arts center. After graduation, Troy didn't want to go home to his overbearing parents in Kansas. So he came here hoping to book gallery shows in D.C., but that hasn't materialized. Now he works in an Alexandria art supply store. Or *worked*. I think the boss has already replaced him. He still paints, is still hopeful." She managed only a stiff smile.

"You have a key to his apartment."

"He's lost his key too many times, so he gave me one. A mailbox key too. When I didn't hear from him after a week, I came and collected the mail. The officers asked me if any letters were missing, but I couldn't tell." She drew a deep breath. "Boyd, were the police right the first time, about his leaving town on purpose?"

"Like you said on the phone, the missing duffel, laptop, and phone suggest it. He left the easel and brushes, stuff easily replaced. May have been in a hurry. And he didn't stop his mail."

"That last is typical Troy." She pressed her hands together prayer fashion. "He must've left here—" she waved a hand vaguely at the disaster area "—just before the burglars arrived." She frowned. "Or maybe he wasn't here at all."

"That makes more sense. He could've phoned from anywhere."

"Even so, something must've happened to him. Like I said, we're—"

"Buddies, yeah." He spat out the word like it was spoiled meat. "But this recent search changes the equation. Tell me exactly what he said on the phone."

"Not sure I can. I was so shocked and upset." She gave him the gist. "I can't figure out what he meant by telling me to watch my back."

"We'll work on that one. Now I have the general idea of what happened, let me look around. Okay if I take photos? It'll help me remember details later."

"Of course." She popped up to watch him search.

No military hair for him. His hair, the tan color of sand, was shaggy on the neck, the right length for a woman to thread her fingers through it. But his chin, which she remembered having a couple days scruff, was clean shaven. Maybe for the high society party. He filled the room with his energy and strength. He wasn't overly tall, about six feet, and *built*. A former Army Ranger, but he must still work out to maintain that broad chest and flat belly. DSF would want their operatives to be fit. She rambled around the room as he prowled.

He photographed with his phone every few steps. He checked in the bathroom and closet, then returned to the kitchen. "This mail on the bar is circulars and ads, a few bills. Some are torn open. You open them?"

"No, the burglars did that. Were they maybe looking for checks?"

"Possible. Can you tell if anything is missing?"

"Not really. Only what you'd expect, like clothing. Other than a new laptop, Troy doesn't have anything valuable, except to him. His sketches and whatever he was working on."

He hunkered down and examined the charcoal and pencil sketches strewn on the floor. The slim tux pants showcased powerful legs. Muscles flexed as he bent and squatted in his search. She imagined those muscles taut and bunched in the Warrior Pose. Pressing her face to the window air unit about now might cool her down.

He rose from kneeling to upright in one easy, fluid motion. "I think they trashed the place to cover a search. Drawers in the desk are partly left open—unless that was the cops?" At a shake of her head, he went on. "The desk drawers, torn envelopes, garbage not tossed around but overturned and shuffled through. Can't say what they were looking for. Ready to go?"

She stifled a yawn and straightened her shoulders. "More than ready. I'll tackle the mess later. Troy shouldn't see this. He'll come back soon. He *will*."

"And you have no ideas on where he might've gone and why?" Boyd's rolling baritone seemed to rumble inside her.

"I've mulled over possibilities. We hang out—*used* to hang out—together unless I had a date or he hooked up with a guy. Maybe he went off with one. But given the warning, that doesn't make sense."

The grim expression smoothed. "A possible new

guy. Anything else?"

"Given all this mess, trouble. He'd have contacted me otherwise. What trouble, I don't know. Maybe with the new guy?" She could guess, but wouldn't go there unless it became necessary. She called him her little bro, and to him she was his big sis. Some big sis, not protecting her bro.

She hooked her tote and they left.

Outside, Boyd told her he would talk to the Linley police and run things by DSF. "Then I'll get back to you. Couple days, tops." He clicked his key fob and a black SUV chirped. "You relax on this, Gemma. I'll get to the bottom of it."

His calm and air of competence eased her nerves. "Thanks. I feel better already."

"Where'd you park? I don't see your car." Her click and the chirping reply turned his head. "A rusty coupe?"

"Yeah, for now. My car's in the shop."

"What's it in for?"

"Sounds like cop talk. 'Twenty years for armed robbery, ma'am.'" His lips curved in that rascal's grin, sparking a little flare inside her. "A week or so ago the brakes failed, and I slid into a ditch. Damage on the bumper and underneath." When his brows jumped upward, she added, "I wasn't hurt."

"When did you last have it serviced?"

"Now you sound like my dad. I keep up with maintenance." The car electronics reminded her, but no reason to mention that. "Odd, but the tow truck driver said it looked like the brake line was punctured. No idea how that happened. It's not like I go off-roading in my little sedan."

His expression darkened like a thunder cloud. "Let

me get my SUV started. I'll follow you home to make sure you're safe. It's late."

****

Boyd shifted in his seat at Thomas Devlin's polished wood conference table. He swallowed a long drink of sweet iced tea. Word was the boss's admin made it special for him. Boyd had met with Thomas Devlin several times, taken part in ops with him, but until now had never been in his office, large enough to swallow Troy Dupree's entire place. Devlin had crossed the expanse to his desk to take a phone call. If things went as Boyd wanted, the boss would take him off the case. Too fucking hard to remain professional with Gemma.

On Friday she'd looked so forlorn and beautiful Boyd had to force himself not to pull her into his arms. He went there intending to be businesslike, but with her close, a tangy scent of some kind in her hair, what he wanted was nowhere near professional. And, *shit*, he hadn't meant to call her honey. While he checked out Dupree's digs, she flitted from place to place, a slim dark-haired pixie in a floaty yellow dress with a blue vine image trailing down one side. Nervous or hopeful? Then she'd started to protest his following her home, but had yielded when he insisted it was on his way. Which it was. Mostly.

Devlin returned and took his seat between Max Rivera and Zach Quinton on the other side of the big conference table.

Devlin swirled the ice in his glass and scanned the notes he'd made during Boyd's report. He'd removed his suit jacket, draped it over the back of his desk chair, but Devlin Security Force's CEO maintained a military bearing even in rolled-up shirtsleeves.

When he looked up, eyes as sharp as an eagle's beneath straight dark brows seemed to bore into Boyd. "Right, Kirby, I agree those men were searching for something."

Boyd suppressed the urge to exhale his relief. "Talked to the Linley Harbor police yesterday. They assume it was drugs, maybe pills. No arrests but Dupree's suspected of buying on the street. Not selling, so I'd be surprised if he left a stash behind. The only fingerprints were Dupree's and Gemma's. Sir."

He probably didn't have to add the *sir*. Devlin treated all the operatives as equals. But he was Delta, and Max Rivera had served with him. No idea of Rivera's rank, but Devlin retired as a captain. Boyd made it only to first sergeant. The *sir* was old habit. As was sitting at attention. Like Quinton was doing.

"Suspicious Dupree left in such a hurry and didn't say anything to Gemma," Rivera said. "Equally suspicious he phoned the way he did, telling her to watch her back." Built like Boyd, he had jet-black hair and unreadable dark eyes. He rubbed his chin. The severe expression on his blunt face was no more encouraging than Devlin's eagle stare.

"*Just* friends, you say?" Quinton asked. Blond and rawboned, with a perpetual smirk, he made a good bookend on Devlin's other side.

"That's it. He's gay. Gemma speculated he'd gone off with a guy." The revelation had untied the knot in his gut. She hadn't called him to help find her lover after all. Not that it made any real difference. She'd given him a photo of Dupree—brown hair, lanky, hooded eyes, face all bony angles—that he included in his report.

"The vandals dumped a portfolio of sketches and

watercolors on the floor. I took photos of these two." He passed the printouts across the table. "They look like preliminary sketches of the woman portrayed in Mickalene Golden's *Cousin Louise*."

Devlin's eyebrows leaped halfway up his brow. "This complicates matters. Maybe ties Dupree to either art theft or forgery. Or both."

"My take on it, too, sir. Can you tell me what's happening with the *Cousin Louise*?"

The boss's grin softened his austere features. "Since it was my aunt who spotted the painting, I went personally to confront the Nicholls about it. To say the least, Aubrey Nicholl was furious his wife had bought art of what he termed questionable provenance, a euphemism for what he really thought. He allowed me to carry it away."

"But?" Boyd shifted in his seat.

"Art Crime's art authenticator hasn't gotten to that painting yet. Specialists have been occupied with other questionable purchases. Mostly here in the District Metro area and around New York City. It's likely more are out there. Given this development, I don't want to wait for Art Crime's guy. I know of one who's worked for us before."

Before Boyd could respond, Rivera spoke. "I just got a text about another painting. This one by Silvio Bellini. A horse painting called *Chincoteague Guardian*. The team that found it is bringing it here now."

Boyd's fists clenched in his lap.

Rivera went on. "Maybe Gemma Bellini is either painting copies herself or having Dupree do it. She might have access others wouldn't to specs on famous paintings. Including her grandfather's."

"Someone could be blackmailing her into it, threatening to expose her past forging," Devlin added. "Somehow connected to Dupree's warning to her. *If* he actually called."

DSF had conducted a thorough background check on her four years ago, which revealed a past connection to art forgery. Quinton jumped in as they speculated further. Boyd's blood pressure climbed, but he kept his mouth shut. Took another drink of the tea. Devlin grew up somewhere in the South, likely why the brew was too sweet for this New England boy.

When the others hit pause, he jumped in.

"Sir, Gemma didn't forge anything. When she was in college, an artist in residence named Morgan Nazaroff assigned her the copying as an assignment. Troy Dupree also. Having art students copy is an accepted teaching approach, a way to learn different styles and techniques. Student copying is not forging. She did *not* profit, so her copying wasn't considered a crime, and it was only a minor scandal at the time." He drew a calming breath.

Rivera's mouth quirked up a tick in what might be a grin. He clicked his pen a couple times. "Does Research have info on this art teacher, Nazaroff?"

"They do now," Boyd said. He'd done the search himself. "Nazaroff was a teenage phenom who commanded high prices for wall-size splashy abstracts. By the time he showed up at the Corcoran and other schools, he was a falling star of the art world, and his lavish lifestyle had shrunk his bank account. He sold the students' copies as real and pocketed the proceeds, except for a cut to Dupree, who profited from the scheme. Gemma was in the dark, like I said. Nazaroff then enjoyed six years of federal hospitality, and Dupree two."

"That puts a different light on her past," Rivera said, folding his hands together.

Boyd leaned forward. "If she's involved now, why did Troy Dupree take off and why did she ask me for help? She's obviously scared for her friend." No point in arguing about the phone call. At this point.

"Possible he's involved," Devlin said, "with whoever is behind this current run of forgeries. See if you can find out where Morgan Nazaroff hangs his hat these days."

"Will do, sir. One thing I didn't mention earlier." He described what Gemma had told him about her car brakes failing. "The tech who worked on her car showed me the brake line. Definitely a puncture created by a sharp, pointed object. I talked the service manager into tagging it and storing it. I'll urge her to call the police."

The other men had been leaning back in their chairs, but his words jerked them upright.

"This changes things," Rivera said. "Dupree blows town, his place is searched, and someone messes with Ms. Bellini's brakes. Can't be a coincidence."

"I agree, but to clarify, her car damage occurred seven days before the break-in." Boyd turned to Devlin. "Don't you want to hand this case off to an art specialist or an FBI Art Crime agent?"

"Not a chance." His boss squared his shoulders. "The Feds are offering us a hefty reward for results. Probably so we tie it up in a neat bow and they take credit. Gemma Bellini trusts you. Get close enough to find out if she's involved. But sound her out about the *Cousin Louise*. Level with her if you have to. You're our man."

Boyd didn't know whether to cheer or groan. "Yes, sir."

Chapter Four

GEMMA STARTED AT the doorbell's gong. Lightness radiated through her. "Boyd's here." *Stop it.* She couldn't let herself be too attracted to this man.

She'd signed a contract yesterday with Devlin Security Force, mostly so she didn't take up Boyd's time for free. This thing with Troy could be worse than she'd originally thought.

Boyd had phoned yesterday, saying he had info for her and could he see her. Of course the Army Ranger would be on time. Now she had no time to clean up. She checked the app on her phone. Seeing him standing at the door jazzed her pulse.

She capped the dauber and set it in the tray before dashing from her studio and down the stairs. A glance in the hall mirror showed her hair was okay, but shoot, she had paint all over. A deep breath didn't slow the wing beats of those butterflies inside.

She punched the alarm code on the keypad and opened up. And didn't he look gorgeous, all those tanned arm muscles on view in his ecru safari shirt. "Hi, Boyd, come in. I'm sorry I'm such a mess. I was in my studio."

"Hey, Gemma." He removed a GO ARMY ball cap as he entered. Stuffed it in a back pocket of his cargo pants. "You look great… colorful." His slow grin sucked the air right out of her lungs. A callused thumb rasped across her cheek, leaving a trail of tingles in its wake. He held it up, smeared with carmine.

"Occupational hazard. I was putting the final touch on a project. Give me a minute to clean up so I don't share more of my color with you. Powder room down the hall has tissues you can use on that paint. Meet you in the living room, to your right."

She hurried up to her bathroom. *Crap*, both cheeks must match the paint. Although the cause had nothing to do with embarrassment. Was she that hard up that a sexy grin and a simple gesture turned her on? Apparently.

Moments later, face clean and paint-splotched, oversized tee replaced with a peach linen tank over her leggings, she descended the stairs.

Instead of making himself comfortable on the sofa, he knelt at her open front door.

"Boyd?"

He levered to his feet. His pewter eyes swept her from top to bottom and back to her mouth. Heat flashed in his gaze before he turned back to the door. "I noticed this earlier. Scratches on the door lock. Like somebody tried to break in."

"What? Are you certain? Maybe I scraped it punching in the code."

"Your fingernails are short, and no nails did this. A pry tool. Somebody either tried to remove the keypad or fu— mess with your code."

"Impossible! I'd have known. Security is tight and—" Her pulse skipped as a memory surfaced. "Something last Tuesday night, maybe eight-thirty. That's my day at Galerie Flora, so I didn't get home until after nine-thirty. TechVA Security said the alarm went off. They sent a car, but the agent found no one and must not have spotted the scratches."

"You have a camera covering the door. What about the feed?"

She heaved a sigh and twisted fingers in her hair. "Nothing. The video doesn't go to TechVA, only to my phone and laptop. When I checked, there was a blip, then a few seconds of blur, but nothing was recorded. Having TechVA watch my door seemed too intrusive, too much like surveillance."

"I hear you. But that company does have a solid reputation."

"Good to know. I need reliable security because Silvio left me three paintings. This neighborhood's no gated community, but it's pretty safe, and I know my neighbors."

"Gated communities aren't as safe as advertised. You're better off where people look out for each other, like in this suburb."

Laughing, she reached toward him, but pulled back before touching his forearm. *Keep it business.*

"Suburb of Linley Harbor? How did you say that deadpan? Even if it's becoming known as an art center, the town's so small its main street is called Main Street. And this area beyond the town limits sort of grew one street at a time, like weeds, a neighbor told me."

He didn't grin again, but gazed at her stony-faced, back to business. Or something else, given the shadows in his eyes. "You want me to take a look around? Just to make certain."

His even tone calmed her nerves. "Your company specializes in art and artifacts. How do you know about home security?"

He shifted his stance and looked down at his boots

before he met her eyes again. "I'm working on a degree in criminal justice at the U of D.C. My coursework covers a wide range of stuff about crime investigation."

"I remember you said you intended to go to college. Very impressive while you're working full time."

Color suffused his cheeks above his beard shadow. "Finishing takes longer is all."

She looped an arm through one of his and pulled him into the living room. She caught his crisp, faintly spicy scent. Cologne or testosterone? "Then I'll give you the tour. But I'd know if anyone had sneaked in and searched or something."

"Not if they knew what they were doing."

"Then it wouldn't have been those burglars at Troy's."

"Don't be too sure of that. They intended to be obvious." No longer relaxed as he was when he arrived, he held himself rigid and vigilant. His jaw worked. "If I suspected an intruder was here, I'd search the place alone."

"What a relief! I chose this condo because of its open living and dining area. Space for entertaining. I seem to know a lot of people, and there's the big Bellini clan."

He covered the room the way he'd examined Troy's apartment. Patrolling like a soldier, noticing everything with measuring eyes. He checked the windows, especially the locks, before he came back to her.

"Clear. Looks like a comfortable space to live in."

The statement of approval made her smile. "Thanks. I don't do formal, to the despair of my mother and sister. It's my favorite room, even before I repainted the walls this warm off-white to better display Silvio's paintings."

The emerald green sectional and chairs weren't new, but she'd added a blue-gray carpet and throw pillows in mauve as contrast. An entertainment center and shelving took up most of the wall opposite the gas fireplace.

Boyd walked over to the shelving. "Nice family photos. I see what you mean about the Bellini clan. And I see your grandfather with his wide smile and white hair. I can never get over you calling him by his first name."

"The man was vain. He said any terms for grandfather made him sound old. But I never thought of him as old, even by the time he died. He was eighty-five." Her throat tightened, and she swallowed.

He turned from her, maybe noticing her emotion. "One of your grandfather's." The painting that caught his eye was as wide as the mantel over which it hung. They crossed to it, and he examined it closely.

"Yes, the wild ponies on one of the barrier islands. It's called *Chincoteague Family*. I'm not a horse lover, but always adored these little colts trotting by their mamas. I reckon that's why he wanted me to have it."

He checked out the other two works, a small one of eighteenth-century Alexandria townhouses, and the other of a child in a blue dress frolicking among the beach grasses.

"It's you. Your green eyes and the way you dance on your toes."

"I was five. Reckon I haven't grown up much."

His gaze, heavy-lidded, swept her again. "I'd say you grew up just fine." When his eyes met hers, the fire in them shot tingles up her spine. Maybe the attraction wasn't all one sided.

Why now? Why this man?

He flexed his hands so muscles bunched in his

forearms, then moved on to looking for signs of intrusion on the French door to the patio. He took a turn in the galley kitchen, checked the lock on the walk-in door to the garage, and then followed her back around to the stairs.

"Second floor, three bedrooms, one converted into my studio. Two bathrooms, one in the master suite. Whoa, I sound like a real estate dealer. Oh, sir, I think you all will especially like the master suite's skylight in the vaulted ceiling."

"I'm sure I would." He slanted her another look that qualified as a leer, and she sputtered a laugh.

He examined the two bedrooms and the hall bath. "I'm not finding anything obvious. I should check the outside too. After the security blip, did anything seem odd or missing?"

"Nothing. I might not have noticed if things had been moved. I don't always keep the place as tidy as you're seeing it now." She'd straightened and stowed odds and ends that morning.

He didn't comment. She started to take his hand, but instead led the way into the studio. He nodded toward the easel. "That what you're working on? Tempera?"

"Yes, rusted anchors at the town docks, and yes on the tempera paint. I'm almost finished, but I want to add some coppery tones to the burnt sienna of the rust. Flora shooed me out of the gallery after lunch so I could work on this. She wants it next week."

"A close study. Exact detail, but stylized. I like it. Do you have more here?" He turned to her, pleasure lighting his gaze.

Delighted, she rose on her toes. "My other recent ones are at Galerie Flora, where I work once a week.

Serious art, which is work. This project in particular."

Tina's tunic hung in the corner to dry, so she directed him over to the new project. "I'm painting daylilies on my friend Pia's dress. Fabric paint's lovely to work with. Decorating fabric is more of a hobby."

Did you paint the blue vine on the dress you wore Friday?"

"Oh, the clematis. Yes. The sundress was too plain without some pop."

"I like this too." Inordinately pleased he'd noticed what she wore, she had to look away. "You have a flower in the anchor one. Always flowers?"

"No, sometimes rocks or seashells. An extra flourish, you see."

He headed for the back wall.

"The sliding-glass door was already here," she said, "but I had the floor-to-ceiling windows installed. More light for the studio. The view is beautiful. I'm up high enough to see the wildlife preserve. The Potomac is too far away, but on a breezy day, I can smell it."

"Where's the camera out here?" He slid open the door and stepped out.

"Lower, to the side. It covers the patio below. And there's another in front on the garage."

Outside, the afternoon heat nearly sent her back into the air conditioning. She squatted by the planter box on a small tarp near the wrought-iron railing. Still wet. At least she hadn't let the plants die. But now it was too heavy for her.

"Here," Boyd said, "let me get that."

"Thanks. Take one side, okay? It sits in the outside brackets." She grasped her end.

"My mom always has boxes like these. Nice

flowers."

"Petunias, geraniums, ivy, and euonymus. A variety for color."

He grinned. "I think you're supposed to hang them empty and fill them later."

"I know that, Mr. Master Gardener. But filling and planting it already hung makes a mess. I usually let it drain enough so I can pick it up. I'm already a month late with these. I've been too busy, but you're here, so…"

"Now you've put me in my place, I'll shut up and hoist." He took the other end, and they lifted it up and over. The planter hooked easily into the brackets.

"Perfect." She reached across the box to pluck out a broken leaf.

Metal groaned and shrieked. The planter wobbled.

She froze. *Earthquake?*

Boyd's arms clamped around her. He hauled her back away from the edge.

More piercing metal screeches. The railing pulled loose. It tilted out and away from the building.

The planter crashed to the ground below.

White noise roared in Gemma's ears. Her breath caught. She registered his heart pounding against her back.

She turned in his arms. "What was that?"

Two red spots marked his lean cheeks. His eyes glittered like iced mercury. He kept an arm around her as he pulled her inside the studio.

Chapter Five

BOYD SWALLOWED HARD, afraid he might spew up the turkey sandwich he'd wolfed down at lunch. Fuck, what if he hadn't grabbed her, pulled her back? She could've fallen head first with the flower box to the brick patio. Sheer luck he caught her.

"Unless this building has shoddy construction," he spat out, "somebody messed with the railing."

He held Gemma away from him. Her gaze swirled with shock, but she shook it off and glared at the space where the railing had stood.

He'd wanted to pull her into his arms from the moment he walked in the door. Seeing the red paint on her cheek and the bright pink braid woven into her thick mass of dark hair had tangled all his circuits. And threatened to again. Not the time.

He swallowed his shock and released his grip on her shoulders. Probably too tight, the reason for that vertical frown line between her brows.

"Gemma, Gemma. You okay?"

"I'm fine. But—" Her eyes widened, and the frown smoothed out. "Oh, Boyd, thank you. You saved my life. I could've…" She swallowed and reached for him.

Shit, he couldn't be trusted to save anybody's life. But he closed his fingers around her slim hand and held on anyway. What could he say? "Hell, it was—"

"Ruined! Smashed!" Not fear or confusion, now it was fury crimping her forehead. Her small stubborn chin lifted, and she shook her other fist at the balcony. "My flowers, the planter. The railing! What a disaster! How did that happen?"

Anger he could handle. "We'll find out. It's better if you wait inside while I check out the damage."

"What? No! It's my balcony."

"Do you really want to get close enough to the edge to examine the brick wall?"

She threw up her hands, but her lips curved in a wisp of a smile that punched in her irresistible dimples. "It's my Italian temper. My anger's not directed at you. But be careful."

"Guaranteed. I'm always careful." If only he'd been more careful in-country.

On the left side of the balcony he moved aside a rattan chair. Propping a hand on the brick wall, he examined the hole where the bolt had been. Photographed it with his phone. Then he moved to the other side. Heat climbed up the back of his neck. *Shit.* He levered to his feet and blocked his temper with a deep breath.

"Well?" Gemma said when he joined her inside.

"Bolts screwed into heavy-duty wall anchors were used to fasten the railing to the brick wall. The usual method. It looks like the anchors on both sides pulled loose."

"What would cause that?" Her slight southern accent deepened to a drawl. Maybe the stress.

His back teeth clenched. "I'll need to see outside first." He nodded toward her bare feet. Something about the toenails painted the same pink as her braid tamped down the foreboding sifting inside him. "Better put on shoes. Bits of the broken planter could be scattered around."

Downstairs, Gemma stepped into barely-there flat-heeled shoes like his sister-in-law wore, while he collected binoculars from his ride. Then they exited through the slider into the late afternoon heat. On either side of the flagstone patio, brick walls extended by wooden lattices separated her from her neighbors. Away from the building, manicured green lawn stretched, bordered by a trimmed hedge and flowering shrubs.

Shadows slanted across the debris. The rectangular plastic box lay in shattered pieces below the dangling railing. Black dirt and broken plants splattered everything—the grass, the flagstone patio, a couple of wrought-iron chairs, and two tall ceramic pots containing more of the same flowers that lay around, small green victims.

"Keep back," he told her. "The railing could go."

Hugging herself, she skirted the damage and shifted from foot to foot in the grass.

The railing creaked overhead as he edged past it, careful where he stepped. A few feet from the side wall, two rectangular indentations in the lawn, the same a few feet farther out. He found similar slots on the other side. As he expected. Knelt and snapped photos of both.

"Come look at this." When she joined him, he said, "Were these marks here before?"

She bent over, pushed curls back from her forehead, placed the other hand on his shoulder. He hadn't forgotten what a toucher Gemma was. An artist's natural sensuality maybe. Distracting, but he could deal. No way would he object.

"I don't know. I set out the flower urns Sunday before going to my dad's for dinner. But sorry, I just didn't notice. What made these digs?"

"One more thing first. Has any maintenance been done out here on the brick recently?"

She shook her head. "I'd have seen the crew. And management always notifies residents ahead of things like that."

"I'll answer your other question first, about wall anchors. They're called that for good reason. They lock into the mortar between the bricks, and the bolts are screwed into them. The anchors would loosen for only two reasons. One is substandard construction. This complex doesn't strike me as inferior."

"I've lived here six years. Nothing is substandard. Dad and my brother Joe—he's a civil engineer—vetted the complex before I bought. So what's the other reason?" One arched eyebrow lifted as if in punctuation.

"These marks in the lawn were made by a ladder. Somebody loosened the anchors deliberately. We need to call the police."

Her pretty green eyes darkened. Normally her cheeks had a healthy glow. Now they lost all color. Her gaze shifted from the ladder marks upward to the anchor holes. "But... that means..."

"Yes."

He ushered her back inside and had her sit at the kitchen serving bar. He poured her a glass of water and watched her drink it dry.

"Boyd, you're saying someone tried to *harm* me." There was that frown line again. Her shoulders straightened and color seeped back into her skin. "What the hell! Are you sure?"

Impressive. Twice he'd seen her rocked and shaken, but come back defiant and swinging. He didn't expect her to be pissed. A woman with spirit.

He hated to level with her. Hated even more what it meant he'd have to do. He walked around the bar and took her hands, pulling her around to face him. This was no time to be delicate. She needed to know the danger she was in.

"They didn't want to just *harm* you. They wanted you dead, but intended it to look accidental. And it's not the first time." He explained about the punctured brake line, another so-called accident. "The service manager saved the brake line. He can show it to the cops, although at this late date it might not count as actual evidence."

"No, no police. Let's go through this again. Couldn't the balcony railing be an accident?"

Denial was natural. He'd seen it among Afghan villagers who insisted their own men who'd left would never return to attack them. He'd heard similar tales from cops and social workers who came to speak to his law enforcement courses.

Or maybe Gemma was still hiding her past?

"Has anybody been in your house since Tuesday?"

She looked at her empty glass for a moment. "Only the cleaning service on Wednesday. They come every two weeks. But I was here. They don't have my key code either. And I doubt those women would know how to loosen the railing."

"Good. Was there another security blip, say Thursday or Friday?" he asked.

She shook her head before her eyes widened. "Shoot, yes. Friday morning. I was at the gallery to schmooze a client when TechVA called. I complained that it was a problem with the equipment, but they said everything was working okay. Maybe it's my phone?"

"No glitch at all. Deliberate, like the brake line. Who knew you'd be gone Friday morning?"

Her brow creased with thought. "Lots of people. Flora, who probably told half of Linley Harbor because she was pumped about my discussing a commission. My friend Pia, who could've told the other half of town. Also my sister Tina and my uncle James. But you can't suspect any of *them*?"

"You just suggested they had spread the news."

"Oh."

"Devlin Security has worked with the Haven County Sheriff's Department more than once. You can trust them to be more thorough than the small Linley Harbor force. Is there some reason you don't want me to call them?"

"No, of course not. It's just, why would someone want to kill me?"

"I don't know. But they've tried twice." He made the call. Identified himself as a Devlin Security operative and explained the situation.

Then to Gemma, he said, "Deputies will be here soon. Maybe a detective too. I need to report in."

She was still resisting reality, but he got her to lock the slider and the front door behind him. His backup weapon was concealed more easily in his hip holster, but he'd feel better having his bigger 9mm with him.

The dispatcher at DSF forwarded his call to Max Rivera. Rivera had the authority to handle this, except he'd been a hardass about Gemma. Boyd sucked in a breath.

"Kirby," Rivera said as soon as he took the call, "tell

me this is an emergency that'll pull me away. Kate's dragging me to a museum fundraiser. I'd rather wear camo than black and white."

"No can do." The man's levity eased the tightness in Boyd's gut. A fraction. "Got a situation, but it's not urgent." He gave Rivera a quick rundown, omitting his hots for Gemma. "Serious shit here. I'll stay for the night. A team should run this, not just me." *Or somebody else, not me.* That ate at him too. Made no sense, but there it was.

"Serious shit is right. Silvio Bellini's granddaughter? High profile serious shit. I'll organize backup in the morning. Any research you need, I'll make sure Marton gives you priority. We're stretched thin. Lots going on. I'll get back to you in the morning when I have something set up."

"Sounds good." He thought the call was finished when Rivera spoke again.

"One more thing. You sounded her out yet on the *Cousin Louise?*"

Boyd suppressed a sigh. "Not yet. Been too busy with the other. Later."

"You'll be with her 24/7. Get closer to her. Find out how deep she is in this forgery scam."

He wanted to say she wasn't, but he'd pushed it in the last meeting. "Roger." The word went to dead air. He grabbed his Go bag, and stuffed some ammo and the other 9mm from his gun safe into it. He locked up and headed for her door.

Get closer to Gemma? Exactly what he wanted and what scared him the most.

Chapter Six

GEMMA WATCHED FROM the open slider as Boyd walked the detective and two uniformed deputies through what he'd found. They'd arrived forty-five minutes ago. First the detective interviewed them both. Boyd explained about the punctured brake line, but the man barely took notes. They toured the damage. The evidence, as Boyd said. Detective Santiago, a thickset fortyish man with a solemn face, had sent the deputies to talk to the neighbors. Maybe someone would remember something significant, but she didn't hold out much hope.

At the moment, the detective and Boyd were bent over the small digs in the lawn.

"It hasn't rained since last Wednesday," Boyd was saying. "The grounds crew mowed the next day. These indents were made afterward by the safety feet of an extension ladder. Took whoever it was a couple tries to get the ladder set where he wanted it. It appears the feet dug in deep because the ground was softened by the rain."

The other man knelt and examined more closely. "Possible."

A man of few words, Detective Santiago. Gemma pressed her lips together. Crap, someone really climbed a ladder to sabotage her balcony railing? She shuddered, hearing in her mind the shriek of metal and the crash of the planter hitting the ground.

She blew out a pent-up breath when Boyd finally directed one of the deputies to photograph the slots. They'd already taken other photos and dusted for prints.

Finally Boyd and the detective came back inside.

"Ms. Bellini," Santiago said, "I will get back to you as soon as possible. You can expect a couple of our techs in the morning. They will examine the scene further." He nodded to her and Boyd. "You have my card if you think of anything else."

After the door closed behind them, Boyd stood there watching her, his muscles tense as if he expected her to fall over. She must look exhausted, but oddly, every cell in her body vibrated. Or maybe she was just too unnerved to calm down.

"It's late, Boyd. Seven must be past quitting time for you." She needed an escape, needed to talk about something other than this faceless threat. She conjured up a smile. "I'd really like a glass of wine. And I keep beer for some of my friends and family. Would you like something?"

A lazy, wicked smile erased the stiff mask he'd worn since the railing fell. It rocked her back on her heels. "A beer would do it." He rotated his shoulders, rubbed the left one, maybe a sore muscle or a war wound. She wouldn't pry.

He let her tug him toward the kitchen, and he settled on the stool with a glass and a beer. "Thanks. This Wood Hills IPA is one of my favorites."

She sipped her Montepulciano. "I have some Bolognese sauce my dad's wife, Jennifer, sent home with me Sunday. I can cook pasta and throw together a salad."

Her breath caught. "I mean… I have all this food, too much for me." Her cheeks were on fire. Shoot, but she wasn't ready to be alone. Was her invitation overstepping? "No pressure. If you have a date or your studies or—"

He held up a hand. "I'm not going anywhere. Especially if you're offering to feed me. About this time of day, I need refueling."

"Well then." She turned and opened the fridge. The chill might cool her jets. She closed her eyes and took deep breaths, centering herself for a sec. Ah, the salami. She grabbed it.

"Jennifer sent this too." She sliced the meat and arranged it with some crackers on a plate. "You can probably handle the calories she insisted she didn't need in the house. It works for me. Must be the Irish side. Like my mom, I never seem to gain." *Stop babbling.*

He grinned at that but made no comment. In quick order, he devoured a few of the appetizers. "How's it going managing your grandfather's works?"

She helped herself to salami and a cracker before pulling out two pots for the sauce and cavatappi.

"Well, I think. His agent John Fitzhugh worked with me for a while. He's mostly retired now, but he's keeping Silvio's estate as his only client," she said as she worked. "The two put up for auction at Christie's sold way above the reserve. And three more are on loan to museums. At least one may purchase."

"A slow release. Is that the plan?"

"Mostly. He never put up a ton for sale. Some in the family want me to sell works faster, but Silvio—and Fitz—insisted scarcity would maintain their value and his place in art history. Even raise it once he… now that he's gone." She blinked rapidly and turned to the stove.

"You've been busy."

She stirred the sauce, then added the cavatappi to the water boiling in the second pot.

"You don't know the half of it. Being executive director of the Silvio Bellini estate is a full-time job. The connections with museums and galleries, the brochures and books, endless offers to buy artwork and license prints. It's allowed me little time for painting."

"Your uncle manages the finances, if I remember correctly."

"Yes, James, my dad's younger brother. He's a financial planner and very careful. I get regular, detailed reports from his bookkeeper, sometimes weekly. I don't have a business bone in my body, so it's been a learning curve these past five years."

"Your grandfather chose you, with an artist's heart. He chose well."

"Oh, Boyd, that's so sweet." Could that possibly be the reason Silvio tapped her?

His rich laugh flipped her pulse. "Honey, nobody has ever suggested I was sweet."

"Silvio taught me, mentored me from the time I was eight. My brothers are both engineers, one civil, the other industrial stuff. Dad's a doctor, orthopedics. My sister's a photographer. She does weddings and portraits. I'm the only one of my siblings who pursued painting." She cocked her head. "Don't I remember that you paint?"

"Not paint. I draw, caricatures and cartoons, but just for fun. Like your clothing painting." His jaw worked. "Some of my courses are art history and art science. Fits in with my work."

Now she was even more impressed. And he'd called

her honey, like the other night. It meant nothing. Some people called everyone honey or hon. It was a Southern thing. Except he was from New England.

During dinner, she ate a little, mostly pushing her food around on her plate, but Boyd finished a second helping. They ferried the dishes to the kitchen. She set the silverware in the sink, heaved a sigh, and lowered her head.

Boyd's warm hands landed on her shoulders, gently squeezing. He turned her to face him and held her loosely. "It'll be okay, Gemma. We'll figure this out."

"We... I do appreciate you wanting to help. Shoot, you saved my life today. But the balcony railing, the brakes..." Her breath hitched. "All that has nothing to do with Troy or the burglars, the reason I contacted you."

"We'll see."

Maybe it was the wine. Maybe it was the man who stood so close in her small kitchen. Maybe it was the heat radiating off him. His gaze, molten steel, stoked fire in her belly. She trusted him in this unfathomable situation. Beyond that, she couldn't, shouldn't. Her pulse clattered. This... this closeness was risky. She'd trusted before and...

But at this moment, for whatever reason, she needed this, needed him.

The intensity in his gaze and his caress on her hair sifted sultry tingles through her. He radiated energy and power, and the circle of his arms offered gentle protection. He didn't press or say a word, merely lowered his head.

"I... I shouldn't. It's not..." Not what, she couldn't say.

"I know. I'll back off if you want."

She rose on tiptoes and cupped his jaw, his beard stubble grazing her palm. His mouth came down on hers and he pulled her tight against his big tough body. His kiss was delicious and devastating, and she clutched his shirt and hung on as his tongue teased the seam of her lips. Opening herself to him was a bad idea, but she couldn't help wanting more than the faint memory of his wild taste. Tilting her head, she danced her tongue with his and let the heat and spicy taste and crisp scent of him wash over her.

"Gemma." His voice thick and rough with desire, he lifted her and settled her onto the serving bar, placing them at about the same height.

His talented mouth feathered kisses along her jaw and down her throat. She pulled him closer with her legs and let her head fall back to give him better access, digging her fingertips into the hard mounds of his shoulder muscles. Her heart pounded and her breath accelerated with the heavy pull of desire. His tongue grazed wet heat at the top edge of her tank before he lifted his head. His lips met hers for one more lightning bolt of a kiss that left her light-headed, and then he pulled back.

He was breathing as hard as she was. "Gemma, you tempt me beyond control. I crave more than a kiss, but—"

"*That*—" she flapped a hand, the only movement she could manage "—was way more than a kiss."

He helped her to her feet. She could see his erection pushing against his zipper. Naked hunger filled his eyes, in their depths the troubled shadows she'd glimpsed earlier. His mouth thinned to an edge as thin as a knife blade.

"No shit." He dragged in a breath. "*But* if I'm distracted—and you are beyond distracting—that could put you in more danger than you're already facing."

Boyd turned away from Gemma, his fists clenched, every muscle, every tendon as taut as stretched cable. What the hell had he been thinking to go for her like that?

Shit. DSF had assigned him to a simple case of art forgery, but fate had set him up to protect *her*. That was his duty now. He'd failed before with tragic results. He wasn't worth the dirt on the bottoms of her sexy little shoes. He didn't deserve her trust. Or her anything.

He couldn't deny how much he wanted her, but he could control himself. Despite the pain eating his soul, he'd do his damnedest to keep her safe. His knuckles were white. He flexed his fingers, rolled his left shoulder. At this rate, he'd need to do his PT three times a day.

Calmer now, he heard her behind him. Faint clinking. She was loading the dishwasher. Carefully, almost silently. Like his mom did when she was upset. Shit, had he scared her?

"You okay, Boyd?" Her voice was thready, not liquid with southern warmth.

When he turned, she was looking at him with concern, not fear.

"Sure. Just pissed at myself for…you know. I—"

"Stop it! Don't you dare, Boyd Kirby. I was right there with you." She shut the dishwasher with a shove of her hip, then crossed her arms.

Dammit, her nipples were still peaked against her shirt. He'd nearly palmed one perfect breast, a sweet handful, when he'd forced himself to stop. He dragged his gaze up to her face.

"I can't deny the chemistry between us. I need to resist acting on it."

Her half smile morphed into a puzzled frown. "That's what you said earlier. You sure it's not something else. Or some*one* else? I'm single, but are you?"

"No, hell, I mean there's nobody. Not for a while." He hung out with colleagues some, but didn't have time for dating. Coursework took up any free time. He hadn't been able to think about any woman but Gemma since she texted him for help.

"So did you mean it when you said you being distracted could put me in more danger? The sheriff's office is on the case. What am I missing?"

"Let's go sit in the living room."

He hustled her away from the close confines of the kitchen. She kicked off her shoes and curled up in a corner of the green sectional. He took the chair opposite.

No touching.

"You're upset," he began. "I feel much the same. Detective Santiago didn't seem convinced anything suspicious is going on. Maybe what else the techs determine will move that investigation along."

"Is there anything we, um, you can do?"

"The situation's more complicated than I thought. We should talk about the main reason I came today."

Her eyes widened. "I'd totally forgotten. The railing and all. Is it about Troy?"

"Could be. I should tell you first what the Linley Harbor sergeant told me."

Her expression went from dark to darker as he explained the cops thought it was guys looking for drugs.

"Troy made some mistakes in the past, but he's a

good guy. Some drug use, weed, maybe cocaine. But that doesn't explain his disappearance."

"I agree. You may like the rest even less." He worked his jaw. Hated what he had to reveal. "When you texted me Friday night, I was in Bethesda to examine a painting. FBI Art Crime and Devlin Security are working together to stop art forgers here and in New York." He scrolled through images on his phone, then turned it toward her. "Do you recognize this portrait?"

She bent forward, tucking hair behind one ear. Peered for a moment. "Could be a Golden, Mickalene Golden. I don't recall the title."

"Yes, it's called *Cousin Louise*." He described its purchase by the party hostess and the effort to authenticate it."

As he spoke, her teeth worried her lower lip. "Is it a forgery?"

"As yet to be determined." He selected another photo and showed her. "I took this and another of sketches on the floor at Dupree's apartment."

She stared, lower lip trembling, then collapsed back against the couch cushion. "I… saw that one but didn't think about Golden. Too eerily similar not to be the *Cousin Louise* woman. The exact pose, the same intensity in the expression. How could he? He… got sucked into forgery a long time ago. He needed money then too. Not again, Troy, oh, no." Beautiful features crumpled, she hugged herself, pressed her forearms against her stomach. Started to reach for him, but pulled her hand back.

Could she be part of the scheme? Is that the reason she resisted calling the cops? The reason she wasn't at this moment fessing up to her past? He didn't want to believe it. Didn't believe it. She seemed genuinely upset about Troy's involvement.

His gut knotted. Rivera had said he could level with her, but only about Dupree and the painting. Now was not the time to confront her on her past. She might shut down. And whatever connection they had would also shut off. *Shit*.

"Boyd, about the forgery gang, have any Bellinis turned up?"

"I was coming to that. I hate telling you, but one has."

She cleared her throat. "Excuse me a minute." With deliberate steps, her head down, she traipsed to the entryway.

Was she going off to cry in private? Boyd shifted in his seat. What should he do? Less than a minute later, she returned with the bag she'd carried last night.

She removed a sketchpad from it and hugged it to her. "Before the police arrived, I leafed through the sketches and watercolors on the floor like you did. I found this." She slid out a paper and handed it to him.

A horse's head, lifted proudly. Other, smaller line drawings of the complete horse lined the edge. "You recognize this." It wasn't a question.

"Sadly, yes. It's a preliminary drawing, but the pattern of brown and white would match a painting by my grandfather of one of the nearby island's wild ponies. Is this the one that was found?"

He nodded. "*Chincoteague Guardian*, yes."

"I know I shouldn't have removed the sketch." She lifted one shoulder in a gesture of defeat. "But I needed to study it and think about how Troy could've copied it."

"And?"

"I don't know. Any images he might've found online wouldn't be large enough to copy accurately. The painting's never been sold and rarely exhibited. It's safe at Worldwide Storage."

"Maybe."

She flinched, but then shook her head. "A forgery, it must be. You and I verified the storage inventory together. I visit Worldwide once a month to make sure everything is in order."

He'd hoped Troy's sketches would force the issue of her past. No dice.

"The attempts on your life, Dupree's disappearance, the break-in, the forged paintings. All of it must be connected. Are the protocols at Worldwide the same as before? Who there has access to the storage unit?"

"Same protocols. Only the manager and only in case of emergency. As before, opening and closing require two codes, the manager's and mine or Uncle James's. I should go check right away. And call my family so they know what's goin' on."

"*We* should go check. And I suggest you not tell anyone, even your family, until we're certain about the horse painting."

"That makes sense. I have some phone calls to make about an upcoming exhibit. I can postpone anything else. Come by anytime. Or I could meet you there. I suppose I don't have to be here when the sheriff's techs do their thing."

"Maybe not, but I do. To witness their efforts, document it for my report." He rose and crossed to sit beside her. Took her icy hands in his. Yeah, touching. What the hell. "And like I said, I'm not going anywhere."

"What do you mean?"

"Gemma, somebody has tried to kill you twice. The sheriff's department might send a cruiser to park out front tomorrow, but isn't doing squat tonight. They can't protect you 24/7. I'm staying right here."

Chapter Seven

AFTER A RESTLESS night, Gemma assumed the Butterfly Pose on her yoga mat. Knees flat, she fitted her bare soles together and closed her eyes. Her instructor said this was the perfect *asana* to ground her when she felt anxious. She'd done the rest of her practice before her shower, but needed this one relaxing pose before meeting the day.

She turned her lips inward. They still tingled from Boyd's kiss. Shoot, her whole body tingled. The kiss still flowed through her body, had painted hot dreams through the night. When she could actually fall asleep. He—and that kiss—made her want more than... well, more.

She felt protected, and not just because he could use a handgun, the one she'd glimpsed when he came back inside last night. Her feeling of security came from the way he carried himself, a sense of vigilance and awareness. Sometimes she caught a look, not just in his eyes, but on his hard features, a haunted look that said he'd seen terrible things.

So yeah, the distraction of sex probably wasn't a good move. She'd been with a few guys since being a damn fool over one, but none had tempted her to throw away caution like Boyd did. She longed for the comfort and assurance of strong arms, the heat and excitement of sex. What would his bare chest look like, how would his skin feel and taste if she touched her tongue to him? But she wouldn't, couldn't. Still…

She'd given him a light blanket and a pillow and left him downstairs to sleep on the couch. During the night, she heard him moving around and talking in a low voice. But his deep tones carried. Checking the doors and windows? Talking on his phone maybe to someone at DSF? He'd gotten no more sleep that she had.

And she wouldn't be able to rest much until this insanity ended. *Chincoteague Guardian* had to be in its assigned slot at Worldwide Storage. It *had* to be there. But that meant someone, maybe Troy, likely Troy, had copied it. Somehow. If it had been forged, her sordid past would be dug up, plastered on the media again. If the painting being examined at DSF was the real one, at least it had been recovered. What if other paintings or sketches were missing? And that would mean Worldwide Storage had failed to protect the Silvio Bellini oeuvre.

Which was worse? She stretched. Not relaxed yet.

After the break-in at Troy's, she'd told Pia about Boyd. Her friend pulled enough from her to know he was a hunk and a half. She texted something vague about the storage company. Pia was a loyal friend, but Gemma didn't want to worry her. Pia could be outrageously dramatic.

The shower came on in the guest bathroom.

She smiled at the image of Boyd naked beneath the spray as she pulled on jeans and a knit top. She would change into a dress before they left. She clipped a blue braid into her hair and wove the mass into a French braid. She dashed down to the kitchen.

****

Boyd rinsed off and turned his face into the hot spray. Maybe that would drive the image of the rocket's explosion from his brain. The memory always ate at his gut, at his soul, but the nightmare brought back the taste of smoke and death, a dark shroud closing in on him. He knew why it returned last night.

Gemma. Protecting her was his new mission.

He drove a fist into his left shoulder. The surface scars were numb, but the underlying muscle felt the impact, a testament to failure. Gemma was a bright spirit who cheered him in spite of the darkness inside him. For this woman, no other option but success. He couldn't let his hunger for her obscure the mission.

When his cell rang with "Wild Thing," he stepped out of the shower. Leaving the water running, he slung a towel around his dripping body and picked up the phone from the vanity.

Great if Jo Cassidy was his official contact. They had worked together before. She was good people. "Hey, Cassidy, how's it shakin'?"

"As little as possible, Kirby. I can still take you," she said, her husky voice a half laugh. Older than him, she prided herself in staying in shape, had dropped him to the mat more than once. "Hear you got yourself in a situation with the Bellini princess."

"No shit." No point in replying to the princess jab. She'd know something was up. Probably already guessed.

"I got a memo of what's going on, mostly about the punctured brake line, but give me details on the railing thing. Lucky you were there."

"Copy that. Here's how I think this went down. Last Tuesday night, one, maybe two guys. They have a blocking device or know enough technology to disable the camera and alarm temporarily. Then they tried to remove the keypad or suss out the code. Maybe their skills failed them or somebody drove by. So they got out of there."

"Then they returned, but around back?"

"Affirmative. More out of sight. The railing seems like the original goal. Sabotage from inside would've been easier. A spotlight on the bolts might've alerted neighbors, so the second attempt was in the daytime, Friday morning when Gemma was at the gallery. She says lots of people knew she would be there. Guys with ladders, maybe even green work clothes to look like the grounds crew. They paused the security feed and the alarm again. Loosened the wall anchors, unscrewed the bolts halfway, and beat it."

"And would be long gone when Bellini leaned on the railing."

"Jesus, yes. Fortunately she procrastinated on the flower box." He shook off the nightmare of Gemma crumpled and broken on the flagstones below. Then updated Cassidy on their schedule.

"Your visit to the storage facility will support the art authenticator's finding either way. I'm your contact and Lincoln Trask is on board too. Rivera pulled him from another team for this high priority case. We can back you up in the field if necessary."

"I hope it doesn't come to that, but good to know. Thanks, Jo."

"The boss is supposed to get back to me later with the art authenticator's report. Mara Marton in Research is working on finding this Nazaroff character. So's Trask. He's also searching for Dupree."

"On both, text me A-sap."

"Will do. While you're escorting the lovely Gemma—yes, I checked on her—I'm looking into James Bellini's finances, background, etc. If he's managing the trust, he may want more out of that fortune than just the fees he earns. I'll keep you updated on that too."

"Plus he has direct access. Gemma relies on him, seems to trust him. Be a damn shame if he's stealing from the fund. Though I can't see why he'd get involved in forging Silvio's paintings. He could just steal from the fund. Check on other people in that office, maybe a bookkeeper."

"Roger that. So how's the shoulder?" Jo's usual no-nonsense tone had warmed, softened. The former U.S. Army Medic was looking out for one of her boys.

"Okay. Long as I do my exercises." He rolled said shoulder. A little stiff. As soon as he got off the phone, he'd perform the stretches. The wounds had meant no more military service, but Devlin Security deemed him fit enough for the job.

"And the rest?"

"I'm a big boy. I'll deal."

"Let me know if you want to talk."

****

Two hours later, Boyd backed out of the driveway. He noted Gemma's stiff position in the passenger seat as she strangled her bag's strap. The drive west to Worldwide Storage would take about an hour, maybe long enough the awkwardness between them would ease.

When he'd come down to breakfast, she'd beamed at him over a big mug of coffee. Artificial exuberance. But still, her smile was full of energy, lighted from within, contagious. She'd done something to her hair, a single braid with another little blue one tucked into it. Sophisticated. Damn, he wanted her. He wanted to undo that braid, bury his fingers in her hair, trace her soft lips with his tongue, gather her in his arms, and carry her up to that king bed in the master suite. Impossible.

"Coffee was my first order of business." She passed him a mug. "The Italian side of my family laments my lack of an espresso maker, but my Irish genes fight having another appliance."

"Espresso's okay, but the cups are too small." He waved away her offer of cream and sugar. Took a big gulp and wished he'd sipped.

"I didn't eat much last night, so I'm starving this morning. I'm about to make breakfast. And I reckon you'd like more than my usual poached egg and fruit. How about I add scrambled eggs and toast to bananas and berries?"

"I understood your lack of appetite, Gemma." He grinned. "And you're right about the breakfast. Unless you mix 'em all together."

She dimpled at him, and his pulse shot off like a rocket.

"I need to call the management company about getting the railing fixed."

He took a drink of coffee, more slowly this time. It would take time for his DSF team to check out family members and look for Nazaroff. And Troy Dupree. He could keep this under wraps as long as the press didn't notice the name Bellini in the sheriff's department reports.

He captured her fluttering hand. "Having that heavy wrought iron hanging out there is dangerous. The sooner that's fixed the better. You can start that ball rolling." It could also be access for another attack. "I'll check with Detective Santiago about the repairs. Yellow tape means it's still a crime scene."

Worry lines appeared in her forehead.

He longed to smooth them with his lips.

Over the food, silence hung in the air with the aroma of toasting bread. Maybe how he'd shut down things between them last night left little to say. Or reality had sunk in and she was afraid.

The sheriff's tech people arrived as he was finishing the last of the coffee. He herded them around the outside. Caught glimpses of Gemma watching them and their equipment while she was on the phone. She had reported afterward that the management company would send someone right away to assess the damage and the risk factor. Whoever had answered must've heard the fear in her voice.

Now on the drive he struggled for a way to open her up. He was no interrogator, only a security operative. With a woman who turned him on just by sitting there. Stiffly.

Silence. That was the problem. The drive would take a little over an hour. "You want some music? I mostly listen to oldies."

"Music would be nice."

He turned on the satellite radio. A Green Day song flowed around them.

When it ended, she said, "Did those tech people say anything helpful?"

He lowered the volume and snorted a laugh. "That they'd send their report to Santiago, and he'd get back to us." Rather to Gemma, but when Boyd had called the detective, he'd insisted on being included. Used DSF as leverage. Apparently the sheriff was a fan of Thomas Devlin's work and the company's policy of cooperating with law enforcement.

Her posture sank from stiff to drooping. His jaw clenched.

A green sedan and a black Ford 250 had stayed behind them the past several miles. A mile farther along, the sedan turned off but the pickup continued back there. A tail? Maybe. This was a busy area, so maybe not. He'd keep an eye on it.

"We don't have enough information yet on the why of the attacks. I can tell you what they probably did."

Gemma straightened and turned toward him. The hem of her fitted blue dress inched above her knees and showcased her legs. Long and shapely. She was small and slim, and her legs... He forced his gaze back to the highway. Adjusted his shades.

"Please," she said.

He checked the rearview mirror. The pickup stayed with them. He veered into the left lane and passed the slower van ahead. The pickup followed, staying farther back. Maybe the driver knew Boyd was testing him.

Gemma cocked her head his way. Probably wondering at his mind lapse.

"Sorry. Here's how it looks to me." He shared the same likely sequence of events he'd reported to Jo Cassidy. "What we need to focus on now is *why*."

"Why someone wants me... dead?" She uttered the last word as barely a whisper.

Chapter Eight

"CAN'T SUGARCOAT IT. Yes. And we're agreed all that's going on is connected to your grandfather's estate, especially the artworks." And maybe the investment millions. "Did his will set up everything? How does it all work? I'll keep what you share confidential."

The information was all in a file, research completed when she hired the company the last time. He asked now in case something had changed. Keeping shit from her ate at him, but he had no choice.

"Sure, if it helps. Silvio's talent and extensive body of work made him famous and very wealthy. So he set up a trust. His two sons received lump sums and stocks outright. The grandchildren and great-grands receive monthly dividends from the fund until age fifty, when that changes to a lump sum and an investment portfolio. I reckon he didn't trust us kids." Her sexy chuckle heated his blood.

He shot her a grin. Noted her fingers gripped together. "And your uncle James receives a salary for managing the trust and other finances connected to the artworks?"

"Yes, and when a painting is sold, he sends us all a cut, himself included, either as a check or a deposit into our share of the fund. It's how I was able to buy my condo. Plus I'm paid for being executive director. I'd do it for free just for that hot title."

"For the record, from what I can see, the job's a lot of work. You earn that salary."

She hadn't hesitated, even once. Still, she'd told him nothing he didn't already know.

He glanced in the rearview mirror. Other vehicles had turned off and new ones entered the highway, but the black pickup remained. It occasionally allowed another vehicle to come between them. When it pulled up closer, he got a glimpse of its license plate. Virginia.

A gas station sign rose above the trees ahead on the right. He had to try something.

"Hey, Gemma, we're a little ahead of schedule. I'm going to stop and top off the tank."

"Okay." But she looked doubtful. Maybe anxious about what she'd find today.

He pulled up to the first pump, but kept watch for the Ford pickup. It kept going past the gas station, but the driver might've looked their way.

He finished gassing up and climbed back inside.

"Boyd, what's goin' on?" She gripped his wrist before he could turn on the engine. Worry darkened her sea-green eyes. "You've been jumpy and watchin' behind us. And now this. The tank was nearly full."

He cupped his hand on her cool fingers. "You should be a detective."

"These past few days have made me suspicious of everything."

"I suspect we're being followed. I wanted to see if the truck would keep going. It did." He hauled in a deep breath. "He could've just been going the same way as us. I'll watch again."

"I'm scared, but I'm angry. I need to *do* something, to help. What can I do?"

Shit. What could he have her do that didn't put her in further danger? He stifled a groan. "Okay, watch behind us for a black pickup with Virginia plates. A Ford 250."

"I know that model. My brother Matt has one. Also black."

Those vertical lines still meant worry, but with determination. Better than fear. He fired up and pulled back onto the highway. They passed a church and a strip mall with a drugstore and a donut shop whose line snaked nearly to the highway. The mall had one entrance and exit, in the middle.

"Parking lot's packed. Good place to hide where you can watch the road. Look for the Ford."

Gemma stared out the side window. As he passed the last store, she said, "There, the pickup was behind a parked garbage truck. It's coming out of the mall now."

"Easy because traffic has thinned in this rural area." A delivery van blocked other traffic from catching up to them and their tail, almost like it was planned that way. Were these guys that good?

"I see it." Gemma scooted around, curling her left leg beneath her. She peered out the rear window.

"Earlier he stayed back too far for me to catch more than a glimpse of the driver. Try to get a look at him or the license plate number."

"Or both."

"Don't let him see you."

She sank a little lower and peered between the seat backs. "He's closing in. The man's wearing a ball cap, so all I can tell is he's big. A little closer and maybe I can read the license."

Maybe one of the guys who searched Troy Dupree's place. Boyd slowed the SUV a little. "Any luck?"

"He's closer," Gemma said. "But there's something, maybe mud, smeared across the license plate numbers." She scooted back around.

He'd rather their tail didn't follow them all the way to their destination. The exit for the Fairfax County Parkway toward Centreville was coming up soon. But he remembered something else before that. Risky, but...

A glance in the rearview mirror revealed a long line of vehicles in the left lane. When a slot opened up, he slid over in front of a white coupe and gunned it. The coupe and other cars behind it trapped the Ford pickup in the right lane. Boyd visualized the guy fuming, cussing him out. He spotted his chance up ahead.

"Gemma, sit tight and hold onto the safety handle above the door. I'm gonna try something."

Her eyes and mouth rounded but she said nothing. She wrapped her fingers around the grab handle. Clutched the seat edge with her left hand.

At the last minute, he yanked the emergency brake. The back wheels skidded, and he wrenched the wheel a hard left. The right front fender just missed taking out the Official Access Only sign.

Horns blasted.

Gemma yelped, but hung on.

Tires shrieked. The SUV shimmied and swayed. Boyd took off the brake, muscled control. The torque gave him no choice but to keep going.

Traffic heading back the way they'd come was just as heavy. The driver of a double-cab pickup in the fast lane must've seen what was going down because he jerked over to the right. Boyd kept his foot on the gas and hung a left into the opening.

More horns blasted. The maneuver probably also earned him some one-finger salutes.

He hauled in a breath and focused on the traffic flow. No cop car in the rearview mirror. No black Ford pickup either. All that mattered was keeping Gemma safe.

"Had to bang that U-ey to lose him. It worked. You okay, honey?"

She nodded and swallowed hard. "That... that was the police lane, where they watch for speeders. How..." She peeled her hand, one finger at a time, from the grab handle.

"How did I anticipate that access lane? From two years ago. Prior to moving the artwork, I scouted all possible routes and ambush points." Among other preparations.

He signaled and eased into the right lane. Felt his heart rate return to normal.

"Impressive." Her grin flashed dimples, and she squeezed his biceps. "Amazing."

She was the amazing one. She'd held tough throughout his outrageous driving, and returned to her normal cheery outlook. A woman who lived her life in color. He couldn't fail her. He wouldn't.

He grinned back. "Thanks for the opportunity to practice my evasion skills. The next exit is coming up. Not a direct route to Worldwide, but taking side roads should get us there on time."

If they found the real painting stored away, for sure the other was a forgery. He'd have to broach the foray into forgery—no, *copying*—in her past. Then neither of them would be grinning.

****

In the Worldwide reception area, Gemma greeted the guards with an upbeat, "How're you all doin' today?" The two returned the greeting with smiles and the expected replies.

She hurried to the guard beaming her a gap-toothed smile. From the start, Gemma had hit it off immediately with Dahlia, who always complimented her painted clothing. The flowers especially caught her eye. The two of them shared a quick hug.

Dahlia had the other guard sign them in while she notified the manager.

Gemma keyed her name and password into the digital ledger and stepped away so Boyd could do the same.

"Dahlia, how's your daughter? The broken arm healing okay?"

"She's doin' fine, Ms. Bellini. Ready to ditch her cast any day now. Thank you for askin'."

"This is for Poppy." She plucked the small gift-wrapped package from her tote.

Dahlia's lips rounded. "You didn't have to do that. What is it?'

She winked. "You'll have to ask Poppy. No peeking."

The two women chatted while Boyd talked with the other guard. The guard hit some keys and showed him the monitor. Boyd nodded, seemingly satisfied, and thanked him.

He prowled the entry space before returning to the desk. Her sentinel, alert, as usual. A frisson of awareness shivered through her.

A few moments later, the manager strode down the hall. He'd come on to her before, so she had another reason to appreciate Boyd's presence. The man advanced, in charcoal pants and an ice-blue dress shirt. His eyebrows arched, and he puffed out his barrel chest when his gaze lit on Boyd.

She glanced at Boyd. He held his body rigid, his eyes glassy and riveted on the man. Neither guard seemed to notice.

Mystified, she fabricated a smile. "Mr. Overton, how're you?"

"Excellent! Good to see you both again." He extended a hand to Gemma. She took it, hoping for a quick getaway, but he didn't let go until she tugged.

Boyd flattened a palm on the reception desk. When she introduced him, his gaze sharpened and he nodded. He then shook hands with the manager.

Overton cleared his throat and led the way to the Bellini storage unit. He left them at the door.

Once the door was secured behind them, Boyd said, "You painted something for the girl."

"She broke her forearm in a bicycle accident. She's a competitive tennis player—or will be again soon—so I painted red poppies on a white tennis visor."

His hearty laugh reverberated around the cavernous chamber. "Perfect. That was a generous thing to do, Gemma."

The admiration and affection in his tone warmed more than one part of her. The moment was lost to ask about his momentary blanking, so she shrugged it off. In here she faced more immediate matters.

She crossed to the vertical racks containing the larger paintings. The temperature in this climate-controlled environment was cooler and drier than outside, a comfortable low seventies and low humidity. Regardless, beads of sweat trickled between her breasts. *Stupid nerves.*

The click of her heels echoed against all the metal. Each rack slid out on a track that held a painting. Most were unframed, but not the one she needed to examine.

"Why was this one never sold?" Boyd asked softly behind her.

"He never put up any of the beach pictures for sale, although they went out on loan to museums. Silvio didn't take criticism well. A few critics called his beach series sentimental and fit only for the mass-market print trade. A possible reason."

She stood at the numbered slot designated for *Chincoteague Guardian* and reached for the handle with a trembling hand.

"Let me get that." Boyd slid out the rack and stepped back.

"Oh, yes, it's here, thank God," she breathed.

"Make sure it's the real one."

She gasped. "You think they could've switched it with the forgery?" She reached for him. When he clasped her hand, she held onto the warm lifeline.

"If thieves could steal it, they could switch it. To delay detection of the theft. But that would require not only forgery, but a sophisticated criminal organization."

Too horrible to contemplate.

He released her hand, and she peered through the magnifying glass she'd added to her tote at the last minute. She examined the detail, the brush strokes, the shades of color, and finally, her grandfather's scrawl. *S. Bellini.*

Stretching, she rolled the tightness from her neck. "Boyd, this is the real one. The broad brushstrokes. How alive the horse appears. Egg tempera has an intrinsic radiance. The sunlight on the horse's mane, on the sand. They seem to glow. Silvio didn't work much in egg tempera, only for his beach paintings. Because of the radiant quality, I think."

He strode to her side.

"I see that. Some of my prep for examining the Golden painting included the qualities of egg tempera. Something struck me as off in the copy. It took me a while to figure out what. Instead of radiance like in this painting, it had the plastic look of acrylic paint."

It warmed her insides that Boyd appreciated that. "But otherwise, it seemed authentic?"

"To my untrained eye, yes." He jerked a nod toward the canvas. "I haven't seen the forgery of this one. *Chincoteague Guardian* has more detail to copy, of both the subject and the island in the background."

"I can't imagine how that could be accomplished except by sitting with it for days, weeks." Like she'd done years ago as a student. *Forger*, a little voice whispered.

"You okay?"

She swallowed hard and banished the accuser. "Yes, just thinking. Silvio kept detailed notes on every work. Measurements and descriptions, paint formulas and thicknesses, you name it, he recorded it." She headed for the cabinets on the other side of the room. "All his original notes in his handwriting, are in those drawers, along with multiple photographs of each work. *I hope*." Her throat closed and she stood there, just staring at the cabinet.

"Easy, Gemma, check before you panic."

His warm, rough palm on her clammy skin and his darkly smooth tone got her moving. She took a seat at the pull-out desk by the cabinet.

Chapter Nine

AFTER SLIPPING ON the white cotton gloves she'd brought, Gemma looked through each drawer. Many minutes later she closed the last one and tugged off her gloves.

"Everything is here, undisturbed. Including the notes on *Chincoteague Guardian*. The photos are on the bottom of each drawer. All still there too. No one has looked through these, let alone removed any."

"Or photographed them?"

She shook her head. "The protective tissue pages separating items are so delicate, even my careful examination crumpled them."

A few minutes later they were escorted out. The overhead sun and summer heat smothered Gemma, but didn't dissipate the cold inside her. While Boyd peered at his vehicle's undercarriage and in the wheel wells, she fretted, shifting from foot to foot. She had to tell him, and she had to tell him now, before they drove away. Before she lost her nerve.

He deemed everything safe and helped her in. Starting the engine kicked on the air conditioning. Maybe the cool air would clear her head.

"While you were signing out," he said, "I got a text from a colleague at DSF. The authenticator verified what you and I already know. The confiscated painting is a forgery."

"Boyd." She knitted her fingers together and stared at her white knuckles. "Because of the horse sketches, we both suspect Troy. But there's more. When… when Troy and I were at the Corcoran, we did some copying in museums. Copying of well-known artists' paintings."

"Gemma—"

"No, don't. Just listen. Please." She looked up and found only gentle concern in his gray gaze. When he remained silent, she went on, forcing a breath past the tightness in her chest. "An artist in residence—his name was Morgan Nazaroff—there for the semester saw talent in Troy and me, he said, and copying would help me learn different styles. The copying… turned out to be a scheme. He sold the paintings we did as authentic. He cheated people out of a *lot* of money. Troy got money from the plot. He was on scholarship and worked part time. If I hadn't persuaded Nazaroff to include him, he wouldn't have…" She bit her lower lip, trying to even her voice.

"I didn't know what they were doing. I just was painting and enjoying the learning." And the attention. The stomach-churning, skin-crawling part she wouldn't reveal. "When I found out, it shocked me no end. I reported it to my advisor. After that, things got crazy. Eventually Nazaroff and Troy got prison terms. The whole debacle was a scandal for my family, but—"

"Enough, Gemma." His warm hands enveloped hers. "I know this. Standard operating procedure, the company conducted background checks on everyone connected to Silvio Bellini before the move to Worldwide. I know weren't a forger. You were a dedicated student artist, that's all. Hell, I should've told you. I didn't because I figured it would upset you that I knew. Thank you for sharing this. I can only imagine how betrayed you felt."

He couldn't possibly know how she felt. More than betrayed, hide under the covers ashamed and humiliated. Of course Devlin Security had researched her. An easy job. The information was on the internet for anyone to find.

And she should've known better, known not to trust. Why Boyd held back didn't matter. Or did it? Was he just being kind? Or was she fooling herself—again?

She lifted her gaze to his. Slid her hands from his and straightened her shoulders. "Just as well it's out in the open. I'd like to see the forgery of *Chincoteague Guardian*. Now."

****

"Fool! You were seen. You let him sucker you." Morgan Nazaroff lobbed his paint brush at his employee. This wasn't the first time Hubik had screwed up. Moving on and leaving him and the other cretins behind couldn't come soon enough.

"He knew the highway better than I did, boss. Like he knew the cop turnout was there." Hubik bent and picked up the brush. He set it on the small table beside the easel but made no comment on the marine-blue paint smeared across his drab t-shirt. Damn right.

"Enough excuses. Is that all you have?" Nazaroff wiped his hands on a stained cloth.

Hubik swiped a palm across his black mustache, yanked off his golf cap. If anyone looked less like a golfer, it was this hulk. "Obvious they were headed to Worldwide Storage. I didn't go there to check. That place has more fucking cameras and security than the

Pentagon."

"And after?"

Hubik sucked in his cheeks. His gaze lowered to his running shoes. "I didn't—"

"Get out of my sight. Next attempt to eliminate her, the three of you had better not fail." He glared at the man. "I don't care if Lover Boy goes too."

As Hubik left, the others in the studio remained silent, continuing their work. Thank God. At least some of his people were competent. Even though tethered, whether literally or figuratively.

So Gemma went to check the horse painting. She couldn't be sure Dupree painted it. Regardless, she'd suspect her old mentor of the worst. Or the best, in this case. Which it would be once he'd amassed enough in his accounts. Even if she connected the dots to him, what could she do? He was well hidden. And his so-called partner was well covered.

Both Hubik and his buddy had been booted from security companies overseas for extortion. Marshak's electronics skills came in handy. Nazaroff knew better than to trust either man.

He went back to work. He needed to finish this painting by tomorrow. It would need time to dry before he could apply his technique to make it look less than recently painted. He should've allowed more time for that on the horse painting.

"I found the guy you call Lover Boy," Marshak said behind him. "My buddy in motor vehicles ran his license plate." The big man consulted his phone screen. "Name's Boyd Kirby. His LinkedIn account says he works for Devlin Security Force in Crystal City. They're—"

"I'm quite aware of them. His turning up at this

moment can't be a coincidence." If Gemma hired them, she was smarter than she used to be.

This Kirby and Gemma working together could cause him trouble, halting this last stage of his operation. The local police couldn't be certain the attempts weren't merely accidents. The delay was making his partner nervous about detection. He had to work faster.

Nazaroff swiveled on his stool, better to address another of his companions. Detection could more likely come from another quarter.

As if she'd felt his inspection as lasers, Lucia Sherbourne lifted her gaze from her computer keyboard. It was her fault *Chincoteague Guardian* had been confiscated.

"You fucked up, Lucia. By now, that painting must be in the hands of the FBI. They know. If they find us or even cause us to shut down, it will be your fault. What have you done with your phone after the Nicholl woman called you to complain?"

She tossed back her coiffed blonde hair and straightened her posture. "It's gone. Destroyed. I have a new phone with a new number. I'm researching new marks."

"No more sales in this area. Word might get out among the level of society you need to ingratiate yourself with." He snorted. "The morons know nothing about art but think they do."

She folded her arms. "It was a fluke somebody questioned that painting. I have more fish on my line eager for Bellinis."

He threw down the cloth and stomped to her desk. "*No*. It's too dangerous. Go farther away. Charlottesville, Richmond, Virginia Beach, up the I-95 corridor to Baltimore. You can find more suckers there, rich assholes who know nothing."

Usually his height and voice intimidated her, but instead, she rose to her feet. Her beauty, albeit a little tired at her age, and patrician attitude might work on their marks, but not on him.

Heavy footsteps behind him announced the return of Hubik. Lucia gave both men a nervous glance as they crossed the room and took positions on either side of her.

"If you have me driving all over creation, I'll have to establish myself in those places. Acquainting myself with galleries takes time. And money. I've made some big sales for you, lots of money. You need me as the face of this operation. From here on out, I'll need a bigger cut of the profits." She held her head high, held his gaze, but her breathing went shallow.

"I'll front you the expenses, as I do now. Then I'll see how you manage out of my sight. Forget taking your time. You'll have to work fast." He never bargained. It didn't hurt to remind the others watching this exchange who was in charge.

Temper flared in her blue eyes, and she opened her mouth. Closed it again. Nodded. Sank onto the chair again. "Understood. One of my customers is ready to make a deal. Surely I can—"

He grabbed her upper arms and yanked her upright. She emitted a small shriek. He shook her until she met his eyes. "Did I not make myself clear? Or do you need to be reminded that the Georgia authorities are still looking for you—*Letty*?"

She shrank into herself. Looked away.

Satisfied, he strode around her to his hired muscle. "And you two, waste no more time. Get rid of Gemma

Bellini. Kirby too. Once he's out of the picture—" he grinned inwardly at his joke "—Devlin Security will be in too much disarray to catch up to us. Do not fail this time."

****

Boyd entered the operatives' common office space and sank down at his desk. Amid the low hum of voices, the aromas of coffee and somebody's pizza filtered through the room. He leaned his elbows on the desk and lowered his face into his hands. Dammit, he'd had another episode. Something in the Worldwide Storage manager's stride or his eyebrows made the dark features of Chaos mask his. Bloody. Accusing. Dead. He lifted his head, shook off the image. He could fucking handle it. Had to. His ghosts weren't going away.

He'd left Gemma in a small conference room to examine the forgery. She immediately charmed Mara Marton of Research and Jo Cassidy. No charm for him today.

He'd wanted to hug her because of that gift for the security guard's daughter. Made himself maintain distance and only compliment her. And then he hurt her, lost her trust. Maybe more. His gut had flash-frozen from the withering frost in Gemma's eyes when he revealed he knew about her past. Should've kept his damn mouth shut. After a fast-food lunch more stilted and silent than breakfast, he'd received a text from Cassidy saying to bring her.

Lincoln Trask ambled over and offered a bottle of water.

Boyd slugged down half the bottle. "Thanks, man. You have anything for me?"

"You're sure Ms. Bellini's not involved in the

forging?" The lanky operative, long arms folded across his chest, held a tablet. Results maybe?

"At this point, I'm more certain of that than I am of my own name. Anything to put us on the trail of these assholes?" The longer this threat went on, the more danger to her. *Shit.*

"Okay, then." Trask's posture relaxed and he hiked one hip onto the adjacent desk. He consulted the tablet's screen. "Here's what else we have. And it ain't much. After serving six years of his eight-year sentence, Morgan Nazaroff hung out a year or two in the Soho section of NYC before coming to Arlington. He worked in a gallery, along with flogging his own work. Without success. Then he disappeared."

"Let me guess. He vanished about the time forged paintings started popping up in the Maryland, Virginia, D.C. area."

"Close. Our Art Crime contact is Special Agent Yasmine Irwin. I've worked with her before, professional, not heavy handed. Forged paintings of dead artists 'came to the team's attention,' as she put it, while our boy was still in Soho. No Bellinis until he came south."

"That's it? No leads?"

"Gallery owner just shrugged when Cassidy asked where he might've gone. We can't find Nazaroff anywhere. No current address. No hits on feelers from Research or IT. No active accounts in his name. No passport. No activity on his Social. No phone. Probably using a burner. Nothing in his name. Anonymous."

"Using a fake identity. More forgery? What about street or security cameras?" More than a trusted operative, Trask was a cyber expert who in college had dabbled in hacking. If anybody could get into the secure eyes of the D.C. area, he was the guy. The company didn't skirt the law much. In this case it might be their only chance. And faster than Art Crime obtaining warrants.

Trask rubbed his shaved dome. "I tried, man. Still nothing." He handed Boyd the folder. "The provenance the blonde provided the buyer of *Chincoteague Guardian*, and Nazaroff's most recent photo. Taken when he set himself up in Arlington. Damn distinctive looking. If he was out in public anywhere inside or outside the Beltway, my software would've picked him out. Might have to range wider."

"I think he's in the area." Boyd had seen his prison photo. In that shot, beneath his bushy black eyebrows, he'd glared at the camera as if itching to strangle the photographer.

He studied this artfully posed image. Still the dramatic eyebrows, but with threads of white in the black. Brush-cut hair also going silver. Wide, unsmiling mouth. His expression that of a predator. Deep-set eyes, prominent bones in a long head. In his black tee—maybe silk—he looked sinewy and strong in his six-two frame. A few years out of prison, he was now fifty-three. Twenty years older than Gemma. Con man, probably narcissistic, could turn on the charisma.

Boyd's gut clenched. Maybe Gemma had shut him out for more than one reason.

"Yeah." Trask consulted his phone screen. "Buyer gave Cassidy and me a description of the woman who sold her the Bellini painting. Seemed to know art and artists, acted professional. Tall blonde, elegant, late forties or early fifties, slight Brit accent. Same description Mrs. Nicholl gave about the seller of the Golden."

"Definitely not Gemma."

"No shit. Suckered Mrs. Nicholl at a D.C. gallery, made like she was a friend of the owner. Fed her a line about the family wanting to sell this one privately. We're sending a sketch artist."

"What about the money? Bank transfer, check, those can be traced."

"Mrs. Nicholl paid cash. So did the other buyer."

"Shit. Money can be laundered through legitimate businesses, but if it's Nazaroff, he's hiding. He wouldn't want to take a risk involving locals. He must have a bank account somewhere. Or accounts. Banks would have to report that big a deposit to regulators."

"We'd need evidence before the FBI would go for obtaining a warrant to look at banks."

"And evidence is in short supply."

He and Trask talked for a few more minutes about the so-called provenance. Then Boyd placed a call to Detective Santiago. Probably more no news or bad news.

Chapter Ten

GEMMA LOWERED HER magnifying glass. She needed a minute before sharing her thoughts with the two DSF people talking quietly on the other side of the room.

She'd so hoped this painting would turn out to be a high-quality giclée print on canvas. They often looked real. But no, it was acrylic paint, and with broad brushstrokes like the original. Just as Boyd said. Her heart squeezed. How did they get so much right, that even she had trouble finding flaws?

The door opened and Boyd entered the room. The other women greeted him warmly.

Jo Cassidy stood and crossed to him. "Just got a text about a new package." She turned to Gemma. "Mara can answer any questions you have, Gemma. I'll be back in a few."

Once she'd left, Boyd took the other seat beside the painting. "How you holding up?"

He could probably tell she wasn't. "Everything you said about this copy is correct. It's nearly perfect. Troy did this. He's better at copying than at creating his own. It breaks my heart."

She beckoned to Mara Marton. A striking woman with silky dark hair and sharp cheekbones, she was high up in the Research Department. Mara pulled her chair closer.

"Mara pointed out tiny details of the painting that

don't seem authentic. I agree, especially this one. The artist's signature is indistinguishable from Silvio's real one." She held the magnifying glass over the swirling *S*. "Except for this. There, in the lower curl, a tiny lower-case *t*. Troy's tell. It was in all the copying he did years ago. He's never divulged whether it meant pride in his work or a sop to his guilt for the forgery money."

"I checked with the authenticator on the *Cousin Louise*," Mara said. "She found the same little *t*."

"I'm sorry about your friend," Boyd said, sympathy in his gaze. He reached for her shoulder but returned his hand to his knee before touching her.

Maybe she'd overreacted to his revelation. His reasons for keeping silent were reasonable. Maybe… "Thanks. Given Troy's in deep here, I'm certain it's Nazaroff he's working for."

"It looks that way. The others on this case have been looking for both him and Nazaroff. No trace of either one. I suspect Nazaroff learned a thing or two in prison about con games and vanishing from sight." He shared with her what he'd learned from his colleague.

"A tall middle-aged blonde. That fits lots of women, even some of my mother's friends, none of whom would have any idea how to carry off such a crime."

Boyd and Mara chuckled, and Gemma's mood lightened a little.

"We're hoping for more soon," he said. "And I have the so-called provenance the seller created to close the sale. See what you can make of these papers. Mara has examined them."

Gemma inspected the first document. "This is typical of what should be included in provenance. A printout of the catalog image and description, probably from WorldCAT."

"A library resource that lists basic facts about artists and their artworks," Mara Marton said to Boyd.

"This one says, correctly, 'unsold.' Next is the receipt with the price paid." She blinked at the number. "$842,000. An amazing amount for a private sale. Still, half as much as I'd expect to get for the real one, although critics don't care for Silvio's beach paintings."

Boyd rubbed his nape. "Yeah, Mrs. Nicholl's husband had some choice words about the cost and for his wife when my boss and two FBI agents visited him."

"These documents are not enough for a knowledgeable collector," Mara Marton said, "but that's not who these scammers are targeting. To the uneducated eye, they seem authentic."

The third paper made Gemma's jaw drop. A letter attesting to the painting's authenticity and the family's willingness to sell, signed by the artist's agent.

"No, this is impossible. It looks like his stationery and his signature, but John Fitzhugh simply cannot be involved. How did they get this?"

Before anyone could answer, Jo Cassidy returned and shut the door behind her. "We have another Bellini copy. This is a small black-and-white sketch behind glass." She laid it beside the easel holding the painting.

Gemma's mind and stomach whirled. Another? This was too much.

"Do you recognize it?" Jo said.

Gemma made herself focus. Moments later, she lifted her gaze from the sketch. "It's one of a few preliminary sketches for a painting Silvio never completed. Signed. He signed everything. Troy didn't create this copy. And it's never been shown, so a listing wouldn't be in WorldCAT." Only in the private catalog she'd checked that morning.

She slumped in the chair. "How is this possible? Are more fake Bellinis out there?"

****

"So that's all we have on Nazaroff." Boyd eyed Gemma in the passenger seat. "I wish to hell I knew where he is." If only he had fucking Nazaroff bound to a chair and eager to confess all.

She didn't reply at first. Still had that shell-shocked expression in her beautiful eyes. No wonder, given all the crap coming at her.

Nobody in the room had answered her question about more Bellini forgeries.

Her tone of voice had twisted his guts into pretzels. He would share all the facts he had in hopes of earning back a little of her lost trust. He needed that to do his job, and no shit, he just plain wanted her to trust him. Hell, he wanted more than her trust, but he'd take what he could get. He cared more than he should, more than was safe. For her.

"I hope these are the only two forgeries. At this point, we simply don't know." They were heading south on Route One from Crystal City. "Detective Santiago didn't have much for me either. A neighbor walking a dog last Tuesday evening thought she saw somebody at your door, but when she came back by, nobody was there. On Friday, a grounds crew was on the property, but not behind your place, and nobody saw anything behind the building."

"So basically *niente*. Nothing." She twisted in her seat to face him and gripped his knee. He nearly jumped but caught himself and shot a glance her way. Her eyes were flinty above red-highlighted creamy cheeks. "Dammit, we have to do something. *I* have to do something."

"We will, and *you* will, Gemma." She was fighting back. And touching him again, both good signs. He covered her hand with his. "Start with this. The guard at Worldwide Storage said only you have accessed the unit. He showed me the records. Nobody else. Not even your uncle."

"I saw you talking to him but then I forgot to ask." She slid her hand away, leaving the sensation of her touch behind. "I'm certain no one examined the hard copies in the drawers. *Chincoteague Guardian* has been on exhibit, so they could've photographed it. But neither that nor researching it on WorldCAT would lead to such a near perfect replica." Her breath hitched. "But the sketch. Silvio never exhibited his trials and errors, his preliminary drawings and plans. And I sure haven't. That sketch is *not* in WorldCAT." She worried her lower lip with her teeth.

He turned west off the highway.

"Wait! Where are you going?" Gemma sat up straight, alarm in her voice. "Are we being followed again?"

"Relax. Our only tail is another operative making sure we don't have unwanted company. All clear." He indicated his Bluetooth headset. "I need some clothes and my laptop from my apartment. Okay?"

"Of course, sure. All you have is a gym bag." She relaxed and looked out the windows.

These were the working-class neighborhoods of Alexandria. Apartment buildings, markets, ethnic restaurants. But she smiled at children riding bikes down the sidewalks and families in a small green park.

While she was distracted, he asked, "If nobody searched the records, how did the forgers do it?" He had a guess, but better if she trusted him enough to spill.

Bleak green eyes met his before her expression firmed to resolute. "The entire catalog—sold and unsold, the specs, Silvio's notes, photos, everything in the drawers at Worldwide—is all digitized. *Everything*. And stored on a secure server at GuardStor.com."

He'd heard of the company, one of the safest, most advanced. "Who has access?"

"Only the immediate Bellini family. Dad—his name's Victor—Uncle James, and my sister. And me. I'm the web mistress, I suppose you'd say. Matt and Joe, my brothers, didn't want the responsibility. They've never been involved."

More people than he'd hoped. "What about personnel in James Bellini's office?"

"Doubtful. I was in his office once when we needed to look up something. He sent his admin out before he logged in. He used his personal laptop, not the company one."

They discussed more possibilities as he negotiated the traffic into his neighborhood. Everybody used the same login and password, she explained. Tracking logins would be helpful now but not a feature they'd deemed necessary at the outset.

"Seems those digital files are the source. Before you ask any of the family, how about this? You change the login and password but tell nobody. We wait, see if that shakes things up."

A long pause. "Okay. But I can't until after Friday evening's museum opening. Maybe later. If there's a sale, Uncle James might need access. I'll wait to tell them about the attempts on my life too. Get it all out at once." Her shoulders moved in a small shudder.

She'd told him about the event. The Washington Cultural Museum was partnering with Maurice Fine Arts, the gallery that gave Silvio Bellini the boost to national prominence. The paintings had already been shipped from Worldwide Storage to the museum, which he knew had excellent security. Several of the stored paintings would hang beside works by peers like Georgia O'Keefe, William Thon, and Andrew Wyeth. The showing was a big fucking deal.

"In the meantime, contact GuardStor. Ask them to check if the files have been hacked."

"Shoot, I never thought about hacking!" She took out her phone. "Calling now."

He listened while she provided verification and all sorts of codes, then explained the situation to their IT guy.

"One of their vice presidents," she said once she'd disconnected. "He'll put a team on it right away and get back to me."

"Let's hope that's the answer." Then they could leave the family alone and focus only on Nazaroff and company.

"I need to go to the museum tomorrow afternoon to check on last minute details. Are you going with me?"

"Absolutely." He turned into the driveway and rolled to a stop in his assigned parking spot in back, jerked a nod toward the white-painted brick building. "Not fancy, but it's well-maintained, safe, and convenient. Easy commute to work and the university. I can run in the big park a few blocks north. Sometimes buddies come run with me. You met one today, Jo Cassidy."

Shit. He was running off at the mouth, like he had to apologize. But that was on him, not on Gemma. She was no snob. He started to reach for the door handle, but stopped at the stricken expression on her face. "What is it?"

"I hate being cooped up like this. I can't take bike rides or go to my spinning class. I just keep imagining horrible ways they can attack me."

Next she'd probably ask about buying a gun or shooting lessons. Bad idea. "I'm not getting my regular exercise either."

She brightened. "Tomorrow morning is the spinning class. You could come as my guest."

"Safe enough. Sounds like a plan. Then I could teach you some self-defense moves."

"Terrific. At last I'll feel I'm doing *something*." Her shoulders bunched, she waved a hand, let it drop. "Now that all this is being investigated, will they, meaning Nazaroff, stop trying to kill me?" She gripped her hands together in her lap.

Terrified, and who could blame her. Damn, keeping her safe was his mission. But he hated seeing her so scared. Some self-defense moves would empower her, give her some control. He had another idea. He'd text Jo about finding the right device for him.

"Maybe, but we still don't know the reason for the attempts on your life or how they connect to the forgeries. We can't be sure of anything. I will *not* let down my guard, Gemma. I *will* protect you with my life."

He wrapped a hand around hers and held on until

she met his eyes.

When she did, her gaze held trust but more. Something flared, heat shimmered in the air between them. She lifted her free hand to his jaw. He breathed in the scent of her hair. His skin fizzed at her touch, and he leaned into her soft palm, lured by her tender mouth, full and lush.

He bent his head, aching to taste her again. And more.

"I know you will, Boyd, but I hope and pray it won't come to that."

Chapter Eleven

GEMMA SIPPED THE beer Boyd poured her as she strolled around his small apartment. He was in the bedroom gathering clothing into a bag. It was getting late, so he'd ordered delivery from the local Thai restaurant.

Why had he pulled away when it was clear what they both wanted? She'd needed his mouth on hers and his embrace, as much for comfort as for pleasure. Had her words doused the flame? Or was it his concern about being distracted? He could be right, for them both. Yet something about him kept her on simmer, and he seemed to feel the same pull. Did he feel their being together would compromise his integrity? A DSF operative with a client? An honorable man worthy of respect, although she needed to be careful. Something more than duty was holding him back.

Something to do with the darkness she sensed in him. She needed to know more about him. And about his momentary zoning out at Worldwide.

The man's surroundings could yield a clue or two.

His space was spartan, but neat. No surprise there. His king-size bed nearly filled the bedroom. Picturing being in that bed with him sparked shimmers within her. On a sigh, she moved on. The spare room contained weights and an elliptical machine. How he stayed so buff. Heat radiated inside as she pictured muscles bulging with each lift. Dammit, her imagination kept turning her on. *Stop it.*

"Boyd," she called, "I have weights in my garage if you want to work out. I use them twice a week. They're old, belonged to Joe when he was in high school."

"Old is still heavy. I'll take you up on that."

In the living room, a merlot sofa and recliner. TV and game device. On the eggshell wall a colorful rug of Middle Eastern design matching the sofa. Maybe from his tour of duty. No real decorating elsewhere. She trailed a finger over the pad where his laptop would live on the small desk. Beside it, bookshelves held textbooks, history books, paperback thrillers.

And framed photographs. *Here we go.* She was studying them when he came out and dropped a duffel and a hanging bag on the sofa.

"Your laptop's at my house. You have homework? Studies?"

"Nope. Not taking courses this summer. I need the computer for this gig."

So he thought of her as a gig. Safer that way, but she didn't have to like it.

"This must've been taken years ago, but I recognize you." She pointed to the portrait of a man and woman and two young teenage boys. Even then, Boyd had a solid build, clearly inherited from his dad.

He joined her, and his heat at her side lured her to lean into him. *Nope, stay put.*

"Dad was a sergeant in the Boston Police Department."

"Was?"

"He was killed in the line of duty." Pride and no little

emotion colored his voice. His mouth thinned to a taut line.

"I'm so sorry. Do you mind telling me more?"

"Drug bust. Big operation. Officers and detectives were there in force. Dad was protecting his partner from one asshole when a second shooter fired on him from the side. Tactical gear wasn't enough to save him. Both got life. I heard they got killed in prison."

"How old were you and your brother?"

"Sixteen. Dave was fourteen."

"Must've hit you all pretty hard."

"Tough days for all of us and family on both sides. Mom took a year off from teaching—she teaches elementary art—so she could pull things together. She didn't want either of us boys to go into law enforcement. After high school, I joined the army. Made Rangers and worked my way up to first sergeant."

"And now you're a protector like your dad."

His shoulders slumped and he waved off her praise. "Hardly, but thanks. Mom's not as worried about us as she used to be."

"And Dave, not law enforcement?"

He barked a laugh. "He's a state trooper. Mom eased up on him after he and his wife gave her a grandson. They have another baby on the way. Girl this time."

The affection in his gaze and in his voice made her smile. She edged over to the next photograph. "And here you are with your Ranger buddies. Judging from your combat gear and the dusty tan landscape, in Afghanistan?"

"Damn good Disney version of it, isn't it? Fooled you."

Neither by that nor by his forced humor, she slanted

94

him an arch look and pursed her lips.

"Okay, that was lame. Yes, my team. The best. As first sergeant, I was in command. A first sergeant usually commands a larger unit, but we were spread thin and had to divvy up."

She watched him. His mouth worked, and a muscle jumped in his jaw. She wanted to ask more but he finally spoke again.

"That's Hugo Lopez on the left, then Rudy Romano."

"An Italian. No wonder they were a great team." She looped her arm with his.

"Damn, so that's why." He knocked the heel of his free hand against his forehead, then squeezed her arm against him.

"Go on. Maybe there's an Irishman too." She jabbed her elbow into his side.

"Sorry." He chuckled, but turned solemn once he returned to the photo. "On my other side are Jamal Santos, Simon Hawkins, and Deion Ritter." He recited the names in an even tone, but the roughness in his voice betrayed his emotion.

"Looks like you all were close." Each had one arm on his rifle, and the other on the next guy's shoulder.

"That kind of recon duty tends to make you tight. Eat together, sleep together, face danger together." He firmed his jaw.

"And this one. A separate photo of these last two goofing around." Their helmets were off and each held devil fingers behind the other's head. "I've read that special ops teammates often have nicknames. Your team too?"

"Nicknames were partly for security and partly for

camaraderie. Hawkins was Hawk, and Ritter was Chaos. And we took a *lot* of photos." He rolled his shoulders and rubbed his nape. Did he feel awkward talking about this? "Off duty, beyond taking care of equipment, not much to do, you know."

"And your nickname?"

"Scorpion." Color crept up his cheeks beneath the scruff.

"Why scorpion?"

"It's about my being the marksman of the team. Scorpion stings but never gets stung."

Gemma wanted to tease him about it, but his tight expression stopped her. "Are they all still in the service?"

"Some are, some aren't."

"Hawk and Chaos?"

"They didn't make it out."

"Oh, Boyd, I'm—"

Two hard knocks sounded on the door. "A youthful voice muffled by the wood said, "Reed Ave Thai delivery."

"Food's here." Boyd hustled to the door.

Saved by the bell. Or the knock. Ooh-kay. A tough loss he didn't want to talk about. She knew what that was like. *Looks like I touched a nerve.*

****

The next morning, Boyd accompanied Gemma to her fitness center. Seeing her in exercise leggings and a skin-tight tee, he barely prevented himself from drooling. A good workout should dial down his hots for her. The place was a nice facility, a little south of the Beltway. After they changed, he followed Gemma through the gym proper to the rear of the building and a classroom half filled with stationary bikes.

When a couple of women eyed him surreptitiously, he asked, "Were they expecting some other guy to show up with you?"

She winked at him. "No guy at all. They're checking you out."

"Should I flex my muscles for them?"

"Dare you."

All he could do was grin.

The instructor, a hard-muscled thirty-something redhead, started them off with climbing a gentle hill, but then the woman got serious with sprints and steeper, muscle-torching climbs. He hadn't done this in a long time. Gemma mopped her forehead and neck during the slowdowns, but otherwise pumped the pedals as hard and fast as the instructor.

His lungs and quads were burning when the class ended. He downed the last drops of his water.

The sweat glistening on her skin made him want to taste it. Her. "Good workout. How are you doing?"

"Workout is right. No wonder you have killer legs and can eat all the pasta you want. Maybe weights and jogging aren't enough conditioning. I might take this up."

She high-fived him. Her burst of laughter flashed more heat through him. Maybe he'd turn the shower temp to arctic.

Afterward they picked up her repaired car, and he followed her home. She patted the hood and practically danced around the hybrid sedan, elated to have her wheels back. The little braid, orange today, in her dark hair danced with her. When he insisted on chauffeuring her until the danger was over, she deflated like a marionette.

"My car's too small for you anyway." Perked up again. Typical Gemma.

He shadowed her that afternoon as she charmed her way through last minute details for the Cultural Museum's opening reception. While checking off her list, she chatted with the manager and guards as old friends, asking after spouses and children. Fascinating how she connected with all kinds of people.

The condo association management company had arranged for the broken balcony railing to be removed and ordered a replacement. He figured weeks, but didn't pop her optimism balloon that the installation would magically happen in days.

He left her locked in his ride until he'd checked everywhere, inside and out. When he returned for her, he found her hugging herself, her kissable mouth tight.

Jo had dropped off the package he requested. Something for her and some smaller items for him. A failsafe.

Her self-defense work started tomorrow. Oh man, that would mean his arms around her.

Chapter Twelve

HE MADE THE evening low key, especially since going out after dark might invite trouble, and a way to reassure her. He cooked a vegetable and rice recipe he'd picked up in Afghanistan. Cooking, eating, chatting about ordinary things, doing the cleanup together, like a—no, he refused to even think the words.

"I played softball in high school," she told him as she wiped down the counter. "I was too small, but it was fun. I love baseball. Go, Nats!"

"Baseball? Really?" He nearly dropped the skillet he was drying.

"Sure. My brothers took me to games every summer as far back as I can remember."

"Too bad you root for the wrong team. Go, Red Sox!"

She flipped dish suds at him.

After they argued about their teams and their chances this season, over coffee on the sofa, she asked him more about Afghanistan. Not about his dead teammates, so he could handle this.

"I'll tell you about one operation. We partnered with Afghan commandos in a raid. We targeted the leader of a militant cell in the mountains bordering Iraq."

She leaned toward him. "Militants. You mean ISIS?"

"ISIS along with some Taliban." He shared only generalities about the raid. But he could still picture the close quarters fighting, hear and feel the intense barrage as enemy fire came at them from three hundred sixty degrees. "Some of the Afghan forces were wounded. Two died later. My team escaped injury. They were the best."

She scooted her chair closer, placed her hand on his where it was clenched on his thigh. Her green gaze was liquid with concern. "Was it always like that, what you did every day?"

He shook his head. "Most of the time we did recon, meaning we reconnoitered an area to make sure militants evicted by regular army had stayed away so the villagers could return." He didn't tell her that could be even riskier.

****

The next morning, Gemma donned a tee, leggings, and running shoes. Boyd's promise of self-defense lessons energized her.

Dammit, she was tired of being afraid, tired of never knowing when the bastard would attack again. Not that she could dispense with Boyd's protection, nor did she even want to, but she needed some way to fight back. Or at least feel she had a chance.

At breakfast, she found a keychain with a heart-shaped fob on the breakfast bar. "What's this, a love token?"

"Early for Valentine's Day." Deadpan, he set a mug of coffee in front of her.

"Good comeback. Thanks for the coffee." She nodded toward the small heart. "So?"

"It's a personal SOS alarm. An innocuous trinket a

woman might carry."

"You don't think your protection and the self-defense instruction are enough?"

"These guys are resourceful. You never know. Redundancy can't hurt."

She inhaled more of the aromatic brew. "Okay. So how does it work?"

He came around the bar and held up the plastic heart. "See this button? Press it, and it emits a hundred and twenty decibel ear-splitting siren."

Impressed, she took it from him and weighed it in her hand. Less heft than a car key fob. "A screech like that could bring half the state's cops. I should've had one when I used to ride the Metro." And before that she should've taken those self-defense classes they'd offered at the university.

"There's more." He pointed to the ring at the end of the chain. "If you yank on the chain, the device emits an SOS message to whatever phone number you program into it via an app on your phone. It also sends that number your GPS coordinates. And it's rechargeable."

"That tiny thing?" She turned it back and forth.

"Directions are in the box." He handed it to her. "Keep the gadget with you at all times."

Her smile spread so wide her cheeks hurt. She wrapped her arms around him and hugged, laying her head on his chest. She inhaled his clean-soap smell and the crisp scent that was uniquely Boyd. Under her ear, his heart bumped a little faster. "Above and beyond. Thank you, thank you." She couldn't stop smiling.

"It'll be on your bill."

In a blur, he bent down and twisted away. His elbow shot up, stopping stopped short of her chin.

"What was *that*?" She jerked away, stumbled back.

He grabbed her upper arms and steadied her. "That, Gemma, was self-defense lesson number one. I defended myself by maneuvering out of your bear hug. If it had been a real attack, I could've rammed my elbow into your chin or nose or throat."

She sucked in air. "And is this a move a smaller person—me—could use to escape from a bigger guy?"

"It's one. An attack is more likely to come from behind. But yeah."

"Maybe we should have breakfast first. I need fuel for what I suspect you're going to put me through."

"Extra fuel. Didn't we buy eggs and bacon on the way home yesterday?"

After they ate, Boyd moved the small end tables in the living room out of the way, setting up their "arena" in the middle.

To begin, he pointed out the areas Gemma should go for if grabbed and held by an attacker. "Somebody your size can't land a hard enough blow on the chest to be effective. Unless you had something like keys in your hand, even a blow to the stomach might not make a man, even a small man, let go."

"I have no keys. Not for the house, not for the car."

"Point taken. Let's start with somebody trying to grab you from the front."

He showed her how to stabilize herself as she drove a knee upward and kicked out. "A hard kick into the family jewels could temporarily paralyze a guy and you could escape. Depending on the height difference, a quick knee thrust can deliver a hard blow."

She lost her balance the first couple of tries, but then drew on her yoga training. He had her practice a few times, with him holding a throw pillow to protect himself. Each time she improved her control.

Of course she wasn't really being assaulted. And she kept longing for actual hugs from Boyd, not a faux ambush.

He showed her how use her elbow if the assailant was closer. "Brace yourself, core—" he slapped his own midsection "—and legs. Use those strong legs, honey, and shift your weight forward. You can strike the neck or chin with an elbow hard enough he'd loosen his grip so—"

"I could run. And scream bloody murder."

They practiced those and a few more moves, including the bear hug, but from the back, until Boyd called time out. "Great work but enough for today. You're a quick learner. You being in shape helps. But we should practice a few more times so you have the muscle memory."

She wiped her forehead with a tissue. "How do you know this stuff? It doesn't seem like what an Army Ranger would do."

The pride in his expression dialed down to neutral. "True. When I came back to the States, I had to wait… for processing. The army assigned me to act as the attacker in women's self-defense classes. I learned along with them."

She considered teasing him about learning how to avoid the groin kick or getting his nose broken. But something, not embarrassment, more of his internal darkness inside, behind that blank mask made her think better of it.

"Instead," she said, "the experience made you a good teacher. But I agree on needing more practice."

"Quiz question. What are the most important things to remember?"

"Aim for the eyes, nose, throat, groin, and feet. And don't panic." *Stay calm?* That would be tough. She didn't feel empowered yet. This was harder than she'd expected.

****

That evening while Gemma painted in her studio, Boyd sat on the sofa and worked on his laptop. She'd impressed him with how fast she picked up the defensive moves. And the pillow came in handy for concealing as well as for protecting his junk. He'd held his breath hoping she wouldn't ask what to do if the guy had a weapon. That would take more than a few lessons in a condo.

He studied photos of the family members who would attend the Friday reception and reviewed reports from Trask and Cassidy. Still no sign of Nazaroff or Dupree. And not much of interest on the Bellini clan.

Given the inheritance from Silvio, the family had no financial woes. Gemma's dad, the orthopedic surgeon, had money of his own and seemed to have a strong second marriage, good relationship with his children and those of the new wife. So far nobody in James Bellini's office stood out as having issues, but he would follow up on something Jo had told him. Tina's husband had cratered a couple of his own businesses in the past but now had a steady job with a commercial realtor. Gemma's brothers were working out west. Those engineering jobs paid damned well. Nothing there.

A relief for Gemma if her family members were all innocent.

His phone played the *Black Panther* theme. Trask.

Gemma had allowed Linc to doublecheck the digital company on whether the server had been hacked. "Tell me some good news, bro."

"Wish I could. Another Bellini forgery showed up, this time in Charlottesville. Far, far outside the Beltway. The couple's insurance company thought it looked suspicious, along with how they bought it. Another private sale. Painting's of a house in Old Alexandria. I'll send a photo."

"Same description of the seller, the blonde woman?"

"Generally the same—middle aged, elegant—but with short dark hair. The seller of the first little sketch was a woman with light brown hair. Wigs, Jo said."

"So we're nowhere." Boyd massaged his shoulder.

"Plus I need more time looking for hackers in those files. Gotta cover my tracks. Nada so far."

"What about Troy Dupree? Any leads on him?"

"No new paintings with the little *t*, if that's what you mean. No hits on his phone or any accounts."

They batted around ideas before ending the call.

He closed the laptop lid and leaned back. Somehow Nazaroff was behind the murder attempts. The aim was probably to delay discovery of the digital files breach. And discovery of the crooks, period.

Bastard must be in a hurry. Probably had a passport in another name, had likely altered his appearance.

If only Gemma would shut off the access now, dammit.

He heard her upstairs humming as she worked. The nights together like this were both bliss and torture. Gemma the toucher squeezed his arm or laid her soft hand on his arm or patted his shoulder or his fucking knee. While he had to struggle to keep his hands off her.

He'd moved into the guest room across the hall from her. At his insistence, both kept their doors ajar. He could hear her sighing or turning over in her sleep. Then later he would wake up aroused and aching from sensations and images of the two of them. Better than his nightmares.

He wanted her but it was more than sex. She made him feel somehow different, like an iceberg inside was melting. Despite the danger, he hadn't smiled so much in years. And he'd never been so aware of his heartbeat, especially when she touched him, even casually.

The longer this went on, the more he got sucked into her orbit, the more he admired her, the more he wanted her. It was impossible. He was too messed up. But by God, he would make sure nobody hurt her.

Except at some point, he might be the one.

Chapter Thirteen

ON FRIDAY EVENING, they arrived early at the museum. Gemma wanted to be there to greet the guests. They passed through the metal detector, and uniformed guards examined the contents of Boyd's pockets and her tiny handbag. She smiled at the welcome-desk attendant as he checked off their names.

"Good evening, David. Looks like a fresh haircut for the evening's event. Very sharp, professional."

"Thank you, Ms. Bellini." The young man looked flustered at her noticing and bent to his list.

Boyd held out an arm, and she laid her hand on the fine worsted of his suit coat. They entered the first gallery. She felt as light as air when she saw it. *Virginia Farmhouse.* Guests would view Silvio's last masterpiece as they entered. The other five were spread among the three rooms. The lighting illuminated the artwork to best advantage. Waiters stood by with champagne and canapes. She spun in a circle before turning to Boyd.

"This'll be such fun." She beamed him a smile. "I do love a party. My brothers won't be here, of course. Their companies send them all over the world. I have no idea where either is this month. I'll introduce you to the rest and—"

"No. Not possible. You can't introduce me to anybody." His voice was low, but his brow was a thundercloud.

"What do you mean?"

"We'd need a cover story about who I am. Did you think of that? Most important, I can't do my job if I have to make nice with people."

She glanced pointedly at the three uniformed men and women within sight. "But there are guards everywhere."

Boyd tugged her off to one side as the doors behind them opened to a queue of people in evening clothes.

"The guards are protecting the art. I'm here to protect *you*."

The words came out low and gruff, not in his normal smooth baritone. Shivers tap-danced down her spine, and not from fear, although he meant to warn her.

"Everyone here for this event has been invited. David will check them all in. Nazaroff will not be one of them. I'm in no danger here."

"Nazaroff may have an accomplice. Or he could send a ringer, a guy in place of an invited guest. I'll take no chances with your life, Gemma."

She brightened. "You'll be with me, so then I'll have to introduce you."

"I will not be with you. I'm not your... date. I'm your bodyguard." His voice sounded like it needed oiling.

Bodyguard. The word stole her breath. This last week, had she fooled herself that she was more than a damn job to him? She refused to believe that. She'd seen the sometimes hungry, sometimes tender way he looked at her. She could see more inside him than he wanted her—or anyone—to see. Inside was something hard and frightening.

As he denied being more than a bodyguard, the muscles in his neck and jaw bunched bowstring tight. His protective nature and thoughtfulness had brought her to trust more than she thought she ever could again, had brought her to let herself want. They attracted each other like heat-seeking missiles—to use a military term he'd appreciate. She'd given up fighting it, but he was still denying the nascent bond between them.

She stiffened her spine and manufactured a smile. Showed teeth. "If you're here to protect me, why won't you be *with* me?"

"I need to scan the crowd. Check for anybody who doesn't belong. Anybody who might not be what they seem. Like that. I should've explained this earlier. I was just bulling ahead. I…" His shoulders twitched.

Poor man, he was struggling to apologize. He was taking care of her, and she was being a brat. She'd worked to rid herself of the Bellini Princess title, and her momentary petulance had nearly recrowned her.

"I do understand. I could've made the evening awkward and potentially dangerous. I wanted a lovely evening here without worrying about… danger."

A slow grin spread from his mouth to his eyes, the grin that always revved her heart and heightened all her senses. "Leave the worrying to me. Have fun and enjoy. I'll keep track of you and those around you."

"Okay, fine. Do the bodyguard thing." She started to turn away, but he caught her arm.

"One more thing. I want you to ignore me, so nobody pays attention to me. I'll blend in, be a fly on the wall. Invisible."

She eyed him up and down, from his serious gray eyes and strong jaw to his broad shoulders and gorgeousness in that indigo suit. He was positively lickable.

"Invisible? You? Not possible." *Here I go, one more brat move.* "Well, if I have to be off on my own, I need a dose of courage."

Even in heels she wasn't tall enough. She planted one hand on his dove-gray shirt and with the other, tugged his head down for a big ol' kiss. Inhaled the scents of clean cotton and crisp aftershave. She held on until he started kissing her back. *Yeah, y'all!*

Lips tingling with delicious pleasure and grinning with triumph at the look on his face, she scurried off to greet the guests.

****

Boyd shadowed Gemma as she smiled and chatted and hugged through the growing throng. Easy duty. As long as she stayed in sight. People taller and wider than Gemma blocked her some. More than one man's hot gaze followed her around the gallery. But otherwise nobody watched her. He kept moving as she weaved in and out.

He'd gotten body-slammed when she came down the condo stairs, that slinky black dress— gown, she'd corrected—hugging her slender curves. No cleavage visible, but the dress was sexy as hell anyway with painted silver roses trailing across the wide shoulder strap. She'd done her hair up in some complicated twist, leaving her neck bare and tempting.

Here at the museum, she'd argued like a damn lawyer until he explained enough so she understood. His fault for putting it off. She'd been so pumped about the reception he hadn't been able to make himself sit her down and go over the ground rules. And then the kiss.

His little head had stood at attention. His big head was still swimming.

No sketchy looking characters, although a few of the artist types were pushing the bohemian look to the wall. Possible Morgan Nazaroff reeled in a starving artist. Just in case, Boyd snapped photos with the tiny hidden camera.

He took a moment to study one framed portrait, of an old man on the docks. Silvio's paintings drew you in, somehow conveyed emotion, even the landscapes. In the babel of voices, he caught snatches of conversation. Gossip, criticism of the art, boasts about golf scores and financial dealings—same shit he'd heard at the Bethesda party.

Gemma was safe enough at the moment. Her dad and his younger wife were introducing her to a white-haired couple.

Victor Bellini looked a lot like Silvio. Same leonine head, his hair dark accented with white at the temples. The financial advisor uncle and his wife stood nearby. James, the younger brother, bore the same resemblance to Silvio. The sister and her husband pushed past Boyd with flutes of champagne. Gemma's sister Tina, the oldest of the younger Bellinis, was more rounded than Gemma, with a brisk manner. Her husband Leo, good-looking and hefty, struck him as flashy in a used car salesman sort of way, and older than his wife. Her mom Erin looked a lot like Gemma. A distinguished-looking man held her arm. Gemma had said she was seeing somebody. He snapped a photo. DSF should probably check him out.

The man turned his way, and his features shifted, darkened. Became Chaos, the lower half of his jaw blown away, his uniform blackened and shredded. Behind him smoke and flames. Around him men's cries.

Boyd stiffened, his arms and legs rigid. Even his lungs seized.

He tightened one hand into a fist. Pressed it against the wall at his back. A moment later, the ghost faded. The man's patrician features returned. Boyd flexed his fingers. Looked around, found Gemma staring at him. He stretched his lips into a smile, managed a shrug. She nodded, but one raised brow said she'd ask later.

Fucking wonderful.

When she turned back to her companions, he again located her mom and escort. They kept their distance from her ex. Painted designs accented her gown too. Both the mom's and sister's gowns.

Gemma spent a lot of time on what she called a hobby.

Yesterday he checked out the paintings, especially the six Bellinis. Antique buildings in Old Alexandria, a second harbor one, a tumbledown farmhouse in the rolling hills, a couple of portraits. In the Washington Cultural Museum, with its polished marble floors and high ceilings, the new showing took up three rooms among the many exhibit spaces. Enormous banners above the paintings performed double duty, Gemma had said. They advertised the museum's major exhibits and hid the acoustic panels.

A relief the rest was closed off. It was hard enough to keep up with Gemma in a confined space.

She hooked the arm of a slope-shouldered man with a ponytail and headed into the next room. Boyd skirted the crowd and eased in not far behind them. He turned away, not wanting to be caught in a photo as art patrons and local artists posed for the press photographer.

Greeting people, Gemma skipped on into the third exhibit space.

He waved away a waiter with canapes and followed. Held up a wall while he checked the scene. A blonde woman trailed in after her, then a couple. Nobody paying her undue attention. He watched Gemma engage one person after another. They laughed and nodded and answered questions. She was a marvel, relating to everyone with ease.

"You're Boyd, aren't you?"

The air backed up in his lungs. He stiffened. Jerked away from the wall. So much for being invisible. He exhaled a "Sorry?"

Maybe he should recognize the redhead looking him over, but he drew a blank.

She waved away his weak apology. "You're just as Gemma described you. No wonder she's kept you all to herself."

Painted metallic swirls jazzed up her blue dress, er, gown. Realization hit him. "Pia."

"Guilty as charged." They shook hands. She sipped from her flute, then tossed her head toward Gemma. "She's something, isn't she?"

"She's amazing." He didn't dare go beyond that. Pia was curious as a cat, Gemma had told him, but loyal. He'd tread carefully. She might have sharp claws.

"She said you were helping her find Troy. Any luck?"

"I'm working on it. We'll find him." He flailed for a new topic. "What is it you do for work? You an artist too?"

Her sputtered laugh said no. "I manage a clothing

store down the street from Galerie Flora. We sell Gemma's painted clothing. Flora sends customers our way, and we reciprocate." She cocked her head. Big brown eyes studied him. "So why aren't you over there with your date?"

"Gemma wanted the freedom to schmooze people without having me tagging along. Fine with me as long as I'm the one taking her home."

"A line from an old song, I believe. Okay then." She turned to leave him alone.

"Wait. Maybe you can help me ID people I should know."

"Sure, as long as you buy me a drink." She held up her empty glass.

He waved down a waiter and snagged a full flute. "Driving," he said when she eyed the water he took for himself.

He half listened as his gaze careened back and forth between people she indicated and Gemma. At least she was visible as she flew among knots of guests. Pia pointed out major patrons of the arts, named the bohemians he noted earlier as up and coming young artists.

Gemma now huddled with her mom and sister. Tina jabbed the air with one hand as she talked, her brow furrowed. The same concern crimped the others' features. He'd ask later.

She hugged her sister and joined a group of women nearby. She and one of them cheek-kissed.

"That's Flora Khalid with the spiky black hair talking to Gemma and none other than the D.C. mayor," Pia was saying.

He sized up the hair and the incandescent outfit.

"The owner of Galerie Flora is herself a work of art."

"Good one. Flora's a trip all right." She fluttered fingers at Gemma, who gaped wide-eyed at the two of them.

He considered winking at her, but then the forty-something blonde he'd noticed earlier approached Gemma. Could it be Nazaroff's shill? So far Boyd hadn't pegged anybody here as a possible in the plot to kill or part of the forgery scam. After a few words with Gemma, the blonde handed her something.

He stiffened, reached for the weapon that wasn't there. Locked in the SUV.

"You know that woman?" He chinned toward the blonde. They were still talking.

Pia tilted her head, then shook it. "I think I've seen her around, but no, don't know her."

A heady mix of guests. Gemma's family and her friends along with pillars of society. And the mysterious blonde.

Pia waved to a guy who was beckoning across the room. "Gotta run. Ritchie has to work tomorrow. I'm sure we'll meet again, Boyd." She blew him a kiss and dashed off.

Boyd left his wall and headed toward Gemma. Blocked by moving bodies, but he couldn't bulldoze his way through since he perceived no obvious threat.

By the time he made his way past people bidding Gemma goodbye, the blonde had vanished.

Chapter Fourteen

"WASN'T THAT A fabulous party? I had the best time. So many lovely people. Nearly everyone invited actually came. A rarity." Gemma kicked off her heels and wriggled her toes. She turned in her seat to better see Boyd's rugged profile, highlighted by the dashboard light. "Sorry if I keep going on and on about it."

"You're entitled. It was first-rate. Now what?" He glanced her way. The indulgent grin tilting his mouth made her catch her breath.

She wanted her mouth on him again, but instead leaned into her seatbelt as he made the turn onto Route One south. "The story and photos in the *Post*'s society pages should make this showing a big success. Maurice said at some point the paper may want me to return for an interview."

Clouds had blotted out the moon and stars. Boyd flipped on the wipers against raindrops. "This was predicted, but I hoped we'd get back before it started."

"Hey, it's *after* the reception." She relaxed, sure of his driving competence, and watched his broad hands on the wheel. She patted his forearm. "You were right, you know."

"About?"

"Me not introducing you. I couldn't have touched base with so many people."

A deep rumble in his chest, then throat clearing. "Can you say that again?"

"What?"

"That I was right. A guy needs to hear that more than once."

A laugh snorted from her. "Couldn't help it, sorry. I've heard my dad say the same thing. Okay, you were right. And not for the first time. How's that?"

"My ego is ecstatic." He chuckled as he passed a slower car. "That huddle with your mom and sister looked intense. Problems?"

"Minor family stuff. No biggie. Just sometimes Leo, Tina's husband, can be such a jerk. He's so controlling. He gave Tina a hard time about her wedding photography business. I think he's jealous of her success, of the family overall. Macho Italian."

"One in every family, I guess. I have an uncle like that. You'd told me your mom was seeing someone. Was that him with her tonight?"

"Definitely. Nice guy, very attentive. Looks like they're an item." She patted his hand. "I know what you're doing. You're detecting. Edward MacMillan is an architect. His firm designed the new wing of the museum. Mom's a docent there. No way he's involved in art forgery." Or murder, but she couldn't bear to say that aloud.

"It's possible in his spare time he knocks off a few Van Goghs."

She chortled and wished the console wasn't so wide. She'd lay her hand on his thigh.

A few miles farther, they exited onto the two-lane leading to Linley Harbor. It wound along beside the creek where she'd sketched a great blue heron fishing.

She ought to do more with that sketch. Rather than on a canvas, that graceful, sinuous body belonged on a long scarf.

What began as a few raindrops now swelled into a downpour.

Boyd's jaw worked as he negotiated around a construction size dump truck stopped by the side of the road.

"Did you send your friend Pia to keep me company?"

"Shoot, no. I had marching orders to ignore you, remember? I didn't tell her you were there either. Pia must've deployed her inner radar to find hot males. What did you think of her?"

"Witty, funny, seems like a loyal friend. I liked her. She ID'd some of the guests for me."

"And she liked you. She's already texted me."

He made no response to that, but she could practically hear his eyeroll.

"Who was the blonde woman? She handed you something," he said after a few minutes.

"Oh, uh, hold on." She fished it out of her handbag. "It was her card. Name's Quinn Rykiel. She's a rep for Sibyl Simone Fashions."

"Which you've heard of?"

"Definitely. Unique and classy. Styles range from high-end women's fashion to moderately priced. The store where Pia works carries them. I've bought a few."

"This rep selling something tonight?"

Gemma grinned at the notion. "The opposite. She said her boss wants to talk to me about creating a line of clothing using my painted designs."

"What did you tell her?"

"I thanked her and said I'd consider it." She scoffed. "As if. I'm not interested. The clothing thing is just for fun, not serious art. Not like the paintings my agent has in a big Alexandria gallery, although I think they took them mostly because of the Bellini name."

"Sounds like somebody doesn't believe in her talent," Boyd said, his tone infused with affection. "You could do both. I can check her out if you want, make sure it's legit."

"Sure, why not. Thanks." She turned the card over and stared at it, then tucked it away.

They drove on in silence. Traffic had thinned to nonexistent, so they ought to be home before ten. *They.* She'd included him. Such a short time together, but it seemed natural.

She'd planned to wait until they reached home to ask about his blanking out, but the dark interior of the vehicle might invite confidence. "I wanted to ask you—"

"Damn." Boyd tipped the rearview mirror. "Truck close behind us with brights on."

The headlights glared even in the side mirror.

"Good. He's passing us," he said.

She peered past him at the vehicle. Huge. All she could see were massive tires. It stayed beside them. Not passing.

"Boyd—"

"The safety handle. Grab it!"

She reached up. Clutched the handle. The truck. Only inches away. Practically on top of them. Her mouth went dry.

Slam!

The impact jerked her sideways in the shoulder harness. Loosened her grip.

"Hold on."

She tightened her fingers. Dared a look. Boyd wrestled the steering wheel.

Wham!

The SUV bounced off the road. Metal shrieked.

The headlights speared darkness. They skidded down the grassy slope. Smashed over low bushes. Slowed in the soft ground and tipped sideways.

She couldn't breathe.

Momentum kept them sliding. Down, down to—*the creek. Oh God!* Her heart clattered. Her fingers ached but she held onto the handle.

Boyd wrenched the wheel to the right. The SUV rocked. Rocked again. His right arm pressed across her chest. He held the wheel in place with the other.

The world tilted. The SUV crashed onto its side. Metal and plastic fractured. Glass shattered.

The impact yanked her grip free. Knocked her against the door. But Boyd held her.

Every muscle tense, she waited. Her heartbeat pounded in her ears. Then the rain and the ticking of the cooling engine registered. They'd stopped. Her head reeled.

"Gemma honey, you okay?" He released his hold on her, cupped her shoulder.

His deep voice, his gentle touch penetrated her fog. She nodded, took a shuddering breath through her cramped throat. And realized she was getting wet. Rain pelted in through the driver side window. The beams of two flashlights were coming closer.

"No, no, no! The guys from the tru—"

"Don't worry, honey. It's the Devlin cavalry."

"Boyd, everybody all right?" The man aimed a

flashlight through the window.

She heaved a sigh and closed her eyes. Took measured breaths.

"Mostly." Boyd turned to her. "Seriously, you okay? Didn't hit your head?"

"I'm okay." All she could manage. She ached in various body parts, but seemed whole.

"That's Lincoln Trask up there, Gemma. He and Jo Cassidy are working with me."

"Don't think I've ever seen a guy deliberately turn over his vehicle," Trask said.

"It was that or hit the tree over there. Figured we had a better chance this way. And it kept us out of the creek."

Gemma squinted out the windshield. A second flashlight framed the rain-swollen creek, only yards below. Shaky and weak as a newborn puppy, she hugged herself. Thanked God Boyd had known what to do.

"Saw the whole thing, but we were back too far to stop it. Fu— Driver beat it, but Cassidy got the license plate. She called in the accident."

"Get us out of here A-sap," Boyd said. "Door's jammed. I'll hand Gemma through the window to you."

"Send her up. Cassidy will take care of her."

She pushed the seat belt button. Nothing. "Dammit, it's jammed."

He punched it, and it released. He took her right hand. "What's this? You're bleeding."

Blood dripped onto her lap from a cut on her forearm. Surreal how the blood mingled with the rain pooling there among glass shards. She blinked away the giddiness. "When we went over, I hit the door. Maybe it's cut from the handle?"

His expression was grim, the set of his mouth tight.

She probably looked worse. He pulled a blue bandana from the glove compartment and wrapped it around her arm.

"I think this is clean. Cassidy will have something better."

His mouth opened again as if he wanted to say more. Instead, he brushed the glass away and wrapped his arms around her. As if she were a doll, he hoisted her from the seat, up and across his body.

Long arms lifted her out and to her feet. She looked up at the lean face of a Black man in a yellow slicker. Smiling, he released his grip, but held out his arms, ready if she toppled over.

"Thanks, Mr. Trask."

"All I did was be in the right place at the right time. And make it Linc."

She blinked furiously. She should've known. The Devlin people had followed them, had their backs like the other day.

Jo Cassidy in a similar slicker wrapped her in something crinkly called a space blanket. Gemma tripped on a rock, stumbled and slid.

The other woman tsk-tsked at her bare feet, then half carried, half herded her up to their SUV. She explained the space blanket would keep her warm and dry.

Before they reached the road, flashing lights and sirens neared from both directions.

Chapter Fifteen

BOYD'S WATCH READ midnight as they arrived at Gemma's condo. Police cruisers, two fire department trucks, and an ambulance had arrived at the scene of the hit-and-run. They used the rescue tool called the Jaws of Life on the door so Boyd could climb out. He answered the county deputy's questions while an EMT saw to Gemma's wound. The deputy had promised Detective Santiago would contact him tomorrow. Which was officially today.

Boyd vibrated all over as he swung open the condo door, nearly banging it against the wall. Fuckin'-A, his fault Gemma was hurt. She could've fucking been killed. He should've suspected something as soon as he saw that monster truck parked beside the road. Should've called Trask and Cassidy then. Should've had them tighten up the space between them. He trooped ahead of Cassidy as they checked inside and out.

"Stop grinding your teeth," Cassidy said. "No recriminations. You couldn't have known what those fuckers had planned. You saved her and yourself. You're both in one piece." She smirked. "Except for the SUV."

"Thanks, Mom."

She swatted his back.

"How's the shoulder?"

"Fine." But he winced when she manipulated his

arm.

"Get your girl and get some sleep. Put ice on the shoulder."

He thought better of saying *thanks, Mom* again. He had to watch it or Cassidy would rat out his wonky shoulder to the others. Or to Gemma.

A few minutes later, Boyd collected Gemma, and the operatives drove away. She picked up her muddy hem and padded up the walk. He took the woven blanket the EMTs had given her, dumped it on the tile floor. It would keep. Still damp, the sexy gown clung to every dip and curve. Her hair dangled every which way, but was no less beautiful.

He raised his gaze to her face. Damn, but she looked lost and scared.

"You saved my life again, Boyd. Both our lives. Smart and brave and resourceful. Thank you. But your SUV, it's probably totaled. I'm so sorry. If I hadn't—"

"Stop it. What happened wasn't your fault. Never think that. And if you hadn't called me in the first place— Shit, I don't want to even say it." He trailed a finger down her cheek and cradled her jaw. "What counts is we're alive and mostly unhurt."

She tilted her head into his caress and sniffed. "You lowered the window before we rolled over, didn't you?"

He rubbed his nape. "Figured otherwise it would jam and we'd have to break the glass." Better not to mention that it would've been an escape route in case they'd gone into the creek.

"Like I said, resourceful."

He shrugged. "Survival training."

"I just realized the airbags didn't open," she said. "Some defect?"

"Airbags don't usually deploy when the impact is on the side or speeds are lower. Injuries from the airbags could be worse than the accident." He shuddered inwardly at the image of airbags squashing Gemma's small form.

"Just as well then." She lifted her hem and headed to the stairs. "Not sure I can save this gown. That little cut bled all over it. I'd love a shower, but the tech said not to get the bandage wet. Time for bed." On the second step, she looked back, expectation in her eyes.

Was that an invitation? Or his imagination? The white tape wrapping her right forearm flashed a stoplight at him. Reminded him of his duty.

He cleared his throat. "I'll take one more look around and turn off the lights."

She turned and continued upward.

He checked windows and doors. Again. Dug an ice pack from the freezer and slapped it on his shoulder. Once the pack warmed, he went up and got in the shower.

When he stepped out of the bathroom in his boxers, he found Gemma standing in the bedroom doorway. In a long tee that hit mid-thigh. She'd brushed her hair out so it rippled across her shoulders. Certain parts of his body leaped to attention.

"Gemma?"

She crossed to him. Her face glowed, bare of makeup and freshly scrubbed. She smelled of something mild like aloe. Rising on tiptoe, she pulled his head down and pressed her lips to his, coaxed his lips apart with her tongue. Shock waves of need jolted through his body. Their tongues slid and stroked, mated. Already he was hard, aching, and... then she pulled away.

"I don't want to be alone," she said in a low voice

that thrummed in his body. "Will you hold me?"

"What about your arm?"

"Merely a scratch. Butterfly bandage. I'm fine."

"If I hold you, I'm going to want more than a kiss."

"I hope so."

His breath snagged, and he picked her up. She laced her fingers behind his neck as he carried her across the hall. He could feel her breath soft and warm against his neck. "Your bed's bigger than mine."

"What was that about being distracted?"

"Honey, you distract me just by existing."

He set her down next to her bed. She peeled off her tee and slid in, naked. Her nipples pebbled, stood at attention. When she pulled up the covers, he stopped her hand.

"I want to look at you." He stood there a moment, taking her in. She was lean and supple, with firmly toned curves and silken skin.

"And I want to see you. All of you." Her voice was low and sultry. "Out of those plaid boxers." She slid over, ran her tongue across her lower lip.

In seconds he stripped down and sank beside her. For the space of about a minute, he let her gaze slide over him and her soft hand caress his damaged shoulder, his chest, his belly. Muscles twitched everywhere she touched. Raw need vibrated through every system in his body.

"Enough. My turn."

A moan of appreciation escaped him as he cupped one high breast, a sweet handful. He nuzzled both breasts, laving each in turn with his tongue. Speared a hand in her glorious hair and took possession of her mouth. Kissed her with his lips, his tongue, his desperate soul, as heat shimmered through him. Her palms flattened on his chest, her nails scraping a nipple, eliciting a growl from deep within him. He cupped one breast and brushed his lips over the other, licked the nipple with his tongue until it peaked and she arched her back and hummed.

"I've wanted you since the first time we met. It was making me crazy."

"I never forgot you and that kiss," she whispered. "Then I wanted more. Now I want it all."

Her lips were wet with his kisses, and her eyelids heavy with desire. The tangy scent of her hair, and the softness of her talented hands smoothing across his shoulders, his back, his butt ignited flames over his skin. He probed her slick folds and caressed as she murmured her need. The scent of her arousal set him afire. She arched up and swirled her tongue around one nipple, wrapped a hand around his erection, and he hardened to such an intense ache he could barely breathe.

He positioned himself above her, ready— Realization slammed into him. He could kick himself. "Gemma, I want to be inside you, but I don't have—"

"—protection." She waved her left arm toward the bedside table. "Bottom drawer. Hurry."

There, he found an unopened box. Ripped into it and tore open a foil packet. Managed to roll on the contents as blood thundered in his head.

"Boyd. Hurry!" She urged him to her.

He propped himself on his forearms. "You're so small. I don't want to crush you."

"You won't." Her strong legs clamped his waist and pulled him into position.

As he sank into her tight, slick heat, she murmured

against his chest and gripped him tighter, clenching her inner muscles and drawing him in deeper. Her lithe body rippled under him, around him with feverish urgency. He stroked, moved within her, shuddering with the sheer joy of finally being one with her. Had to make it good, make it last. Gritted his teeth against the building tension burning through his blood. Reached between them and swirled a finger on the most sensitive spot until the grip of her legs on his waist went lax. She cried out and shuddered her climax, spasming around him. He powered one last thrust before his entire being seized up and a torrent of pure molten pleasure ripped through him for a long, satisfying release.

Moments later, he eased away and collapsed on his side, used a bedside tissue to clean himself. He pulled up the light cover and snuggled her close. Waited for his heart to calm. He'd wanted hot sex tonight to burn away all the demons that owned his soul. He got that and more. New sensations swamped him, possessive urges he didn't need, didn't want.

Those feelings were just chemistry, and the danger threatening her gave sex that extra edge. Yeah.

****

Gemma floated in a sensory pool of pleasure. More than mere sex, shattering. He was tender and physical, smart and sensitive, and so… male. Something about him warmed her heart and gave her confidence. He made her feel she wasn't a fake, just playing the role of an artist and all the rest. Somewhere deep in her bruised heart, something bloomed, something like hope. Now that they'd made love, she ought to tell him what had plagued her, eaten at her insides since Troy's connection to the forgery.

But she couldn't spoil tonight. And desire could wait while she acquainted herself more with his lightly tanned body. She rubbed her fingertips over the sprinkling of dusky hair on his chest, darker than the hair on his head, and breathed in the scent of soap and what she could name only the essence of the man.

She considered licking his flat nipples, but too quickly she'd be on her back. She wasn't finished inspecting the contours of his muscles, the hard pectorals banding his chest, the bulging deltoids on his rounded shoulders, and the taut biceps beneath her head. He was dozing, or she'd ask about the tattoo covering scars on his left shoulder. Maybe a military symbol, a lightning bolt slashing between a sun and a star.

He turned toward her, nuzzling her hair. Being wrapped in his heat made her heart beat faster, her skin tingle, warmth pool between her thighs. She reached between them and walked her fingers down his taut belly. She cupped him, petted, and he sprang to attention in her hand.

"Gemma?"

"You know, that box is still mostly full."

He responded with a deep, rolling laugh that rumbled through her body. He lifted her on top his big body and kissed her, and she let her hands glide over his skin, smiling against his mouth as his muscles clenched and leaped at her touch. She pulled from his grasp and slid down his body, closed her fingers around his thick erection. It pulsed, straining against her grasp. She trailed her fingers down its length and back again, but lost her focus when his thumb and forefinger rolled one of her nipples. Sparks of desire shot straight to her center. His other hand reached between them, and precise and insistent, he stroked her. Anticipation built low in her belly and raw electricity thrummed through her entire body.

His heart hammering against hers, his muscles quivered with need. He brushed away her hand and sheathed himself. He lifted her above him and lowered her in one smooth move, and she shuddered as her body adjusted again to how completely he filled her. As he thrust then, she strained to meet his strokes with hers, bent to press her lips to his chest, feel their hearts hammering in tandem, their hips pounding against each other, the slap of heated flesh against flesh. Her thoughts dissolved into sensation building on sensation until pulsing shocks from their joining surged to liquid fireworks. He stiffened beneath her and groaned as his climax shook him.

****

Boyd lay on his back, hands stacked beneath his head, as Gemma slept curled against his side. It should've been just sex between them, physical release, and comforting her after the crash. Not Fourth of July pyrotechnics, followed by a rush of tenderness. And a dangerous need to connect with her in every way.

Their second time had been equally electrifying. He'd let her explore, a bit, all while hunger drummed through him in a steady beat. And then she rode him, and they took each other to climax.

Afterward she slept, and he could not.

He rolled off the bed and stepped into his boxers. Went down and stood at the patio doors. He stared into the darkness.

Was he so wrapped up in her that he'd missed something? He went through the preparation for the evening, the drive, the various scenarios, places he should've spotted trouble. Other than the obvious monster truck, nothing.

The museum reception was no secret, publicized in the *Post*, even though closed to all but invited guests. Was the guy in the dump truck some thug hired by Nazaroff? Or somebody else?

That wasn't the main puzzle eating at him.

How did their attacker know when they he and Gemma left the reception and would come back down the road to Linley Harbor? And another thing else bothered him, but the hour was too late to talk to Trask about a new search he wanted the man to do.

He heard Gemma mumble in her sleep and went back up to pull her into his arms. He wouldn't sleep, but he needed to hold her.

Chapter Sixteen

GEMMA EYED THE lemon linen top she'd just paired with long shorts. The three-quarter sleeves would mostly cover a bandage. The cut on her arm stung. Though not bad. Rolling her shoulders, she preferred to think her other achy muscles resulted not from the crash, but from their late-night activities. Her yoga routine this morning helped ease some stiffness, regardless of the source.

Boyd had watched some of her yoga practice from bed. As he left to shower, he said, "Now I know the other way you keep so fit. You can wrap those great legs around me anytime you want." She smiled at herself in the mirror as she clipped a braid—white blond today—to her hair.

"So that's the secret. Fake braids," Boyd said from the bathroom door. He passed her one of the mugs of coffee he carried. "What's so funny?"

"Thanks. Nothing." Just feeling the warmth bloom again, like a beam of morning sunlight. He wore cargo shorts, but no shirt. Could she talk him into going shirtless all the time? If only they had more time this morning…

He planted a coffee-flavored kiss on her lips. "Detective Santiago phoned. He'll be here in an hour. About the crash."

"He say anything else?"

"Nada. The silent detective." He placed his mug beside hers. He pushed up her sleeve. "Starting to bruise, but doesn't look too bad. You ready for bandaging?" He tipped his head toward the first-aid items she'd laid out on the counter. She had no butterfly bandages. He'd assured her he'd done enough field dressing he could rig something with gauze and tape.

Facing him, she folded up her sleeve. This seemed like a good time to ask him about the scars, and then maybe she'd have the courage to tell him the rest about Nazaroff.

She caressed the ropy scars on his shoulder. "Would you tell me about these and the tattoo?"

He lifted a shoulder in a *why not* move. "We were doing recon like I told you, checking a village. Our mission was making sure it was safe for the villagers to return, that none of the militants had sneaked back. We separated, inspecting homes for signs of bombs. Maybe wires hidden in the dirt by the door. Like that." Each word sounded scraped past his vocal cords.

He cleared his throat, then swabbed ointment on her cut. His gaze was on his work, his breathing fast. "The rocket came out of nowhere. The explosion killed two men."

"The photo. Chaos and Hawk."

He nodded, busy for a minute cutting tape and folding over parts of the tape strips. "The rest of us were wounded, some more than others. Lopez, 'Lobo,' lost a leg. I just got this. Muscle and nerve damage from shrapnel. Healed okay but not enough to be mission ready. My ticket out of the army." He grimaced as if he wished he could go back.

She pictured his tight expression when he'd shared the reason for his being nicknamed the Scorpion. On that mission, he got stung, but only in the shoulder, while two others died.

Guilt.

"And you honor your men with this tattoo over the scars. What does the design signify?"

"Our regiment. 75th Ranger, Third Battalion. Goes back to earlier days, World War II."

He placed one end of each of the three altered tape strips on her skin. When he stuck the tape on the other side of the cut, it pulled the deep opening together. He covered it all with gauze and more tape.

When he looked up at her again, guilt or grief bracketed his gaze. Maybe both.

She smoothed out her sleeve. "Very professional, Dr. Kirby. Thanks." She rose on tiptoes and kissed him lightly. "Do you wish you were still in the Army?"

"At first I did, but I have a good life now. My work is worthwhile, challenging. Up to now it's been less dangerous." His laugh was a jagged one that bared teeth but held no humor.

Not happy, maybe because she'd quizzed him and taken him back to that painful time. He clearly hadn't dealt with the attack and the losses. She knew about guilt, although not his kind of survivor's guilt. She did know about the sense of honor and the loss of it. And he'd been in charge, the first sergeant. Maybe she had no right, but something urged her to press him.

"Twice I've seen you sort of blank out, go into a zone, and then snap out of it. Flashbacks?"

He placed the unused bandages back in their container with deliberate care and closed the lid. His bland expression darkened to a scowl. She feared he'd shut her off, but he nodded.

"Not exactly. Hawk, Chaos, one of them, his ruined face superimposes on somebody I see. I failed my men. They're my ghosts. I deserve their haunting."

Ghosts? What could she say to that?

He snatched up his untouched coffee mug and hit the stairs. "I'll wait downstairs for the detective."

****

Boyd opened the door to Detective Santiago and ushered him into the living room. Gemma beckoned him to the seat opposite her. Boyd sat beside her on the couch.

Santiago held a go cup and declined her offer of more. Either the man had a favorite brew or he wanted it clear this was an official visit. He told Boyd, "Once the department is finished processing the Jeep, you can collect your belongings and have it towed. This should not take long."

His square features a mask, he sat straight, stiffly, in the plush armchair that invited napping. He adjusted his sheriff's department windbreaker and took out a notebook and pen. When they assented to his request to record the interview, he set up a small recorder.

Official then.

Boyd leaned back against the throw pillow and spread his hands on his thighs.

"Detective Santiago," Gemma began, "can you—"

He held up a hand. "Ms. Bellini, I'll address your questions in a while. But first I would like an account of what happened in the hit-and-run. I already know you were headed home from a reception in D.C. Please start from there."

"Boyd saw more than I did." She placed her hand on his knee.

After last night—and this morning—the mere touch of her soft hand on him set him on fire. Loose cargo pants were the only remedy. He shifted a hand to cover hers.

"The rain began as we were leaving," he said, "but picked up when I turned down the Linley Harbor Road. Soon after that, I spotted the dump truck parked on the verge." He described how the dumper overtook them, hit them with the brights first. Then paralleled the SUV.

Gemma's fingers tightened on his leg. Not a sexual touch, a grip of fear. Probably be a long time before she worked through the terror she must've felt, especially having no control.

"Could you see inside the truck cab?" the detective asked.

"Not enough to see anybody. Not in the rain and the darkness. And a construction-size dumper's a high monster. He veered close and then slammed sideways into me. Twice. Likely his intent was to force a rollover. After the first bump, I slowed so his second crack landed mostly toward the front fender. That shoved me off the road and down the slope toward the creek. You'd have to ask my colleagues who were right behind us. They called 911."

"Deputy interviewed them last night. I have their numbers." The room went silent, except for the scratching of Santiago's pen as he wrote something in his small notebook.

"Can you tell us about the dump truck?" Gemma drew a deep breath, relief in her pretty eyes the retelling had ended.

"Yes, ma'am. Found early this morning on a side

road. Homeowner getting ready for work called it in. Construction company reported it missing about the same time. Techs are processing it now. Likely the same dump truck."

He turned to Boyd. "Black paint on two locations fits your description of how you were struck. Odds are it will match your vehicle."

"Detective," Boyd began, "you have to admit after this blatant attack that 'a person or persons unknown' have tried to kill Ms. Bellini. Three times. All are attempts at murder."

Santiago's mouth thinned. He smoothed the collar of his sport coat. "It looks that way, but we still have little evidence and no suspects. Maybe we will get lucky and the techs will find fingerprints in that truck cab."

The would-be killers had been careful so far. Boyd wasn't counting on a slip next time.

"Then there is the question of motive." The detective's gaze slid to Gemma. "Why would somebody want to kill you?"

Gemma glanced at Boyd.

"Go ahead," he said.

"It probably has something to do with artworks by my grandfather, Silvio Bellini. He—"

Santiago held up a hand. "I know who your grandfather was."

"Of course. I recently learned about forgeries of two unsold pieces of his, a sketch and a painting. Since I'm the executive director of the estate, the art forgers might think I'm a threat."

"Detective," Boyd said, "The two Bellinis aren't the only forgeries. FBI Art Crime and Devlin Security are working together on cases in the D.C. area."

The corners of Santiago's mouth turned down, and he shifted in his seat. "I did not know about DSF, but the FBI alerted the sheriff's department about the forgeries."

"We like to coordinate with local law enforcement where possible," Boyd said evenly.

"An old friend of mine, Troy Dupree, has been missing for three weeks," Gemma said. "Last Friday, he phoned me with a cryptic warning to be careful." She described racing to the apartment, but finding only burglars. "At the time, I thought his warning was about the men who searched his place. But after learning more, I think it was about the art forgery ring. Those men must be part of it. At Devlin Security I discovered it was Troy who copied the two paintings just recovered."

"The Linley Harbor police haven't conducted much of an investigation into Dupree's disappearance and the burglary," Boyd said. "They seem to think it's all about drugs. Those events and the attacks on Gemma must instead be connected to the forgery ring." He described the search and his finding the sketches that led to more on the art forgers.

Santiago stared at him for a long moment. "I will reach out to the Linley Harbor PD."

He turned to Gemma. "Ms. Bellini, I am aware of your past and your connection to Dupree at that time. Are you again involved with art forgery? Could these attempts be the result of a falling out? Could your accomplices fear you will turn them in?" His harsh tone hardened the accusations into steel.

Gemma stiffened, her spine as straight as a bayonet. She removed her hand from Boyd's leg and folded her hands in her lap. Lifted her chin. Sea-green shards of ice speared the detective.

Boyd held his breath.

"Since you apparently have looked into my past, you must know the facts, that I was *not* involved in art forgery but was copying museum paintings as a student assignment. And that also once I discovered it was my teacher, an artist in residence, selling as authentic the copies Troy and I created, I reported it. And him. I would turn in the forgers today if I knew who and where they are."

She rose to her feet. "Now I would like you to leave my home."

****

Gemma turned her back while Boyd escorted Santiago out. He closed the door behind them. She remained standing there, the tension inside her a giant bubble that threatened to choke her. Vivid images reeled through her mind. Of Nazaroff glaring into the news cameras, his blazing eyes accusing her of betraying him. Of mics shoved in her face and voices taunting the Bellini Princess.

None of that compared to his trying to kill her.

When she heard Boyd return, she scrubbed her hands down her burning cheeks. All she could do was move ahead. Starting now. She'd do whatever it took to stop Nazaroff, no matter what, or she would never be whole.

"Impressive. An air of command worthy of a general." He held up his hands and applauded.

"Damn him, accusing me." She turned to face him. "I should've known the police would dig up my past. Now all that mess will be splashed across the media. Again!"

"And you'll triumph over it again. We'll stop

Nazaroff. This time he'll go to prison for longer than a few years."

"Triumph?" She shook her head. "I was considered complicit until after the trial. Only then did the district attorney go on television stating that I'd been duped and was innocent."

"DSF research must've missed something. Didn't you testify to that in court?"

She stomped around the room, the white braid flapping behind her. "I didn't testify at all. They had enough evidence against him without me. Troy and the buyers, along with the paintings. Most of which were Troy's."

"You've lost me again. He didn't sell the ones you copied?"

"One, as I recall." She shrugged, adjusted the braid's clip. "My copies were a bit… off. I did fine with the original artist's style, the brush strokes, the colors. But it seems I added, um—"

"Flourishes? Touches? Like flowers or seashells in the corner?" The corners of his mouth ticked up.

"Not that, just my own interpretation of the subject. A wider smile on one portrait. Oh, and I changed trees in a landscape to look windblown. It needed a more dynamic feel."

His initial snicker escalated into a howl. "First thing I've had to laugh so much about since this began."

She managed a smile. "I'll do whatever it takes to stop the forging and *him*."

Boyd reeled her into arms, and the warmth of his kiss on the top of her head drew a sigh from deep within her chest. "I'm sure you'd object, but I'd like to lock you in a human-size gun safe until we nail Nazaroff."

"I'm safer with you." A frisson of heat sparked through her, urging her to stay in his powerful arms. It might be the last time once he knew her shameful secret.

She hugged him and drew a deep, calming breath before stepping back. "There's something else I need to tell you about Nazaroff." *And me.*

Chapter Seventeen

SHE CURLED UP in the armchair, locked her fingers together. If she sat beside him, she'd want to lean on him, and she needed to be strong. She waited until he took a seat opposite her.

As always, he gathered an aura of stillness about him. No finger drumming on his knees. No tapping a foot. His was an air of quiet control. But in a manner that didn't put her on the defensive because his gaze remained cloud-gray soft. After this, he might not want to protect her or want *her*. The thought ran a hot knife into her belly, but she had to tell him. Now.

She forced herself not to look away or down, but to meet his gaze.

"I've never told anyone this. Getting caught up in Nazaroff's scheme isn't all I'm ashamed of. The college staged an exhibit of his work, had a reception to open it, the works. So I looked up to him as a famous artist—not as successful as my grandfather, but well known. And someone I could learn from. Anyway, he was older than me, sophisticated and good looking in a dramatic sort of way, and I fell under his spell."

She sucked in a breath for strength. "And fell into his bed. He seduced me with compliments and wine. I was a fool."

Boyd leaned forward and held out a hand, but she

shook her head. Unable to sit any longer, she pushed to her feet and paced to the mantel. She gripped the wood and stared at nothing. She couldn't look at Silvio's painted ponies.

"I think now he wasn't so much seducing *me*, but the granddaughter of Silvio Bellini. Bragging rights. Except as far as I know, he has never revealed the affair to anyone. Not when I reported the forgery to my advisor. Not at the trial or afterward." She'd waited for years for the shoe to drop. Now it might. With a great thud.

Revealing her long-kept secret ought to unburden her. But that weight bubble still filled her chest, making it hard to draw an easy breath. She couldn't look at Boyd, to see the revulsion he must feel. "How I could have…"

His arms wrapped around her. She hadn't heard him cross the room. She sank against him. His body heat and the steady thump of his heart reduced her racing pulse a notch.

"When exactly did this happen? How old were you?" He tipped up her chin, forcing her to look at him.

"Sophomore year. Spring semester. I turned twenty in March."

"Barely out of your teens. He was more than just older than you. *Twenty* years older. He played you, targeted you."

"Later when I looked back, I figured that out. Dammit, he laid it on thick, and I gobbled it up with a ladle. The shame has twisted my insides for—"

"*No. No more*. The guilt, the shame are his. Not yours." Boyd kissed her, taking his time, saturating her senses with his wild taste, his tongue painting his assurances into her.

A long minute later, he released her and paced around the room.

"Here's how I see it going down. Nazaroff's prominence in artistic circles had skidded down a slope. Obtaining artist in residence gigs gave him more than prestige and a paycheck. It gave him access to impressionable art students. He used his position and a slick line of bull."

"You think he might've started art forgery before he came to the Corcoran?" The notion had never occurred to her. She perched on the arm of the sectional.

"Possible. I didn't look up other gigs at art schools and colleges, but it wouldn't surprise me because of how fast he moved in on you both. Troy because he needed money—and his ability to copy perfectly. He targeted you as beautiful and talented. That you were also Silvio Bellini's granddaughter was a bonus. I'm betting he played everybody. Not just you."

He flopped onto the couch and pulled her down beside him. He curved an arm around her and tucked her close.

For a long time, the memories of what she'd done, of how Nazaroff had used her, lurked within her, invading her dreams. All that faded over time, but the attacks, the forgery brought back all the pain in scarlet and obsidian.

Boyd's insight, especially his acceptance and support, siphoned away the worst of the torment. He knew her deepest, darkest secret and didn't reject her. He liked her, cared about her. And the evidence he still wanted her had pressed against her when he kissed her.

His casual affection and tenderness like this warmed her heart. Finally, here was a man she could trust and respect. She'd told herself her prior occasional relationships were enough, but in reality she was always separate. Boyd made her feel no longer alone.

His trust in her, his belief in her buoyed her. She was ready to fight. Perhaps Silvio was watching with approval.

"I want the bastard stopped. I want him behind bars. I'll testify against him, and he can say whatever he wants about the past." A bitter laugh burst from her. "Dammit, at the time his attention seemed real, so genuine. Genuine all right, genuine *fake*, like the copied paintings."

"You ready to move on the login and password then?"

"I'll change the login and password today. *Now*. I don't have any idea how he gets into the archives. I've made mistakes in learning to manage Silvio's estate, but not the password and login. They're secure." Although her family might disagree once they found out.

"It's not on you. Either he has a hacker, or somehow he's learned about the archives and has obtained the login and password."

The possibility a hacker could access the files spiked prickles down her spine, but the other possibility could mean grief and scandal for her family. She drew as deep a breath as she could manage with a vise-tight chest.

"So unless it's a hacker, ending his access that way has to shake things up."

"It should." With stiff fingers, Boyd scraped back his hair. "He could always pull up stakes and move on. I don't think he will. He may have two motives for going after you. Worry you'll shut down access before he's finished in this area. But also because you reported him back then."

Her stomach flipped. "Revenge."

****

On Sunday, when Boyd greeted Trask and Cassidy out front, Gemma remained upstairs on the phone with various family members arranging meetings.

Trask climbed out of a pickup, a big crew-cab. More than a couple years old from the looks of it, but it would do. He handed Boyd the key fob. "Here you go, man. Your chariot for the duration. She's a little beat up from a gig in the back country a couple years ago. The company will reimburse you for whatever the insurance wouldn't cover on yours."

"Thanks, Linc. Good to know." Boyd pocketed the fob. When Cassidy joined them, he asked for an update.

"Nothing concerning on the family members so far, except for the uncle." She gave him a brief rundown.

He asked her to sit on the info. "I'll confront the man himself when we meet with him this week. In the meantime, could you look deeper into the brother-in-law, Leo Parisi?" He told them about Gemma's little conference with her mom and sister at the art reception. "Gemma described him as controlling, jealous of Tina's success in her business."

"You think jealous might mean more, like resentful?" she said.

"Possible. He hasn't done well in any business. Working as a rental agent can't pay all that much. Some commercial spaces might serve a forgery gang as both a studio and a hideout. Could you put a tail on him for a few days?" A stretch from being jealous of the family and teaming up with art forgers, but checking on the guy further couldn't hurt. Gemma's life was at stake.

"Sounds good. I'll take care of it."

"And I ought to be able to find out what properties Parisi's in charge of." Trask made a note.

"How's it going with the tracker buttons?" Cassidy asked.

"Fuck, it's hard, Jo. The woman has too many clothes. Today I managed to slip one inside the hem of her shirt." Anytime she wasn't in sight, his gut tightened. Like now. If she knew, she'd be paranoid about it and refuse. The strategy was bound to come back and bite him on the ass.

"You're not getting too close to the client, are you?"

His back tightened. "I'm doing my job, keeping her safe."

And spending the night in her bed, getting in deeper and deeper. Last night he'd followed her up the stairs and waited, not wanting to push. Then after he checked her bandage, she kissed him and stepped into his waiting arms. He held her hard against him, carried her to her bed, and made love with her until they were both breathless.

In spite of all the crap she was going through, she could still smile. Her smile made the world seem right. He had to keep her safe. And when the danger ended, he'd have to walk away. Somehow. *Shit*. He banished the twist in his gut.

He managed to hold Cassidy's gaze, but her scowl said she didn't buy what he was selling.

****

On Gemma's day to work at Galerie Flora, Boyd sat in front of the store in the pickup. He'd emailed a copy of the police crash report to his insurance company. This truck was okay, but when he got the check, he'd buy another SUV.

He scanned the vicinity as he stretched. Again. Shoppers, locals chatting on the sidewalk. Like every time he looked around. Except the same pickup passed three times. He was about to photograph the license when the driver pulled over and a woman hopped in. Just tooling by waiting for her. Not a threat.

Four days since those assholes rammed his ride. No attempts since on Gemma's life and nobody following them. Two days since Gemma changed the login and password to the archive. Hard to know if that had been detected yet. One thing he really hated was waiting, not knowing what Nazaroff would try next.

He drummed his fingers on the wheel. Pulled his ball cap lower. Peered into the store. She and Tolu, the full-time employee, mingled with the art shoppers. A backgrounder on Toluse Sayed, abstract painter and the son of South African immigrants, said he was clean.

Gemma was still in sight. Still fine. Damn fine, in a hand-painted white dress and heels. Until all the mess was cleared up and Nazaroff jailed, Gemma was working at the shop only until five. No evenings. Too dangerous for her to be in there alone at night.

A couple passing by on the sidewalk looked askance at him. *Shit.* They must think him a pervert. He let the glasses drop and dangle on his chest.

Yesterday workers had installed a new wrought-iron balcony rail at the condo. Boyd watched the process, playing the interested bystander. They ignored him. Gemma wasn't fooled.

Then a call from the detective informed him the construction company owner's son often left the keys inside the dump truck and bragged nobody'd steal it because they wouldn't be able to handle the monster. The truck had been wiped clean, even of employee fingerprints.

Gemma's calls to her family roused everybody's curiosity, but she revealed nothing. Get it over all at once, she said, like pulling a tooth. But her mirthless grin meant the calls pained her like a wisdom tooth extraction without anesthetic.

Then she went with him to the towing company. He took pictures of the damaged SUV using an app from his insurance company. The buckled and smashed body, the mangled chassis, the shattered windows.

She stood by, clutching her shopping bags to her chest and pressing a hand to her mouth, while he retrieved his tactical kit and tools. After they left Friday's reception, he'd moved the big 9mm from his gun safe and into his hip holster. If the hit-and-run assholes had come down the hill for them, he'd have been ready. Last, he removed the gun safe from the console space and unbolted the cable from the frame. The safe and other loose stuff got dumped into the bags.

"When you see what totaled looks like," he said, "it hits you hard. Lucky we made it out."

She shook her head, and maybe shook away her shock at seeing the damage in daylight. She had smiled then. "Not luck. It was you who made our survival possible."

Boyd turned toward the shop and lifted the binoculars, focused on Gemma smiling and gesturing at a painting. Her client, a woman in a sparkly tank top and jeans tight enough to pop the seams, beckoned to a bored-looking man. Boyd knew the picture in question, one of Tolu's abstracts—er, works of abstract expressionism, Gemma had corrected. Not to his taste, but if she was selling it, hell, he'd buy. These tasteless fools ought to look closer at her painting of the anchor, two works to the right.

This morning while she and Tolu had welcomed shoppers and regular clients, Boyd hung around inside. After lunch, she'd banished him to his vehicle, saying his predatory stare made their clients nervous. Looked like he didn't blend into the wall this time either.

Chapter Eighteen

WHILE GEMMA STOWED food after a supermarket run, she stewed about their next steps. In the living room, Boyd was setting up another self-defense session. With him in the house, she'd had to revise upward her usual grocery list. Thankfully, he was an easy roommate. Roommate? Lover? She refused to think too deeply about their relationship, whatever it was or could be. Instead, she needed to focus on protecting herself and stopping the thieves in the digital archives. Soon Linc Trask would stop the hacker. Had to be a hacker. A Bellini would never...

Her brain whirled with questions as she rounded the breakfast bar out of the kitchen. When would Nazaroff send the next thug to try to kill her? And where was poor Troy?

From behind, iron-hard arms banded her shoulders.

Her adrenaline surged. She bent forward from the waist.

Twisting her torso, she yelled, "No!" and drove her right elbow upward toward his face. The blow struck flesh and bone with a *thwack*.

"Shit!" Boyd's arms dropped from around her.

She pivoted away.

He stumbled backward a step and held a hand to his face.

She hurried to him. "Oh no, did I hurt you?"

"Your pointy little elbow just clipped my nose. Hit my cheek." He lowered his hand and blinked. Sure enough, a red spot flagged his left cheekbone.

"Sorry, but you surprised me."

"Don't be sorry, honey. You were supposed to be surprised. And you did what I taught you." Grinning, he looked her up and down. "You're damn near close to graduation."

She smiled back and stepped into his arms, no threat, only safe and protective. "You're lucky I didn't zap you with my SOS alarm."

They spent an hour practicing some of the other moves. But they needed to talk about Troy again. Boyd had said Devlin Security was working on it. But what were they doing to find him?

****

Later Gemma made a pitcher of iced tea and herded Boyd onto the patio. He plopped onto a wrought-iron chair, all grumpy, although cushions softened the effect. His guard dog mode, like with the gallery patrons, made her cleaning service women nervous.

A mere half hour after they arrived, Betty Lou and Sarita had come to the studio, their hands folded prayer style, brows creased in distress. Boyd had confronted them, all sweaty after his workout with weights, and asked to see their IDs. He then followed them from room to room. Betty Lou protested they did not steal or break things. Gemma reassured them. After she promised *her man* would leave them to their work in peace, the women had looked skeptical but returned to cleaning.

Gemma understood what Boyd was doing, more than he probably realized. *"I deserve their haunting,"* he said about his dead comrades. He felt he'd failed his men, so he was terrified of failing to protect her. She could do little except show her trust in him.

"I don't want to lose them." She handed him an icy glass. "I could clean my old apartment in an hour, but I don't have time to keep this much house more than neat. This service pays a living wage, and these women are the most thorough cleaners I've had. They're honest and hard working."

She tipped her head toward the plate on the small table holding the pitcher. "Besides, Sarita makes yummy cinnamon cookies. In Spanish, *polvorones de canela.*"

"I'll stuff my mouth with these and tell her later how delicious they were." He popped one into his mouth. "They look like donut holes but taste even better."

They sat in the shade drinking tea and munching cookies. The summer heat made her wish she could relax enough for a nap.

"These past few days have kept us busy," Gemma said after Boyd devoured half the cookies.

"No shit. You're thinking about Troy." He straightened and reached for her. The tension in her eased as his hand enveloped hers. "Trask reported earlier they've found no trace. Let's look at the situation again. Maybe he phoned you that night because he'd gotten cold feet about the forgery and split. Maybe he was hiding out."

"He was afraid to stay on the phone, and when I called back, it was turned off. Could he have feared Nazaroff would trace his location?"

He rolled his shoulders. "That's a level of technical sophistication I wouldn't expect of an art forger. I'll ask Trask about the possibilities. So where could Troy have gone?"

"Maybe he's been paid for his forging and rented a room."

"Without using a credit card? Doubtful. Our techs found his card numbers and accounts in his apartment. He hasn't used either card. What about that house of Silvio's?"

She straightened. "Troy went there with me twice when Silvio was alive. The place is part of the estate. One more thing to deal with."

"Could he have broken in and be staying there?"

"Not the house, because of the security system. People broke in a couple of times looking for souvenirs, but we've removed everything valuable or personal." As she thought, she gathered her hair and lifted it off her neck. "Troy could've gotten into the guest cottage. Only the lawn service was there recently, but those guys wouldn't notice or care. The caretaker checks on the property occasionally. He hasn't gone in a month. I could ask him to check."

"Better if we do it ourselves." He kissed her hand and released her, reached for his iced tea. "What about Silvio's agent? Another person we need to talk to."

"His house is on the way from here to the beach house. We could do both Friday." A sigh escaped her lips. "I don't look forward to tomorrow, sharing everything with my family."

"Not *everything*."

"Yes, yes. The minimum. No details." Parroting their agreement betrayed her anxiety. The police were keeping a lid on the investigation, but at some point the press would find out about everything. Better the family heard it from her. With Boyd's support.

"I have news for you on something else," he said. "Quinn Rykiel, who gave you her card from the fashion designer—"

"Sibyl Simone Fashions, yes?" She expected the worst.

"She's legit. Has worked there for ten years. Personnel records and her company portrait prove she's the same woman who approached you. "You could consider her idea and call—"

The theme from *Black Panther* erupted from his phone. "Trask. Maybe he has something for us."

Gemma tightened her grip on the chair arms. She leaned forward, hoping for a clue, but Boyd merely murmured or listened. *Please.*

Finally he lowered his phone. "Any word from the digital company about hacking?"

"No. I'd have told you. Nothing." She'd called earlier as she had every morning when she'd first asked them to check.

He relayed that, listened another minute, and disconnected.

By the guarded caution bracketing his eyes, she knew. She didn't want to know. Her chest tightened again. "Boyd?"

"No hacker. If Lincoln Trask can't detect intrusion, it's not there. That's not how the forgers are obtaining their information. It's got to be the login and password."

Hearing it in such a matter-of-fact tone delivered a quick, vicious twist to her heart. Tears burned her eyes. "My family, it can't be anyone in my family."

"Wait, honey. Maybe not. Somebody got a look at the screen at the crucial login time. Or one of the family shared accidentally."

"So someone like my mom's house cleaner found it and shared it with Nazaroff?"

"He seems to have some local thugs. Hoping for just such an opportunity, he could've used them to target people connected to the Bellini family."

Her brain reeled. She dragged in oxygen past the ever-present tension balloon and rubbed her temples. She longed for what Boyd suggested to be true, but his scenario didn't work.

"I should've told you this before, but I kept thinking the culprit was a hacker. The digital storage system requires an app on the user's computer. It must be installed by GuardStor and verified. Otherwise, the login and password are useless."

****

The next day, Boyd drummed his fingers on the steering wheel as he sat outside Gemma's mom's house. Damned hot in a tin can with no breeze through the open windows. Almost as hot as he'd been after the spinning class with her earlier. He'd need a second shower. He started the engine for a shot of conditioned air.

This big pickup belonged like a stray mutt at a dog show in this Alexandria neighborhood of upscale brick homes boasting luxury rides and limos. Wouldn't surprise him if somebody called the cops. Trask and Cassidy were in the office today, so two other operatives had his back. Their SUV waited at the end of the block. Another operative was keeping an eye on Gemma's condo. So far no new attacks. He wanted to keep it that way.

He checked the time. Gemma was spending a long time in there. She'd arranged to see her mom and sister together since they lived in the same neighborhood.

Before she left, she pressed a hand to her stomach—nerves—but set her mouth in a hard line. He had to trust her determination not to cave to their questions and blurt out too much.

"Wild Thing" started playing on his phone. He swiped the screen. "Hey, Jo."

"Hey yourself. Wanted you to know the Feebs have decided they want to be kept in the loop. Mr. Devlin says they may step in at some point."

"Step in? More like step on or around us. Anything on Leo Parisi yet?"

Big sigh. "Four of us tag-teamed him. Monday and Wednesday, he helped Tina load photo equipment in her SUV, but left for the office at ten. Home, office, meetings with potential renters at a warehouse and a boarded-up restaurant on Brandon Avenue in Springfield. Tuesday afternoon he browsed sports cars at a dealer. Lunch at the Elks Club two days, every day after work. Five o'clock brewskis. Nothing there. I called it off this morning. Sorry. I thought you were onto something."

Checking out cars might mean he expected a windfall, yet the Bellini money might pay for classy new wheels. Damn, Boyd had thought ol' Leo would pan out. On the other hand, maybe he just liked to look at cars.

"Yeah, me too. On my end, we're still fishing. When I have something, I'll get back to you. Gemma's inside talking to her mom and sister. I'm in the truck. Waiting." Sweating it. Literally.

"Why aren't you in there too?" Humor laced Jo's words.

"Gemma didn't want them focused on the two of us as a couple. More pressure than she could deal with. I don't get it. Once she starts laying out the forgery and attempts on her life, she has to explain my presence inside or out here."

"Baffled, are you?" She snerked a laugh. "Come on. Tina's a wedding photographer, and Erin is Gemma's *mother*. If you're out in the truck, they can't size you up. You're just the security guy, the bodyguard. So what's she telling them?"

"The minimum about the attempts on her life and the art forgery. That the police and Devlin Security are investigating and don't want details released. She's not mentioning blocking the archive." Clear to see she felt like a traitor, but she acknowledged secrecy was essential.

"Sounds good. Then what?"

"We wait for who reacts and how to being blocked from the archive."

"Let me know how James Bellini handles your show and tell today."

"Will do. He's our last appointment." He'd see how his private chat went before he decided what to tell Gemma, if anything. The front door opened and closed, and she flitted down the steps. "Here she comes. Gotta go."

Once inside, she leaned back against the head rest and sighed.

"You okay?" He pulled away from the curb. Started the GPS, set to take them to the orthopedics clinic where Victor Bellini was a partner.

She blessed him with a wobbly smile. "They took the news about like I expected. Tears and hugs. Both asked a ton of questions. I told them only what we decided."

"Dress rehearsal for your dad."

"Sharing more would've been harder. Now the first one's behind me, I can see that. Oh, and they wanted to meet you. I told them you'd rather keep watch outside. Bodyguard and all that."

A sniff from her sent his glance her way. She straightened and lifted her chin. "I had to promise to bring you back to meet them when this is all over."

Not going to happen.

Chapter Nineteen

"WHAT'S THIS ALL about?" Victor Bellini said, giving Gemma a brief one-armed hug and shaking hands with Boyd. His eyes widened when she introduced Boyd as a Devlin Security operative.

"It's a serious matter, Dad, but I can't tell you much."

She intended to conduct this as an official meeting, putting on her executive director persona, the one she donned for gallery owners and art patrons. But this was Dad, and she was his youngest. His baby, as he often reminded her.

He rolled his desk chair around the desk so he faced them. Shoot, no physical barrier between them.

She asked him to listen without interruptions until she finished her explanation. She folded her hands atop her handbag, too small for much of a shield.

"There have been three attempts on my life made to look like accidents." When Victor opened his mouth, she shook her head. "Thanks to Boyd here, and others in the company, I have not been injured. Also, some of Silvio's works have been copied and sold to unsuspecting buyers. Forgeries. It's likely the crimes are connected. The appropriate authorities and Devlin Security are investigating. That's all I can tell you." She braced herself for his questions.

Victor swept a hand over his head, his expression nearly as dark as his shock of ebony hair. "Why have you kept all this from me? And I assume, from your mother?"

His roughened voice and clipped tone meant he was afraid for her. She wouldn't let him tuck her away for safekeeping.

Head high, she kept her voice even. "Earlier this morning I told Mom exactly what I just told you."

She turned to Boyd, who was sitting at military attention. "Would you mind clarifying?"

He angled a nod to her. "Dr. Bellini, figuring out what was going on and if the crimes might be connected took some time. Much is still not clear. The authorities, including the FBI, insist the details be kept quiet."

"The FBI. Because of the forgery. What paintings have been forged? Were any stolen? Who's after my daughter? And why isn't she in a safe house or under protection?" His gaze shot back and forth between them, pleading.

Gemma needed to take back control. This meeting was hers, not his.

"I can't answer that. Law enforcement and FBI Art Crime and Devlin Security all feel it's important the details not be shared. I'm asking you to tell no one. Not my brothers and not Jennifer. No one. For the integrity of the investigation and... for my safety. Will you do that?"

His mouth quirked in either a smile or a grimace. "Doctors know how to keep confidences."

She'd have to accept that as a yes. "So far the media haven't learned about any of what I've told you. I hope this can all be cleared up before they do. Silvio entrusted his estate to my care. I won't allow any of this to damage his legacy. And I *am* under protection."

Victor glared at Boyd. "You?"

"Yes, sir. With backup. Mostly my job is protecting Gemma, but also investigating the art crimes. With her help."

She rose to her feet. "That's all. I won't keep you, Dad. You must have patients waiting."

He stood and wrapped his arms around her. Hugged her tight. He would worry, but at least he'd dealt with her one adult to another.

Victor turned to Boyd but didn't shake his hand again. "You look like a man who can handle himself. I'm counting on that. If anything happens to my baby, it's you I'll hold responsible."

****

Boyd finished his second pork taco. Gemma was picking at her taco salad. Both knew the place as a popular Alexandria Mexican restaurant, and it was on their way into D.C. She'd hardly spoken since they left her father's ortho clinic. Silence and no appetite meant something was bugging her. A happy Gemma was a chatty Gemma. He crunched into his third taco and considered his battle plan. No point in being subtle. A frontal assault it was.

"Was it the 'baby' remark?"

She lifted solemn green eyes to him. By her fixed expression, he knew he'd nailed it. She puffed out a breath and stirred tortilla shell bits into the meat and salad.

"I really wanted him to see me as a competent adult, but..." She hiked a slim shoulder.

"He did. Didn't he listen and agree to do what you asked? He understood, but hearing bad guys want to kill his daughter scared him. He was in full daddy mode then."

"Thanks. I suppose you're right, but I hate it when he calls me his 'baby.'"

"Look. it's the same in my family. Dave and I are only two, but to Mom, he's her baby. Yeah, her baby, the big bad state trooper. Same thing in my cousins' families too. Chill."

When she grinned and forked up a chunk of spicy beef, he awarded himself a medal. A small one, but hey.

She ate with more appetite for a few minutes. Then, "Did you mean what you said, that you'd protect me with your life?"

"I meant every word. They'll have to go through me to get to you." He set down his half-eaten taco. "Then you can take 'em down with your self-d moves."

"Or deafen them with this." She flicked the alarm dangling from the strap of her bag.

They laughed together, and she dug into her lunch. He could've told her she was more than a job to him, way the hell more. Better not.

After lunch they met with her uncle James in his North Capitol Street suite at Baker, Cowell, and Bellini Capital Management. The twelfth story window behind his polished walnut desk offered a distant view of the Capitol Building. A side table held fresh flowers in a vase. Boyd inhaled their scent and something else. Oh yeah, money.

While James Bellini kissed Gemma on both cheeks and asked after her mother, Boyd sized him up. Fifties, fit looking, custom tailored trousers—the jacket hung on a rack in the corner—and light-blue shirt with matching tie that probably cost more than Boyd's entire wardrobe, including the tux. Aside from the money angle, still good looking enough to attract women. Damn, Boyd really wanted this man to be the breakthrough to end this threat—*these* threats.

Unlike her dad, James exhibited not an eyelash blink of reaction when Gemma introduced Boyd. After a handshake, James escorted them to a grouping of upholstered chairs.

Gemma placed her handbag on her lap and made her intro. She waited for his assent to listen to the end. As she spoke, disbelief and then horror registered in crimped lines across his brow and a downturned mouth. When she finished, he shook his head, saying he couldn't believe this possible. He agreed to keep what she told him to himself, then asked many of the same questions as her father.

"So there's a team, Mr. Kirby, not just you, protecting my niece?"

"A team on backup, but I'm on watch 24/7, sir. Devlin Security fully appreciates the severity of the recent attacks."

"Then I think we're finished," Gemma said, rising from her seat. She slung her bag onto her shoulder. "When this is over, all the details will come out."

James rounded his desk and hugged her, kissed her cheeks again. Shook Boyd's hand. "If either of you need anything, anything at all, just ask."

They walked out into the reception area, and the door closed behind them with a soft snick.

"So nice to see you again, Ms. Bellini." The dark-haired woman, James's administrative assistant, smiled broadly. Administrative assistant, Boyd huffed inwardly, another name for palace guard.

"Wonderful to see you, Grace. I don't make it here as often as I'd like." Gemma then inquired about the woman's family.

Boyd had counted on her doing exactly that. He patted his pockets. Excused himself, saying he'd left his phone inside.

They barely paid attention as he opened the door to the inner sanctum and slipped inside.

"Yes?" James said, shooting to his feet from behind the desk.

"Gemma thinks I've left my phone in here, but it's an excuse to talk privately." He strode to the polished desk. "A colleague observed you a week ago having drinks with this attractive young woman." He withdrew his ammo from his inner jacket pocket and laid one of the photos on the desk.

James's features flattened to blank, but he swallowed. Twice. "This means nothing. Meeting with people all the time is part of doing business."

Boyd withdrew a second and a third photo and placed both alongside the first. One showed James handing the woman a thick envelope. The last showed the woman at a teller window removing a wad of cash from the same envelope.

The other man's face paled a shade or two. "You... you have no right."

"Devlin Security is assisting FBI Art Crime in the forgery investigation. Would you rather I'd taken these to the agent in charge? When it comes to protecting your niece, I'll do whatever it takes. And didn't you offer your help only minutes ago?" The photos couldn't be used as evidence in court, but they sure as hell provided leverage.

"But this—" James tapped a finger on the photos "—has nothing to do with the threat to Gemma or the paintings." His voice sounded brittle, less in command.

"We'll see. Blackmail about an affair could've led you to do anything to cover it up. Or this woman could be an intermediary with the art forgers. Along with money, did you share specific details about Silvio's paintings?"

He started to push to his feet, but fell heavily back into the seat. "No, never! My uncle's paintings?" He shook his head over and over. The hand touching one of the photos trembled. "That's not what it's about."

"Then tell me what it *is* about."

James raked stiff fingers through his hair. "Whitney—her name's Whitney York—used to work here but left to go back to college full time."

That much Boyd already knew, thanks to Cassidy. He placed his hands on the desk and leaned forward. "And?"

"Money is tight. I ran into her in the restaurant where she was waiting tables. We talked, had a few drinks… and one thing led to another." His features sagged in defeat.

"An affair."

"It was. Past tense. I ended it with that envelope. Along with the money, it contained the contact information of someone who can help her obtain a grant to pay for her education." He managed to stand this time and firmed his expression. "But she has nothing to do with any art forgers. Impossible."

"We're still investigating. If she is involved, your affair with her is sure to come out."

"She's not involved. And I've confessed to my wife.

She may eventually forgive me." He swept up the three photos and shoved them at Boyd. "Get these out of here."

Boyd pocketed them and headed to the door. He wasn't convinced. Or did he want to believe the man was the leaker so he had a lead?

****

"Finally. Took you long enough." Nazaroff smacked his palm on the table. The other man's eyes shifted away. The reason became obvious. "Your hands are empty. You were supposed to bring me the next printouts."

Marshak and Hubik had entered behind him and took positions to one side of the door. They folded their ham-size arms. Marshak's eyes rolled above his bulbous nose. Echoes of keyboards, of shoes shuffling and easels scraping on the cement floor vanished. The other three were listening.

"I couldn't get them. Couldn't get in."

"*In*? Into the website?"

His head jerked up and down. "It wouldn't let me. The login didn't work. A technical glitch. Maybe."

"She changed the login, you idiot, probably the password as well."

A sour odor mingled with the tang of paints. Fool was sweating and not just from the piss poor air conditioning they'd rented. Let him.

This eventuality was exactly what Nazaroff had feared ever since learning that Gemma had charge of the estate. He needed more time. Time enough to complete more paintings. But this man and the other two failed to rid him of the threat before she—and Kirby—figured it out.

"Your incompetence and one delay after another

have cost me. Cost *us*. All of us. No payout for me means no payout for you." Not that the craphead would be around to collect more than he'd already been paid. "You're of no use to me anymore."

"But… these guys—" he jabbed a thumb over his shoulder at the two men to his right "—screwed up all my arrangements." His eyebrows jammed together, sculpting wide wales in his broad forehead.

"Hey, wait a fuckin' minute," Hubik began.

Nazaroff held up a hand, and the thug subsided.

"Ah, but the *arrangements*, the plots were all yours." Nazaroff waited a beat, then smiled. "What is it we need to move forward?"

"Access to the archives, of course. The new login and password. But with that Kirby guy there all the time, we can't get into her house to search."

"Exactly. You won't have to. Bring me Gemma Bellini."

"Holy shit! No, I can't. She'll see me. She'll know."

"She won't be going home afterward. She'll disappear. You want her out of the way as much as I do. Time for you to fucking show you mean it. Understand me?"

The other man looked as if he'd swallowed a live toad, but he nodded. When Nazaroff had begun his arrangement with his so-called partner, the man had swaggered and bragged, and bought into the forgery. Now he drooped, his cockiness scraped away. A man who could crack.

Nazaroff's gaze encompassed Marshak and Hubik as well. "The three of you work out something. Soon. A plan that must not fail."

He didn't need to add *or else*.

Chapter Twenty

WHEN THEY RETURNED to Gemma's condo, she went upstairs. To clear her head, she said, with her paints. Boyd took his phone out to the patio to check in with Jo Cassidy.

"Gemma said mom and sis cried. Her dad ordered me to take care of her or else." Then he detailed his chat with the uncle. "He claims the affair is over and he told his wife. Maybe."

Before he could go on, she said, "I have something that may cheer you up. We've found Nazaroff's shill. Art Crime did a search on known female con artists involved with art and artifacts and compared them with the descriptions from the bilked buyers."

"Photos?"

"You bet. Trask showed the buyers an array of photos, and all three ID'd the same woman. She used the name Lucia Sherbourne for a couple of sales, Lydia Simmons for a third. Real name's Letty Boggess. She's wanted in Georgia for bilking galleries, selling them sketches supposedly by Picasso and Braque. I'm sending you her picture now."

The photo popped up in his messages. "As described, attractive, late forties. Distinctive high cheekbones set her apart."

"Identifiable despite the wigs. FBI has the photo and

info. I may know more from them after our gig tomorrow." Throat clearing on Cassidy's end. "I have a little more on the York woman since we spoke."

"Thanks. I think."

"Chavez followed her yesterday. I'm sitting on her today. In classes at Marymount University for most of the day. Waits tables at an Alexandria restaurant until nine. Then home to an efficiency near the college. Mailbox had York, but no first name or initial. She didn't leave until this morning. Same routine both days. I'm parked in the lot near her car at the college. Dead end, bro."

He thought about it. "She may be, but the uncle, I'm not so sure. He needed a pile of cash to give her the other day. Could've gotten that from Nazaroff. Untraceable."

Grumbling noises over the phone. "Look, Boyd, I know you want this solved, everything over with, but this is an unlikely scenario. Ol' Uncle James is stinkin' rich, with multiple sources of cash. But hey, in the interest of thoroughness, I'll get Chavez to follow him again. After our gig tomorrow, I'll stick with her."

"In the interest of thoroughness. Thanks. See you in the morning."

Tomorrow, Cassidy in a long, brown wig and another operative who resembled Boyd enough from a distance would switch vehicles with him. The idea was for them to lead Nazaroff's guys toward Worldwide Storage. Boyd and Gemma would head south to see Silvio's artist agent.

Boyd stared at the silent phone. Did he want everything over with? Hell, yes, he wanted the danger and the art forgery over with. But *everything*? Not Gemma's happy smile that punched in her dimples or…

His knuckles blanched white around the wrought-iron chair arm.

****

As soon as Gemma hopped out of the truck, John Fitzhugh opened the front door of the sprawling white frame house. A formal man, he'd dressed to greet his guests in navy dress pants and a crisp snowy shirt.

Slipping her sunglasses into her tote, she could almost smell the sun's heat on the stone walk. Her first steps faltered. Boyd cupped her elbow and gave it a light squeeze. His support steadied her.

"You ready?"

"I am, but I worry how all our bad news will affect him." She drew a deep breath and then waved to Fitz. She skipped up the steps into his embrace.

His thinning gray hair had turned nearly white, but he was lean and seemed as fit as ever. Now watery with age, his thoughtful blue eyes might perceive the concern on her face. But his gaze rose to Boyd, behind her.

"Fitz, it's wonderful to see you. It's been way too long." She turned aside and drew Boyd closer. "This is my... friend, Boyd Kirby."

"Sir, it's an honor. Gemma sings your praises."

Fitz chuckled as he shook Boyd's hand. "Call me Fitz. Everyone does. And pay no attention to her. The girl's the most enthusiastic person I've ever known."

He beckoned them in and led the way through living and dining areas to a covered veranda. A ceiling fan provided a breeze, not cool, but at least moving air that brought the scents of the water and freshly mowed grass. Gemma loved this house. Gaps in the dune bushes allowed glimpses of the beach. The view might make an interesting painting, a different angle on the seaside.

They took seats around a low table on which sat champagne flutes and the ingredients for mimosas. Oh boy, he thought this was a celebration of romance. Boyd would probably prefer beer, but he smiled and thanked their host as he accepted a glass.

She and Fitz chatted for a few minutes about family and work. His daughter Megan was Gemma's agent and took on many of Fitz's clients when he retired.

"I brought you something." She plucked a soft package wrapped in tissue paper from her tote.

His eyes sparkled as he unwrapped it. He lifted up a pale blue necktie. "You know me too well. Wonderful. You have such a way with movement. They truly seem to be flying." He thanked her profusely while tying on the gift.

On its pale blue silk she'd painted a small flock of piping plovers in flight. A dedicated bird watcher, Fitz loved those small shore birds.

He turned to Boyd. "Are you an artist too?"

A rumbled chuckle. "An amateur at best." At Gemma's nod, he went on. "I'm an operative for Devlin Security Force. You may remember the name from the transfer of Silvio's artworks to the new storage. We provided the security."

"I do, of course. But…" His gaze darkened.

"Fitz, I must apologize," she said. "It's lovely to see you and get caught up, but this is more than a social call." She explained the forgery of Silvio's works, but, not wanting to frighten him, omitted the attempts on her life. As she spoke, he sank back in his chair and blinked rapidly as processing the revelation sank in. "The biggest sale so far was of *Chincoteague Guardian*. FBI Art Crime is looking into the matter, but Boyd and a team at

Devlin Security are helping me."

"Horrible! How could this happen?" the old man said. "You have everything secured."

"I thought so. But somehow the art forgers have accessed the digital records. That's how they created paintings that passed for authentic."

That was Boyd's cue to step in. "Buyers are targeted by a woman who approaches them in a gallery or museum where they're looking at works in the same genre. She tells them the family wishes to conduct the sale privately. This woman." He held out his phone.

The older man took reading glasses from his shirt pocket and put them on. He peered closely at the image on the screen and frowned. When he met their gazes, his expression was even more puzzled.

"She's a writer for *Art & Artists*. She came to see me a couple of months ago. Her name's Diana Rountree. Except the woman in your photo has blonde hair. Diana's is red. Same age, about my daughter's forty-eight. Odd that I still haven't seen the article. This is all very strange."

"Strange doesn't begin to describe it, I'm afraid." Gemma scooted her chair closer and clasped his cold hand. "This woman is no writer for any journal. She's an experienced con artist who calls herself many names. I know you are not involved, but maybe you can help explain *this*." She nodded to Boyd.

He unfolded a copy of the fake provenance letter. "The woman selling the forged Bellinis provides the buyers with letters like these. This one was for *Chincoteague Guardian*." He handed it to Fitz.

The agent blinked harder. "But... but this is my stationery. Except it hasn't the embossed letterhead."

"This is a photocopy, but the letter she used did have the embossed letterhead," Gemma said. "I saw it myself."

Fitz collapsed back into the chair cushion and downed a healthy swig of his mimosa. He shook his head again and again. "And that looks like my signature at the bottom. If you have more to tell me, I'll need something stronger than champagne."

"How could she have obtained your actual stationery?" Boyd said.

Fitz stared at his lap as he sipped more champagne. He set down the glass and pushed to his feet. "Follow me."

He led them back the way they'd come and down the hall to his home office. Gemma admired the memorabilia on the walls, along with a painting of this shore Silvio had given him.

Fitz rolled out his desk chair. "We met here in my office. It seemed more appropriate for an interview from a prestigious journal." His mouth thinned. He had likely realized that was no interview anyone would ever read. "But I have her business card, from *Art & Artists*. It's real. I know their cards. Here. It's still tucked into the desk blotter pad." He held out the card.

"Did you leave her alone at any point?" Boyd accepted it and took out his phone.

"Yes, she had a bit of a cough, so I went to fetch iced tea." More blinking. He wiped his eyes with a tissue. "Oh."

"Yes, I'm afraid she helped herself," Gemma said gently. The poor man had still hoped he hadn't been duped.

He withdrew a stationer's box and set it on the

desktop. "This should be almost full. It's missing a couple dozen sheets. She must've tucked them into her briefcase while I was gone."

Boyd's thumbs were still busy on his phone, so Gemma said, "Did she have you sign anything?"

"A release to print the interview. So that's how she—or one of this *gang*—copied my signature. Damned clever, these crooks. But the card, was that forged too?"

Boyd looked up from his phone. "Forged or lifted at a gallery, but the name is real. Diana Rountree is a writer for *Art & Artists*, but she's not the woman who stole from you. This is her photo from the journal's website." He held out the phone.

"Diana Rountree is young enough to be my granddaughter," Fitz whispered. Scarlet flagged his papery cheeks. He shook his head. "That... that woman really snookered me, didn't she? Damn."

****

Seeing the fixed sadness on Gemma's beautiful face made Boyd want to punch the guys responsible for this entire mess. He flexed his fingers on the steering wheel. She was mangling the straps of her bag as she stared ahead at the highway. Hadn't said a word since they left John Fitzhugh's. At lunch she kept conversation going despite Fitz's dark mood, and her own. She described her current painting project, another dock scene, and last Friday's reception. She'd drawn Boyd in to add his perspective on the crowd. Whatever made her—and Fitz—feel better.

Was her mood because of him or anxiety about the possibility Dupree was hiding out at Silvio's place? Gemma could stand tough for herself, but other people's woes stung her tender heart. If they actually found

Dupree in that guest cottage, maybe he'd give them a location, a lead, something that would end Nazaroff's racket.

"Honey, you're not dealing with all this shit alone. I'm here for you." He held out a hand.

"I know, and I can't tell you how much that means to me." She linked fingers with him, and her delectable mouth curved in a half smile. "When Fitz curses, bless his heart, you know he's really upset. He feels guilty and ashamed he was taken in."

"Didn't you catch what he said as we left?"

She tilted her head. "Something about catching the damn crooks. Oh. He swore again."

"Exactly. And there was fire in his eyes. He'll be okay."

"I hope you're right. And we *must* catch the damn crooks." Gemma turned toward him, curling one leg beneath her. She laid a hand on his shoulder. "It's been nearly a week since that dump truck rammed us and days since I shut off access to the archive. I'm going nuts wondering when Nazaroff will try something else, and imagining all sorts of horrible things he could do. Nothing so far. What's going on?"

"I wish I knew. It's like that line in old movies. It's quiet… too quiet. Art Crime has alerted galleries in the D.C. area and beyond. My team is scouting known thugs for hire." He covered her hand with his right one. "Waiting for a break is the hardest part."

On the outskirts of Rimini Beach, the town where Silvio's house was located, they stopped at a market for supplies. Not knowing how much time the visit to Fitzhugh would take, they'd packed for the night.

The nav screen displayed the turnoff to the house,

but without Gemma's excited pointing, he might've missed seeing the narrow private lane shaded by big pine trees.

"Before Silvio bought this house, it had been a small farm for a few years. The pines are a good buffer between the property and the highway. Beyond the boxwood hedge behind the house is a small pond and the neighbor's vineyard."

A sprawling two-story house came into view on their right. Boyd negotiated a curve past a small cottage with a porch on the left. No tire tracks on the lane or here, no footprints in the sand and gravel path leading to the cottage. He parked in front of the separate three-car garage.

"This has always been called the beach house," she went on, chirping forced optimism, "but the beach is actually a mile back down the road. Silvio wanted seclusion for his work and a house big enough for the family. He and Nana added the wings. The guest cottage was here."

If Dupree was staying in that cottage, he was more than roughing it. "I'll—"

"—*go check around the outside. You stay here with the doors locked.*" She grinned, but her eyes betrayed her anxiety.

He grinned back. "If you see anybody but me, lay on the horn."

His tour—cottage and main house—turned up no tracks, no trash, no nothing except signs of a well-maintained property. Possible the recent rain washed away tracks or footprints, even those of the local contractor in charge of the mowing and hedge trimming.

"No signs of anybody," he told her when he opened

the passenger door. "Ready to check inside the cottage?"

Nibbling on her lower lip, she joined him. Her hand already held the key ring. She flipped to the key as they crossed the lawn.

"Troy? It's Gemma, Troy. Are you here?"

No answer.

She climbed the two steps to the porch and unlocked the door before stepping aside for him.

His hand on his holstered 9mm, Boyd turned the knob. Pushed the door inward. "Troy Dupree, if you're here, come on out. We're here to help you."

Silence.

The guy had never been known to own a weapon, but frightened men did desperate things. Boyd jerked his head sideways, and Gemma eased farther to the side. He unholstered the weapon and clicked off the safety.

Stepped inside. Mold and dust tickled his nose. Dust covered the tables, and evidence of mice dotted the hardwood floor. He quickly cleared the bedroom and tiny bath.

"You can come in if you want," he called. "Doesn't look like anybody's been here."

She took a few steps inside and looked around. Apparently drew the same conclusion. Turned and went to the porch, held onto one of the pine posts.

Boyd pulled her into his arms. Held her while she cried. She seemed to blame herself for Dupree's getting involved in art forgery, but the guy had made his own choices. Now was not the time to bring that up.

"Where the hell can he be?" she murmured against his chest.

Unless Troy had some secret hideout, he could come up with two possibilities. Neither was anything she'd want to hear.

Chapter Twenty-One

GEMMA WAITED IN the truck again while Boyd went through the house. She'd unlocked the door for him with her code. That was twenty minutes ago. She tapped fingers on her knee. *Come on, Boyd, it's a big house, but still...* Except for a few pieces of furniture, the place was empty. Troy wasn't there.

Was he with Nazaroff? She couldn't believe Troy had anything to do with the attempts on— *No, don't even think it.* Her pulse scrambled as a whisper of fear chilled the back of her neck.

And now she'd dragged Boyd all this way for nothing. But here they were. At this wonderful house. They should both relax.

When he came around the corner of the house and gave her the all-clear sign, she opened the passenger door and hopped out. "Nothing and no one, right?"

"Nothing but ghostly furniture and some dust." A wry grin crinkled lines beside his eyes. "Six bedrooms?"

"And four and a half baths. For all the family and kids, sometimes other artists too."

As he collected their bags from the back, he jerked a nod toward the sunroom addition. "What's with the wooden balcony at the end of that wing?"

"Nana liked to go out and look at the stars before bed. She enjoyed it a few years before a stroke took her

180

life. Silvio never used the balcony again."

Boyd curved an arm around her and kissed her forehead.

They carried in their bags and the cooler. Although it had been closed up, the Colonial wasn't hot, due to central air conditioning, but she turned it off and opened windows throughout to invite in fresh air. At sunset, she'd crank it up again.

When she looked longingly toward the studio wing, he said, "Go ahead and commune. Great space in there, lots of light."

"Thanks. I agree." She stroked his beard-shadowed jaw and brushed a kiss on his chin. In his arms, she could forget everything, but she backed away and went down the hall.

He was right, she needed to visit Silvio's spirit. The studio took up the entire addition. Skylights and tall windows on both east and west sides provided that light. *Silvio, if I can stop these forgers, maybe at last I'll feel less like one.*

Nothing in there, no easels or canvases or tarps, just the late-afternoon sunshine dancing shadows across the wood floorboards. Still, Gemma fancied she could smell turpentine and gesso. Even hear her grandfather's smooth voice. But it was only the echo of her sandals scraping the wooden floor.

She marched out before she let herself get maudlin.

After she'd made the bed in the master suite and changed into shorts and a tank top, she found Boyd in the sunroom enjoying the breeze. He'd uncovered the porch furniture and sat sprawled on the loveseat cushions. The lowering sun's rays filtered through the louvered blinds, splashing the Adirondack chairs in gold.

"Great view out this way, the lawn sloping down to the pond," he said.

She sank onto the other cushion and laid her head against his arm, a comfy muscle pillow. "We can sit here and watch the sunset if you want."

"I want."

"Oh, I forgot to put away the groceries." She jerked erect and pushed to her feet.

"Whoa, Gemma."

Boyd's arms encircled her. He turned her to face him and pressed his lips to hers. Not passionate, or a prologue to sex in the master suite. A gentle, tender kiss, as if he knew she was faking her upbeat attitude. He released her with a peck on her forehead.

"You've had a rough couple of days. I want you to stay here and just *be*. Food's already in the fridge. I'm grilling, remember?"

She rose on tiptoes and returned the kiss. She wanted more, but would wait for later. "Thank you. Then I'll go open the wine."

"Wine'll be good with the steak, but I'll crack a beer for the cocktail cruise."

He too had changed into shorts and one of his countless Army t-shirts. A bulge at his hip meant he carried a holstered pistol. No need for it here, but he wasn't a man to take chances. The thought shivered a little thrill through her.

A quick trip to the kitchen and Gemma set out crackers and a mix of crabmeat, mayo, and lemon juice on a tray. They snacked and sipped while the grill heated.

"I *am* relaxing, per orders, but I have to ask," she said. "Do you think Troy is still working with Nazaroff?"

"That would explain why nobody can find him. Or

maybe he wanted out and is hiding. We know where he's not. Is there anywhere else you can think of he could've gone?"

Her chest tightened. Maybe he was afraid he could go to prison again. That would explain his sudden disappearance and his warning to her. She should've seen before it was too late that he'd gotten into trouble.

"I don't. He wouldn't have gone home. His parents kicked him out when he came out to them. But they could have a suggestion where to look."

She might need to write down something, so she took her phone to the kitchen. It rang four times before a woman's voice answered.

"Hi, Mrs. Dupree, it's Gemma Bellini, Troy's friend." The woman asked if Troy had returned, which made her task easier. As they talked, the weight in her chest eased, and the zing of adrenaline energized her.

A few minutes later, she raced back to the sunroom.

"Troy used to go fishing with his uncle in the Blue Ridge foothills. Troy's mom says the uncle's cabin is still there. It doesn't have an actual address, but it's up a dirt road behind this farm." She handed him the paper with the address and bounced from foot to foot. "Is that our next trip?"

He gave a slow head shake. "I'll send this info to Cassidy. Devlin operatives will go. Better if you don't get too far from civilization."

She slumped sideways on the seat. Of course he was right. It could be dangerous.

"Sure, that makes sense. Now about those steaks?"

The ribeyes were perfect, medium rare and tender, accompanied by a foil packet of sliced potatoes, onions, and green peppers. They ate at the picnic table in the sunroom and watched ducks gliding on the pond. As the sun sank, deer materialized out of the pines to graze.

After he checked inside and out as he always did and locked up, they climbed the stairs.

Gemma yawned as she entered the bedroom behind him. "Sorry, it's that delicious dinner and the wine. And all that relaxing. I'm used to being busy."

He turned, his gray eyes heavy-lidded and his rascal's smile devastating. "I plan on keeping you busy a while longer."

He captured her hands. Her heart thumped in response. Her senses leaped to attention, rousing her to hyperawareness. He captured her with his eyes, sooty dark with desire, and filled her every breath with the clean cotton scent of his t-shirt and the potent heat of aroused male. No other man had ever caused this instant heat, this rise of need. She'd come to crave his touch, his full embrace, the feeling of utter possession. He was a fever in her blood.

"So what do you have in mind? This late at night I hope it's not more self-defense training."

"Depends on your definition."

She freed her hands and speared her fingers in his hair. Rose on her toes and licked the hollow of his throat where his pulse beat. "Show me what you've got."

"I do love a challenge."

He reached behind his head and yanked upward on his t-shirt, pulled it up and off, tossed it, and kicked off his shorts and boxers. He pulled her flush against him. He was a marvel of both smooth and ripped muscles. Against her, she felt the steel of bunched muscles, his erection insistent against her belly.

She smoothed her palm down his hard chest with its

dusting of dusky hairs. Before she could delve lower than his belly button, he scooped her up and sank onto the sheets, taking her with him. She hummed her pleasure at being enveloped in his heat and strength. He removed her tank and bra and cupped one breast, brushing his thumb across her nipple, the rasp of the callus so erotic she arched off the bed. He lavished attention on the other breast, and in short order the rest of her clothes disappeared.

His kisses were hungry and drugging, and his tongue met hers in a lush and lazy sweep. She returned the favor, eliciting a moan from him. She knew only his dark taste, the heat of his mouth. Conscious thought fragmented.

Ripples of heat washed through her as she melted, mindless. His hands spread over her torso, each finger marking her with his heat. He moved down her body then, kissing and licking and nibbling as he went, as if savoring her as dessert. He spread her thighs and settled, teasing her with his tongue until she clutched at his shoulders, reaching for him.

"Hurry!"

He paused for protection, then she went boneless as he entered her. He took his time moving, pressing, all while kissing her with thoroughness and tangling all her circuits. She lost herself in his powerful strokes and the encompassing heat of his body as she climbed toward completion, filled with exhilaration. Heat flashed within her, spread through her belly and thighs, and her whole body tingled. He groaned her name and surged against her as his climax took him.

****

Gemma woke to silence and the lack of a heat source and deep breathing beside her. Light from the moon filtered through the eyebrow window. The hallway nightlights. No sounds in the bathroom. Did Boyd have one of his nightmares?

She punched her pillow and flopped onto her back.

Neither had said a word about their relationship continuing after Nazaroff and his thugs were "rolled up," as Boyd put it. She knew little of his feelings for her other than desire. And he did seem to like her.

For years, she'd kept men at arm's length. Not willing to trust, she kept relationships casual and brief. But Boyd... one look from him and her body softened and her heart raced. She couldn't recall feeling like this for anyone else, and had from the beginning. She'd resisted letting herself admit anything but desire for him, but being together constantly had changed things and changed her. It wasn't just that he was tough and a protector to his bones. He was more, attentive and kind and genuine. She cared for him. A lot. And making love with him was both sweet and sizzling.

They were attuned to each other's bodies now so the joining was richer, more intense. It frightened her. He made her want more than she'd believed she could ever have.

She slid out of bed and turned on the bedside light. After slipping on the long tee she'd brought to sleep in, she padded barefoot downstairs. She found him in the sunroom. Wearing only his boxers, he stood staring out at the moonlit pond, his arms rigid at his sides.

"A soothing sight," she said, by way of announcing herself.

He spun toward her, every muscle, every tendon tightened like iron bands. Fists clenched and jawline taut. Not soothed.

"Yes," he bit out. He scraped back his hair in a harsh motion.

"You had the nightmare again."

"Didn't mean to wake you."

"You didn't." Would he welcome her embrace? Or was it the kind of hurt he wanted to nurse? The latter, but she bet he *needed* touching. She walked to him and curved an arm around his waist, kissed his scarred shoulder. "I've heard counseling can help soldiers deal with PTSD."

He remained silent, not rejecting her touch but not moving and still staring out. She stood with him in silent support.

Finally, a rumbling sigh escaped him. "I had counseling before I left the Rangers."

"If you try again, you might find peace."

"No. I didn't keep my men safe. I don't deserve peace." He turned and walked away into the darkened house.

Gemma hung her head and let the tears fall, tears for this man who hurt so much. His nightmares plagued him more often because of his fear he would fail to protect her.

Did she want more than she could have? Maybe. But she couldn't deny she'd fallen in love with him. Acting on her feelings was another matter.

No escape from worries. For either of them.

Chapter Twenty-Two

LYING ON HIS side, Boyd remained still when
Gemma returned to the darkened room. The mattress
barely moved as she climbed in bed. On the far side, her
back to him. The idea she might be afraid of him
delivered a vicious twist to his gut. She was brave and
strong in many ways, but her tender heart, already
bruised, didn't need more blows.

His head was a war zone, the nightmare more
violent and bloody than usual, waking him in a cold
sweat. Counseling wouldn't make it all go away, but if
he could protect Gemma until the danger ended, maybe
he'd earn a respite from the worst. For now, if he held
her while she slept, he could pretend he was keeping her
safe.

"I didn't mean to scare you," he said in a quiet voice.

"You didn't. But I do worry about you." She scooted
closer, made his bent arm her pillow.

When she fitted her curvy little behind against his
lap, his body sprang to attention. As always, his reaction
to her was intense and instantaneous. She was warm and
soft and smelled of shampoo and lotion. He wrapped her
in his other arm and held her. "Gemma?"

"Yes, oh, yes." She wriggled around and hooked her
right leg over his hip.

He found her mouth and tasted her sweetness and

heat, her sunshine to his darkness, kissed her with his lips, his tongue, his soul. Did she know this was what he needed? Or maybe what they both needed. He stroked between her thighs, and when he slid inside her, she sighed and urged him deeper. They moved together until she uttered a soft cry and pulsed around him and his climax exploded in a tsunami of pleasure.

****

Boyd was awakened early Saturday morning by a call from Jo Cassidy. The summons to Devlin Security for an update came as no surprise. He'd texted her the info about the cabin and that he had more from John Fitzhugh. He and Gemma ate a quick breakfast and packed up. Any reassurance by him about the search for Troy fell flat. She fretted and vibrated with muttered worry and hope. Hell, her worry was justified.

An hour and a half later, Boyd joined Cassidy, Trask, and Marton. The aroma of everybody's morning joe hovered around the small conference table. He swallowed a gulp of his brew and opened his laptop. Turned out the main reason for the confab was prep for Cassidy and Trask's meeting later with Detective Santiago and Art Crime Special Agent Irwin.

Marton asked for his report first, saying it might inform her search for how the art forgers convinced buyers the paintings were authentic. Not his priority. Dupree was. He could be the key. Then the threat to Gemma could end. But he waited. He was low man here.

No matter. His report on the fake Diana Rountree aka Lucia Sherbourne aka Letty Boggess, the stolen stationery, and Fitzhugh's signature took all of five minutes.

When he finished, Cassidy asked, "Any flak from

Gemma's stopping access to the archive?"

"No reaction from family members, no attempts on her life, zip. I'm holding my breath."

"The Sherbourne woman's all over the place," Marton said, tapping a finger on her laptop screen, "first in the Washington area and now Charlottesville and Richmond. A possible in Baltimore. The recovery of the *Chincoteague Guardian* might've have spooked the gang."

Before anyone could speculate on that, Boyd said, "I'm more concerned that we find Troy Dupree. If he's found, he could blow the art forgery case wide open. Any word?"

Cassidy shook her head. "Interstate goes only so far into those hills. Winding two-lanes where Chavez and Wing are now."

A ping announced a text on his phone. He glanced at the screen. "They just arrived at the farm, headed up to the cabin now."

Marton received a call and had to step out for a moment.

"Where'd you stash Gemma?" Trask asked Boyd.

"In the staff café with her sketch pad. When I alerted Mr. Devlin's office, Francine said the boss would send somebody to hang out nearby, keep an eye out for her safety." Not necessary here, but he appreciated the gesture. Unless Devlin still suspected her involvement. "Gemma texted me a few minutes ago that Francine brought her a plate of her lemon bars."

"Not the ones she makes special for Devlin?"

Boyd grinned. "You got it. I told her if she doesn't save me a few, I'll leave her there."

Marton returned and the others gave their reports.

Boyd made notes on his laptop, hoping to connect some dots.

Cassidy's check into James Bellini's erstwhile girlfriend verified her student and waitress status and found no connections to art of any kind, let alone forgery or Morgan Nazaroff. No history of nefarious anything. A dead end, as she'd predicted. No dots to anything.

"Look for hints that James would like to wrest control of Silvio's estate from Gemma," Boyd said. "A power grab."

Cassidy agreed. They discussed the possibility of interviewing his staff. Or persuading Detective Santiago to try that angle. Trask said he'd bring it up at the meeting.

"I looked deeper into Leo Parisi." Trask ran a finger down a printout as he talked. "Failed businesses—used cars and window cleaning, for two. Not a hard charger. The current job, commercial building rentals, appears on shaky ground, likely for the same reason. The other employees of that firm received bonuses last year. Nada for our boy."

"Parisi strikes me as somebody who looks for the big score but doesn't work to make it happen," Boyd said. If we had evidence, the Feebs might be interested in obtaining a warrant."

"A lazy bum in every family," said Cassidy. "Except mine." Chuckles around the table. "So we're agreed that's a dead end?"

Everybody agreed. Boyd nodded last, but with reluctance. Shit, they still had nothing on how Nazaroff and crew were getting into the archives. This was taking too fucking long.

"You might as well have the rest of what I dug up.

Sending now." Trask hit keys.

"Why not. Thanks." Probably nothing there, but he would look at it later.

"It's—"

Cassidy's phone vibrated on the table, interrupting Trask. She swiped the screen, tapped. "Hey, Chavez. You're on speaker. Kirby, Trask, and Marton are with me. Sit rep."

Throat clearing. Then, "Nobody at that cabin."

Boyd's gut clenched. He resisted shifting in his chair, instead fisted his hands on his knees.

"That it?" she asked. "No signs of anybody?"

"Didn't say that." His voice sounded hollow, probably on the truck's speaker. "Just spoke to the farmer at the foot of the hill. We had to come down to get cell service. He says Dupree arrived there early June. Went out about once a week for supplies."

Trask and Boyd exchanged a look. Marton tapped keys on her laptop.

"What's the scene there now?" Cassidy asked.

"Car registered to Dupree is parked by the cabin. Tire tracks of a second vehicle, probably a pickup. Cabin door busted in. Table, wooden chair overturned, other signs of a struggle. Artist's paint brushes, paint tubes on the floor. Big cooler on the floor, moldy food and rancid liquid inside. Couple articles of clothing in the bedroom but no suitcase or duffel."

"Any idea how long ago this invasion happened?" Boyd flexed his fingers, worked his jaw.

Chavez muttered something to Wing.

Wing's lighter voice replied something unintelligible and then, louder, "About two weeks ago— the farmer doesn't recall what day—two men in a black

Ford pickup stopped to ask him if he knew where Dupree was. Claimed they were friends of his. He directed them up the narrow track leading to the cabin. Didn't see them leave. Hasn't seen Dupree since that day."

Boyd swallowed the acidic lump in his throat. How was he going to tell Gemma? How much should he say?

****

Gemma shoved the cookie plate aside. The lemony aroma no longer appealed. A few DSF people occupied tables, chatting among themselves. One man had gotten up and left when Boyd arrived. She gripped his hand.

"Now we know where he's been, right? And he left with those men. You said there was no luggage in the cabin." She sniffed back tears, drew a shuddery breath. "What could it mean?"

"It appears to be Nazaroff's men, maybe the ones who searched Dupree's apartment. Could be the same black Ford that followed you and me."

She shivered, remembering those thugs. "Somehow they traced him?"

"His phone would be the only way. Nazaroff must've had a tracker bug planted in it. One of his people seems to have tech skills. Illegal tech skills. Those guys didn't know about the cabin. They ended up at the farm, probably where Dupree used his phone."

"When he... called me." She started to release him, but his hand remained wrapped around hers, an anchor against the headwinds.

"The time frame is right. My guess is he got cold feet about continuing the forgery. Maybe shame because it was Bellinis he was copying. Maybe fear of going to prison again. So he packed up and split. Looks to me like they did the break-in to search for a clue to where he went. All they had until that phone call."

She nodded. "I should've known something was going on with him. I should've done something." Only when a warm thumb swiped at the wetness on her cheek, did she realize she was crying. She plucked a tissue from her tote and blew her nose.

"C'mon, honey. We're finished here. Let's go home." He stood and picked up the plastic-wrapped lemon bars. "Thanks for these."

"You can thank Francine. She brought those for you." One thing she could smile about.

They walked in silence through the building and took the elevator to the basement parking garage. Boyd handed her up into the vehicle and went around to the driver side.

Once settled in their seats, he started the engine but didn't pull out of the parking slot.

"Boyd?"

Turned sideways, he was studying her, his expression tight, his gray eyes cold as sleet.

"Gemma, you care more for this guy than just as a friend. He did call to warn you, but otherwise the concern and caring seems damned one sided."

Did he distrust her? Or even suspect her involvement? No, impossible. But his unspoken question hung in the air. *Why?* Only her shame had prevented her from telling him.

"Why do I feel responsible for Troy?" She wiped away more tears and puffed a breath. Dropped the tissue she'd shredded into her tote. "Because it was my doing that got him involved with Nazaroff to begin with. I wanted a buddy to go with me when I was copying paintings. My girlfriend wasn't interested. I liked Troy, saw he had talent, so I asked him."

"And then Nazaroff took advantage and reeled in the guy who needed money."

And me, who was infatuated with him. At least Boyd didn't add those words. "Yes. But if I hadn't gotten Troy involved with the copying, he'd never have gone to prison. And he wouldn't be in trouble now."

Boyd leaned across the console, cupped her chin, and kissed her lightly. "People make their own choices. When you learned about the forging, you reported it. When Nazaroff offered Troy money for crossing the line from a little student copying to criminal forging, he could've made the same choice. And for damn sure his choice to join Nazaroff again years later is not on you."

"But I should've seen that Troy was involved in something bad. And I can't deny the fact that I was partly responsible back then." Enough that she still felt like a forger herself. Irrational, but there it was. Still.

Boyd's mouth turned down, and he shook his head. "Hard to let go of old guilt. I should know. If it's any comfort, if Troy is with Nazaroff's forgery crew, he's probably okay."

She nodded her agreement, but in her head she heard what Boyd didn't say—*for now.*

****

On the way home, Gemma considered Boyd's comment about old guilt. Could he be right that she inflated her responsibility for Troy? Not just for the art forgery, but recently for taking on a big sister role once he came to Linley Harbor. She couldn't solve that conundrum now. New revelations and changing dangers wrenched her one way, and the good news she had to share with Boyd the other way, so she was stretched tighter than a canvas,

After they settled in at her condo, Boyd informed her this morning's meeting had ended with an order to lie low, stay put. He had to check in every couple hours. The company had too much else going on. They'd continue posting somebody to watch the neighborhood overnight.

"When will it end?" She jabbed a fist at the world in general and stomped around the room. Looked for something to kick or punch, but found only things she loved. "I was hoping to go to the Sunday spinning class, burn off my, what, frustration, fear, rage. Dammit!"

Boyd caught her flailing hands and pulled her close.

"Whoa, honey, what about this? Since we're stuck here, we could stay in bed for three days. That should burn off… something."

She jumped him, wrapping her legs around his waist. He kissed her with a lazy sweep of his tongue that flashed liquid fire through her veins. If only she could take him up on it. He spread his hands on her behind and took the kiss deeper.

But then she said against his mouth, "Maybe two days," before she slid to her feet. "I have to work." She swayed her hips and did a couple of dance steps in the tiny celebration she allowed herself. A big grin leaked out too.

"Work? What's up?"

"My agent came through with a painting commission. She called when I was in the café. I told her I'd start on preliminary sketches. The client liked the beach grass painting at the Alexandria gallery, but would prefer one that included shore birds. I agreed to do that. When Megan told her I also paint fabric, she added shore birds on a tunic to her commission."

"See? The clothing thing in combo with your canvases could work."

She hiked one shoulder. "Perhaps." But she didn't want to think about that, only this new project. She bounced on her toes.

"A *major* commission, Gemma, congratulations. Go for it. I'll be here when you need a break." His eyelids lowered and his lips contorted into what might pass for a leer.

"If only you had a mustache, you could twirl it." She laughed and kissed him before dashing up the stairs. "First I have to call Pia. And then Mom and Tina. They'll want a report on Fitz and the beach house. I intend to push them on selling the place. It's time."

Chapter Twenty-Three

BOYD TOOK HIS laptop to the dining table and booted up. He used his notes from the meeting to make a list of what they knew about Nazaroff's operation, what they suspected, and what they didn't know. Shit, the last was the longest. They didn't know where he stashed the money paid for paintings or the location of his base of operations or who else was involved beyond Dupree, Lucia/Letty, and the two muscles. Or when or how Nazaroff would make another go at Gemma. The last thought crawled like cockroaches in his gut.

He opened the file Trask had emailed him. A spreadsheet. A note at the top labeled it the list of rental properties assigned to Parisi. Trask hadn't lost his hacking chops. On the right, addresses, descriptions, rented or not. Of the twenty, Parisi had rented out only seven. Of the available ones, Trask had crossed off the warehouse and boarded-up restaurant Cassidy mentioned when she tailed Parisi.

Boyd stared hard at the screen. He couldn't just sit around waiting for DSF or the authorities to get some kind of break. He wanted to stop these assholes before they went after Gemma again. Maybe a waste of time, but a search of these properties meant being proactive.

Would any of the unrented properties suit Nazaroff's purpose? Or the rented ones? Shit. He could've used a phony business name.

Boyd spent the next hour checking on the renters' identities.

The first three checked out. Real business websites, owners members of the Chamber of Commerce. The buildings as seen in Google Street View—office building, restaurant, garage—were either open already or in the midst of renovations.

When Gemma came downstairs, he closed the laptop lid. No reason to upset her about following a trail to her sister's husband. A trail that might lead nowhere.

****

By Monday afternoon, Boyd had narrowed his search to three unrented properties. One had been a call center, another a furniture store, the third a small manufacturing business. More than once, Street View picked up vehicles parked behind the third and in front of the others. He hadn't caught sight of anybody nearby, coming or going. Could be people carpooling and that was their rendezvous. Could be homeless people not wanting to sleep rough.

Or not.

He tapped Cassidy's number on his phone.

"Yo, you tired of quality time with her already?" she said.

"I'll pretend you didn't say that." He gave her a rundown of his internet search, omitting where he'd obtained the list. She could probably guess. "I figure any one of these three might serve Nazaroff's purposes. Big open space for setting up easels and desks and computers. Smaller offices where the non-locals could even camp out. Likely internet ready. Back doors for privacy."

"Seems possible," she said slowly.

"More than possible. It's damn plausible and probable that Leo Parisi was targeted by Nazaroff and set him up in one of these buildings. The power and water have stayed on in all three. Apparently makes a place easier to rent."

"It's also possible that since Gemma blocked Nazaroff from the archive, he has moved on. Maybe he mined this area for all he could."

"Jo, back in college, she's the one who turned him in. He wants revenge. He hasn't stopped. Didn't they just find another painting in Baltimore?"

"Copy that. Worth a try. I'll run it by Max Rivera. Send me the addresses."

****

Gemma waited until the last two customers left Galerie Flora. They'd expressed interest in one of Tolu's abstracts. A shame he was taking so long bringing back the lunch orders. It made a big difference for sales when the artist talked with the prospects. The noon hour was usually slower, no one even browsing the window display.

She kicked off her high heels, picked up her phone from the desk, and read her sister's text. She and Mom were at an Alexandria Greek restaurant. Tina asked if they could bring her anything, souvlaki or baklava. Clearly a pretext. They were just hoping to meet Boyd. She texted back thanking Tina, but she had just finished lunch. Hah, if only.

She glanced at Boyd. Like last Tuesday, he was keeping watch for her safety from his loaner truck. When Tolu returned with the sandwiches, he'd join them inside. The morning had been busy, so her stomach was sitting up and begging. Boyd's too, she bet. But at the moment, he wasn't looking this way. Busy on his phone.

Tolu had been gone a good half hour. Was Sammy's Café super busy today or did the cooks have a meltdown?

A shuffling sound from rear of the gallery announced Tolu's return. After stepping into her heels, she hurried that way. She yanked open the door. The heat from the un-air-conditioned back room hit her in the face.

The glare of the overhead bulb revealed two men. Not Tolu.

"Leo, what are *you* doing here?"

****

Boyd powered down the windows and turned off the truck engine. At least Mother Nature supplied a breeze. He observed two customers leave the gallery. Empty-handed. Brisk sales that morning kept both Gemma and Tolu busy, but now Gemma was alone.

She strolled the floor. Her long yellow top floating with each sexy sway of her slim hips. She was texting on her phone. Set it down on the desk, adjusted the rack of prints, straightened a painting. Kept glancing toward the back room. Impatient for lunch. So was he. Impatient to be with her. His gut didn't trust she was safe unless he was touching her soft skin, hearing her lilting voice, seeing her smile. Was he doing everything he should to protect her?

His phone played "Wild Thing."

He answered on his headset. "Hey, Jo. Any news?"

"Good news for a change. The FBI has just arrested Letty Boggess at a gallery in Annapolis."

"No shit!"

"My reaction when I heard. This time instead of a

customer, her mark for a fake Bellini was the gallery owner. He recognized her from the Feebs' warning circular and called it in."

He turned toward the gallery again. No Gemma. The door to the back room stood ajar. Probably back there because Tolu came in.

"Any details?" He kept his eyes on the gallery.

"When she returned with the painting, they were waiting. Called herself Lydia Symes this time."

"This is big, Jo. Whether she talks or not."

****

The man with a black mustache beside Leo looked vaguely familiar. Broad forehead pleated in a fierce scowl beneath his baseball-team cap, he said nothing. He leaned forward and shoved the door closed.

"Leo?" she repeated.

Her brother-in-law's ruddy features glistened with the sweat she smelled emanating from him. He grabbed her arm. "Tina's been in a terrible car accident. You have to come with me to the hospital. Now."

His words made no sense. Tina? She took a step backward, tried to pull from his grasp, but he held on.

"What? No. Impossible. She's at lunch with Mom at the Taverna Mediterranean. I just texted with her." What was going on? This was bizarre. She looked from one man to the other.

A black pistol appeared in the mustached man's hand. He aimed it at her.

Gemma's mouth soured with an odd metallic taste. The horror of realization rattled her heart in her chest and pulsed in her constricted throat. *Boyd.* She had to alert Boyd. He could do something. He could—

Another man wearing a baseball cap stepped from

the dark storeroom. Mouth tight beneath an outsized nose, he also held a black pistol, but pointed low. Light through the half-open door spilled onto a man tied up on the floor. A dirty white cloth gagged his mouth. His eyes were wide with fear. *Tolu!*

Her heart hit a higher gear as adrenaline burned through her. "Damn you! Don't hurt him. He's—"

"Come with us quietly," the first man interrupted, "or your friend here dies." He jabbed an elbow toward the mustached man. "*He* will stay here in case you cause me trouble."

She firmed her chin, the fury raging in her body sharpening her tone. "Leo, you? You're the one? Why?"

He recoiled as her acid-tipped words struck home. "You… you heard him. Move." But the hitch in his voice betrayed his fear. He opened the outer door.

"I need my purse. It's just inside the gallery."

"Nice try, bitch. Forget it."

"But—"

The mustached man held her upper arm in an iron grip and manhandled her outside.

White-hot pain scraped her chest. Adrenaline roared in her ears. She had no way to alert Boyd. No SOS alarm. No phone. Nothing.

Chapter Twenty-Four

"IF NAZAROFF AND company find out their shill has been picked up, they could split before we find them," Boyd said. "What's being done about scouting out those three buildings? I can't leave Gemma or I'd fucking do it. The clock is ticking on this one."

"Cool it, Sergeant," Cassidy said. "It was only yesterday you brought it up. Rivera is organizing a team to scout out those places. I saw them from above, same as you. Looks more promising than I thought."

"Thanks for that. Okay then." How long would scouting those buildings take?

He looked over at the gallery. No Gemma. No Tolu either.

His nerves tingled, itched with foreboding. "Hang on, Jo. I'm going in to check on Gemma. She's been in that back room too long."

He turned on the engine just long enough to power up the windows. Checked the weapon in the hip holster. Locked up and hustled in the front door. Her phone lay on the desk, tote with her handbag beneath it.

"Gemma?"

No reply. And where was Tolu? Boyd's nerves flashed a warning beacon. He flicked loose the strap on his holster. Pulled open the door to the back room. "Gemma?"

The room was empty but for a bulging bag from Sammy's Café on the floor. Muffled thumps sounded from the storeroom. Then banging on the closed door. Sweat trickled down Boyd's nape and by his ears.

Hand on his weapon, he stood to the side and opened the door. Thumping, louder and with obvious agitation. Nerves on hyperalert, he chanced a look. Tolu Silva lay on the floor, bound legs raised, poised to kick the door again.

The breath whistled from his lungs. A sick cloud spread through him. *Gemma, they had Gemma.* He forced himself to breathe, to act. He flicked on the safety, holstered the weapon.

"Tolu, I'll get you free, man." He started with the cloth gag.

The other man spat out the wad of material while Boyd released the duct tape from his wrists. Tolu worked his jaw and started on the tape around his ankles. "Those men… they took Gemma. Held guns on her. Made her go."

"Jo," Boyd said. He gestured at his ear for Tolu's benefit. "You heard?"

"Yeah. Alerting Devlin and Trask now. Get her location and we'll coordinate with the sheriff's department. FBI will take too long."

"How long ago did the last guy leave?" Boyd asked, helping Tolu to his feet.

"Hard to say. Fifteen minutes maybe."

"Tell me all of it."

"Three men. Soon as I opened the door, bringing back lunch, you know, two guys, almost as big as you, jumped me." He shook his head, a ruddy flush coloring his dark cheeks. "Then they made a noise so Gemma would come back here."

Each word hit Boyd like a bullet to the gut as Tolu continued his tale with the third man's name. Parisi, fucking Leo Parisi. "Do you need medical treatment?"

"No, no. I'm fine here. Those men could hurt Gemma. Go, go, find her."

Boyd clasped his hand. "I'll do my damnedest."

His heart pounding so hard it hurt, he raced back to the truck. Gemma's purse remained at the gallery. She had no way to alert anybody. No way to contact him. He shouldn't have pressured her into changing the login. They could've found another way. His fault. His failure.

He lowered his head to the steering wheel for a moment. *Hang on, Gemma.*

His years in the Army had taught him to master his emotions. He had to do that now so he could act. Gemma needed clear thinking from him. Clear thinking would save her. He would find her.

He had to save her.

He opened the app for the tracker buttons he'd tucked inside the waistband of her capris. "Jo, I'm tracking her location now. Hang on for the address."

Got her. Deep, even breaths. The vehicle was moving on streets, not highways. They'd had a good head start. Where the hell were they taking her? He stared at his phone screen, willing them to stop. When they did, he blinked, focused. Checked the addresses of Parisi's open rentals.

"Got her, Jo. It's that small manufacturing building in Arlington, other side of I-395 from Arlandria. Still has the name on the building, Erdwell Fabrications." He gave her the address and started the engine. "Call my backup team somewhere behind me too."

"Wait there, Boyd. It's the login and password they want. We have teams ready to go. I've got Santiago on the phone. He's calling in deputies."

"Not waiting. It's Gemma."

****

The mustached man pulled Gemma out of the van. The other thug with the bulbous nose and Leo followed. No one spoke.

She staggered a couple of steps, squinted at the sun as she adjusted from her bumpy ride face down on the floor. That ride had clarified a few things. The two hulks in baseball caps were the men who'd searched Troy's apartment. And the ones who took him from that cabin. The hope that Troy might be here kept the tightness in her chest at bay. She had to stay calm.

They were parked behind a brick building. Distant whirring of machinery might mean an industrial park. A huge rusting trash bin tilted to one side. Weeds beside the building's steel door straggled toward the sun.

Before she could look around more, Mustache, who seemed to be in charge, hustled her into the building. Leo followed. Window air conditioners hummed in windows at her back, but didn't do much to cool the cavernous interior. Perspiration immediately beaded on her forehead. Beneath odors of paint, turpentine, other chemicals, lurked the sourness of mildew.

Once inside, Big Nose removed the dirty bandana from her mouth. He wrapped a rough hand around her upper arm. In case she made a break for it. Here?

She worked saliva into her mouth to dispel the taste of stale sweat. She spun on Leo.

"How could you betray our family this way?"

He ran a hand through his thinning hair. The deep

lines in his meaty face indicated strain. Or guilt. His mouth twisted, and he spat, "You think you're so high and mighty, doling out shitass amounts from one painting at a time, running everything. More like *ruining* everything, when you could sell that whole estate. Millions for each of us. With you out of the way, Tina will take over."

"It comes down to greed, doesn't it? Not the family or Silvio's legacy."

His gaze slid away. He said nothing more.

No one else seemed to be here. Not the woman who was selling the forgeries. No Troy. Only the three men standing by in silence. Waiting. For Nazaroff, she guessed.

Fluorescent lights glowed and fizzed overhead in this area. Electric cords from floor outlets snaked to standing lamps at three easels. Two held canvases in progress. Troy must be here someplace, another artist as well. But where? This appeared to be only one big room.

Other canvases leaned against a big heavy-looking metal cabinet, maybe the base for other equipment. Painting supplies and takeout containers littered two folding tables. Two other tables held laptops and a printer. The area beyond lay in shadows. To her right spanned a huge garage door, both wide and tall.

The waiting pressed down on her shoulders, tightened her stomach. She was in the middle of nowhere. Outside, she'd heard no road noises or voices. If she called for help, only her captors would hear her.

Bile rose in her throat, and she willed it down.

No one knew where she was. Boyd would go inside the gallery to check when she didn't come out of the back room.

He'd find Tolu. *God, please let Tolu be all right.*

She sucked in a steadying breath. Tolu would tell him what happened, maybe remember the name Leo. Would that be enough? Maybe the backup team saw the men take her away. But no, wouldn't they have been parked on Main a block behind Boyd? He would be frantic, would blame himself.

So how could he find her?

She had to buy time. Her knees and her insides might tremble, but she would keep her chin high. She was a Bellini.

A door opened and closed in the gloom beyond this lighted circle. Maybe an office?

Shoes crunched dirt or debris on the floor with each step toward them.

Chapter Twenty-Five

"WELCOME, MY DEAR Gemma. It's been too long," he said in that distinctive raspy voice that sounded like he'd swallowed sandpaper. He held a black pistol.

Not long enough. She waited a beat, studying him, while Nazaroff's deep-set ebony eyes appraised her. Long-limbed and rawboned, he looked much the same except for the lines beside his mocking mouth and the silver at his temples that matched his gray silk tee. Not his painting clothes.

Dressed to impress?

Gemma lifted her chin. "Being kidnapped at gunpoint doesn't make me feel welcome, Professor."

Chuckling, he stowed the pistol in his jeans pocket. "Better?"

She didn't respond or react.

"Hubik, let go of the lady's arm. You might cause a bruise." He turned back to her with a crocodile smile. "Professor? You used to call me Morgan."

"You've come down in the world if this building is where you call home." She rubbed her arm to erase his flunky's sweaty grip.

Anger flashed in his eyes before he banked it. "Au contraire, I'm told the previous tenant built high-end custom furniture. We're quite comfortable here."

"Where's Troy? I know he's been forging paintings

with you."

Nazaroff, his brows raised, looked behind him, then to either side as if searching for Troy. He shrugged and smiled. "He's not here. I have no idea where he is. The boy's not that reliable."

"I don't believe you." Flames ignited, burning up the back of her neck to her ears. She drew on her yoga practice, taking cleansing breaths, then bit the inside of her cheek, hard. The sharp pain cleared her head and doused the fire. Calm, not fury, would see her through this. One finger at a time, she relaxed her hands, clenched at her sides.

"But enough. I suspect you know why you were invited."

Gemma glared at him.

Leo had been leaning against the edge of a table. Now he pushed away and got in her face. "The login and password. Just fucking give it to him."

She took a step away from Leo and faced Nazaroff. "And then what? Do you believe I'm still that same naïve fool?" Once he had what he wanted, he wouldn't just let her go.

"Not at all. I believe you are much more practical now. Your youthful self was into learning and... pleasure." Three long-legged strides to the first easel and he returned with a palette knife in his hand. "Maybe learning persists, but practicality should take precedence here."

He gripped her shoulder, slid the sharp blade down her neck.

She flinched, but swallowed the cry that crowded her throat.

Blood trickled onto the neckline of her butterscotch

yellow blouse, the thought popping into her head that it would blend into the crimson embroidery. The sting of the shallow cut stifled the hysterics that threatened to bubble up into giggles.

Calm, remember. Calm.

Playing along might create more delay. Delay was her only weapon. She could identify all these men. If Boyd didn't come in time, Nazaroff or one of his hoodlums would kill her. Leo wouldn't have the guts.

She pressed a hand to the cut. "I see, your stay in prison taught you new ways to manipulate people. Fine. I'll do it."

"I'm pleased you're seeing reason." Nazaroff gestured to the nearest table. "Leo, you're on. Your big moment."

Sweat streaming down his temples, Leo hurried to the laptop.

It was hot in here, but not that hot. Her brother-in-law's future was probably in as much jeopardy as hers.

And now, he was about to find out how he'd screwed up. He pulled up a chair and opened the lid.

"GardStor.com, Leo. Go ahead," she said.

He bent over the keyboard for a few minutes, his brows beetled in concentration as he typed and worked the touchpad.

Nazaroff took her by the arm, pulled her around the table to stand with him. In bird of prey mode, he peered over Leo's shoulder. "What the hell is the matter?"

Leo slumped back in the chair. "This is the public site of GardStor. I can't find the login page. It doesn't look the same."

"No?" Gemma folded her arms. "What a shame."

The backhanded blow caught her across the face.

Her head snapped sideways. Pain exploded, sharp and vibrating in her skull. Darkness painted the edges of her consciousness before it cleared. She staggered, tasting blood, and placed a palm on the table to steady herself.

She made herself face her tormentor.

Big Nose, whose name she knew now was Hubik, stood nearby, but didn't grab her.

Leo remained at the useless laptop, his ruddy complexion the color of clay, probably paler than hers.

"No more games, bitch. How do we log in?" Nazaroff stalked back and forth close to the easels, away from Leo. Away, mercifully, from her.

"*We* don't. Not on this device. The laptop must have the GardStor program on the client's computer. It's installed and verified by GardStor. Otherwise the login and password are useless."

She stood now facing the door, but too far away to consider making a run for it. She wouldn't make it five feet. Movement outside past the grimy window above one of the air conditioners tumbled her pulse.

Boyd?

She schooled her expression, touched a hand to her aching cheek. She turned away from the window. Nazaroff wasn't watching her, but was menacing Leo.

"You fucking idiot, you didn't know this about the login?"

Leo shook his head. Flopped a hand at the computer. "No, it was just there on Tina's laptop."

"Go then, get your wife's laptop. And make it quick."

"I… I can't do that. She'll know. I could get *her*—" he jerked his chin toward Gemma "—laptop, but I need the code to get in her house."

"It's on my phone, which is in the handbag you made me leave at the gallery." She hugged herself, counting on Leo's round trip being a long one.

Nazaroff yanked him up on his feet. The folding chair clattered to the floor.

"Bring that laptop from your house. Get going."

"You want me to escort him?" Mustache said.

"No, Marshak. I need you here. He knows better than to fuck up again. Don't you, Leo?"

Nodding hard enough to break vertebrae, Leo jogged to the door.

****

Boyd kept low as he picked his way among the weeds and trash. Three vehicles were parked beyond the big wheeled trash bin. The black Ford 250 that had tailed them, a minivan, and a BMW sedan. He took photos of all three license plates. Had just finished letting the air out of the truck's front tires when the Erdwell Building's door opened.

He dived behind the trash bin and peered around the corner.

Wheezing like an old man, Leo Parisi jogged past the bin, juggling his key fob.

Boyd jumped him. Grabbed him by the throat and jammed the big 9mm in his ribs.

"You call out, you're a dead man. The slow and painful way." He tightened his grip.

Parisi shook his head, or maybe his head was just shaking. Either way, he stayed silent except for choppy breaths.

Boyd muscled him over behind the trash bin, out of sight. Yanked his hands behind his back and secured his wrists with zip ties. Shoved his shoulders so he sat down hard.

"Y-you're him, aren't you, her bodyguard?"

"Where were you going?"

Parisi's gaze slid away. He heaved a shaky sigh.

Boyd grabbed his throat again. "*Where?*"

"Okay, okay. To get my wife's laptop."

Boyd didn't need to ask why. "Who's inside?"

"Nazaroff, his two local guys, and Gemma."

"Nobody else, you swear?" He squeezed, then removed his hand from the man's neck.

"I s-swear."

"Is Gemma okay?"

Parisi shrugged. His breathing panicky, he remained mute.

Pain ripped at Boyd's chest. *No, they need the login.* Sucking in a breath, he lifted his hand toward the man's throat. "Out with it."

"Wait. No. Nazaroff slapped her some, but she's okay."

"She'd better be."

Boyd quizzed him on the men's weapons and the inside layout, Gemma's location. Then zip tied his ankles and slapped tape across his mouth before flipping him facedown. He picked up the key fob from the ground and pocketed it.

"You can hope it's the cops who find you when this is all over. Thanks for coming outside, asshole." He drove away in the Beemer.

Chapter Twenty-Six

AFTER THE DOOR banged shut behind Leo, Gemma remained where she was, away from Nazaroff and the computer. At a nod from Marshak, she sank onto a metal folding chair. Her knocking knees could use the respite. Her head felt better, but her cheek ached, starting to swell, probably bruised. She touched the shallow slit on her neck. It ached, but at least the bleeding had stopped.

Her gaze fell on the other easels. Troy and another forger, then. On the floor beside one easel lay a metal chain connected to a ring in the floor. On the other end what looked like a... manacle?

Oh God, Troy. Tears welled, clogged her throat. The tension in her already tight chest cranked to a vise. If he wasn't here, where could he be? Was he even alive?

She'd known Nazaroff to be manipulative and prone to explosions of temper, but years ago they were only verbal attacks. If a student didn't execute a style following his instructions, his criticisms cut deep. So gullible and selfish of her to have ignored all that because of his attention and flattery. Greed and perhaps prison turned him ruthless, sadistic. He was no better than his henchmen, just cleverer.

He sat at the table, focused on the laptop. He hit keys, grumbling to himself. After a few minutes, he shoved the chair away and slammed the laptop lid. He crossed to an easel and cleaned a couple of paint brushes with enough ferocity to reduce them to bare handles. Tossing them down, he strode away toward the front of the building and paced the shadowed empty floor beyond the lights.

She didn't turn to watch his progress, but his footsteps echoed in every thud of her pulse.

He was plotting something, she felt it. Whatever he conjured didn't bode well for her. After a turn past the tall garage door, he came back and sat at his easel. He stared at the canvas but didn't pick up a brush.

"Why the forging again?" Leading him to talk about himself might divert him while they waited for Leo's return. "You're extremely talented and could command sizeable prices and commissions for your own art."

He looked up at her. The smirk curling his lips made him look more dangerous. "Nothing like what I'm getting now. Copying a few canvases goes quicker than creating my own. It also pays much more."

"So honest sales aren't enough? Notoriety can mean fame and fortune. You could work your experiences into publicity."

He threaded fingers through his hair. "Publicity's the last thing I want."

"You seem to have… churned out a lot of Bellinis, and I assume other copies, in a short amount of time."

Ignoring her dig at the quality of the paintings, he laughed. "Quality staff."

"Why the rush?"

"No rush. Just padding my retirement."

"Your retirement? How so? You're still a young man."

"Flattery, Gemma? What do you expect sucking up to accomplish?"

She lifted one shoulder in an oh-well shrug. Anything to give Boyd time or *someone* time.

Had that movement outside the window been only her imagination? Leo could return soon with Tina's laptop, and— *No, don't think. Just keep Nazaroff talking.*

"And your thugs here, are they going to have their retirements padded as well?"

"Thugs? My dear, these gentlemen are protecting all our assets. Marshak here—"

CRASH!

The huge garage door exploded inward.

Then pops of gunfire. Blinding flashes of light. The vroom of a revving engine.

Whitish smoke billowed, obscuring everything.

Gemma shot from her chair and pelted toward the door.

"Stop her!" Marshak yelled from somewhere in the murk.

Hubik grabbed her from behind. She struggled in his grip but he held on, one arm tight around her, the other holding his pistol.

She couldn't see the others through the smoke veil.

The thuds and grunts of a fight reverberated from where the monster vehicle had crashed their party. Then another blast like a gunshot.

She couldn't see much, but she could see her captor's lime-green running shoes. She stomped her heel, hard, on his instep.

Hubik shrieked and bent over. His grip relaxed.

She ducked from his hold and powered her right elbow upward.

The crunch of cartilage and another scream were her reward. The heel of her shoe remained stuck. She stepped out of it and its mate, held up the remaining spike heel, ready.

The thug had sunk to the floor, moaning. The pistol dropped from his grip.

She scooped it up.

The smoke was clearing. The remnants of the garage door covered the ramming vehicle.

Was it Boyd? Or someone else?

If she could see better, so could Nazaroff. Where was he? He could attack her at any minute. And he had a pistol. Gasping for steady breaths and trembling in every limb, she searched the lighted area, the dark corners for safety.

The metal cabinet.

She raced past the easels to the black bulk. She grasped the cool metal handle. Didn't turn it. Her heart raced. If she hid inside, she might be trapped.

Bending over to look small, she scurried behind the metal box and crouched in the shadows.

****

Boyd yanked the zip tie a notch tighter around the man's wrists. "Where is she?"

The fucker said nothing.

Boyd fastened his ankles the same way. Propped one foot on his back. Added pressure. *"Where. Is. She?"*

Grunts at the pressure on his spine. "Back there… the tables."

"You better hope nobody has hurt Gemma, asshole, or I'll be back."

Blood dripped on the zip ties.

Boyd stepped away. He dug out a wound-clotting

pack and slapped it on the gash beneath his left armpit. Pain spiked through his left side, jolting his breath. He couldn't manage tape one handed, so he pressed the pack against his side with his arm. He lifted the 9mm from where the fucker had kicked it away, stowed it in a pouch in his body armor.

He took out his phone, hit speed dial, then dropped it in a chest pouch. Bluetooth was easier.

"Yo, sit rep," Cassidy said.

He spoke just above a whisper. "I opened up the can for your grand entrance. Side of the building. One gorilla inside neutralized with zip ties. Same with Leo Parisi, outside behind the trash bin. No sign of Nazaroff. Gemma either. Another gorilla down farther into the room, so she may have done some damage."

"Good for her. We're five minutes out. Sheriff's deputies and Santiago too. FBI is on the way."

"Sooner the better." He ended the call.

The smoke was clearing, so he sidled along the wall as he scanned for Gemma—and whoever else might be here. In the lighted area, the second man sat on the floor, moaning. If Parisi hadn't lied, Nazaroff was the only remaining threat.

Weapon drawn, Boyd crossed to the man.

He was clutching his foot, his sneaker soaked in blood. More pooled on the floor. One of Gemma's shoes lay on its side, the spike heel glistening red. *WTG, honey.* Guy looked up at the footsteps. His outsized nose matched the bloody foot. *Double whammy.*

"By dose," the creep said. "Bitch broke by dose."

"You're lucky she let you live." Boyd patted him down. Ammo clip, but no weapon. He needed both hands to zip-tie the man's wrists, so let the clotting pack fall to the floor. He stowed the other zip tie. With that impaled foot, asshole was going nowhere.

The movements set off flares of pain. Boyd swore long and loud inside his head. Pushing to his feet, he reapplied the pack to his wound. Held it tighter. Set his jaw. Listened, but heard only the wind rattling the remnants of the garage door and the rasp of his own breath.

What was Nazaroff waiting for? Or had he made a run for it? Boyd had to risk it.

"Gemma?"

She popped up, her green eyes wide, from behind a dark cast-iron cabinet. "Oh, Boyd, Boyd. You came. I was afraid you wouldn't find me."

On a sob, she raced barefoot around the side and past an easel. A purple bruise puffed one cheek. Blood spattered her clothing. Gathering momentum, she was about to throw herself at him.

"Honey, I booked it here as fast as I could." Stowing his weapon, he braced himself and circled her waist with his right arm. Pulled her hard against his side and buried his face in her hair. Inhaled her unique scent. Thanked God she was alive and whole.

"I heard your footsteps. I was afraid it was Nazaroff or Marshak."

"Marshak? If that's the big goon with a mustache, he's tied up back by the big opening I made with the truck." She nodded and he kissed her lightly. Keeping his breathing shallow, he stepped back. "I'll take that." He lifted the pistol from her hand, flicked on the safety, stuffed it in one of his pouches.

"Good." Her shoulders moved in a small shudder.

"Bastards hurt you." A quick boil churned inside

him. Damn, he might hurt her further if he even touched a finger to her injury.

"Nazaroff's handiwork, but I'm okay," she chirped. "I took out my revenge on Hubik." She pointed to her victim. "Most of the blood is his. I lifted that gun from him."

He glanced at what she clutched against her. "You gonna stab *me* with that thing too?"

She held up the spike heel. "Cinderella could've used one of these on the ugly stepsisters."

Her brows drew together. She leaned across him, her mouth rounded in concern. "You're hurt. Did Marshak shoot you?" She reached toward his injury, but he caught her hand.

"Just a graze. More blood than damage."

She looked skeptical, but subsided and let him hold her with his good arm.

He told her about her brother-in-law, tied up outside. Spread his lips in what he hoped was a smile and not a grimace of pain. Waited as she fretted about telling her sister what Leo had been doing. He told her about finding Tolu, that her friend was worried about her.

"Where's Nazaroff?" he said.

"No idea. When you crashed through that wall and all the fireworks exploded, he disappeared into the smoke."

Shit, the flash bangs and smoke bombs were meant to disorient them all, but might've given Nazaroff cover to split.

"Troy's not here. I don't know..." Gemma swallowed hard, then continued. "Nazaroff was deliberately vague about him. There's an iron shackle by one easel."

"So he couldn't run again." He spotted the chain and manacle. "Bastards."

"There must be a third copier, but I haven't seen them." Her gaze searched the room. "No one else came? This was all *you*?"

"I had to find you fast. The cops and DSF are on the way."

His heart punched against his chest wall. Until Gemma, he hadn't known what he was missing in his life. She filled that hole with her generosity and spiky energy, and they'd made a sort of life together these past weeks. The power of his need for her scared him. He'd have to walk away, but how?

She blessed him with a soft smile and patted his cheek.

Voices from the garage door end turned them around. Cassidy, Trask, and other operatives streamed in along with Santiago and sheriff's deputies. Weapons drawn, they spread through the room. Boyd started toward Cassidy.

"Wait." Gemma crossed to one of the tables. "Nazaroff's laptop is gone."

"Shit." He beckoned to Cassidy.

She jogged over, a medical backpack hooked over one shoulder.

"Gemma needs a little bandaging. That guy over there too. Nazaroff may have taken off. Give me a minute." He squeezed Gemma's hand and started to run, but thought better of it.

He walked out the back door. The van was gone.

Nazaroff was in the wind.

He rounded the trash bin. "Hey, Leo, rise and shine. The cops want a chat." When the man didn't move or react, he looked closer. A bullet hole decorated the back of Leo's head.

Chapter Twenty-Seven

GEMMA FOLLOWED JO outside past the crumpled truck. The front end was all "stove up," as her Nana would say, from bulldozing into the building. She inhaled the fresh air, lifted her gaze into the breeze, relieved to be free of fear and out under the summer sun. She'd spent the last half hour answering questions about being kidnapped and what had happened since. An Art Crime agent quizzed her about how the forgers were able to copy Silvio's works so precisely.

Boyd had to remain in the building answering questions and filling in events, he told her, before he joined Detective Santiago and Special Agent Irwin.

Jo directed her to a table beneath the awning set up for the investigators and forensics staff. Gemma took a folding chair and stretched out, wriggling her bare toes.

"Here you go." Jo carried two bottles of water and a pair of hot pink flipflops. "These'll be too big for you, but should be better than my boots."

"Thanks so much. I seem to be barefoot whenever you come to my rescue." She slipped on the sandals, then drank great gulps of the icy water.

"Let's hope this is the last time," the other woman said. "I can't leave, but the chief deputy said he'd free up somebody in a while to drive you home."

"I'll need to go to the gallery instead. My handbag,

my phone, everything is there." Except her car. But Tolu would give her a lift if Boyd wasn't free by then.

Two ENTs carried Nazaroff's henchman Hubik out on a stretcher. His foot was bandaged and he held an ice pack on his nose.

She winced and hugged herself. "Oh dear, he's in a lot of pain. I really hurt him, didn't I?"

"Don't feel guilty. He'd have done worse to you if he had the chance. Boyd's self-defense lessons paid off." Her phone rang. She excused herself and walked away.

Jo was right. Boyd's lessons helped her survive. That man might've shot her if she hadn't acted. Boyd saved her life. He changed her life. She wanted a real relationship with him without the threat hanging over her head like a guillotine blade.

Jo returned and pulled her chair around beside Gemma. "No easy way to tell you, hon. Deputies found Troy Dupree's body out back in a shed."

Gemma's stomach pitched and tears fell. She bent over and rocked, hugging herself. The guilt descended, the big bad wolf with claws. She'd feared this outcome, but forced it to the back of her consciousness. *Oh, Troy, my sweet little bro, I'm so sorry.* A sob fought to escape her throat, and she gritted her teeth. Straightening, she met Jo's concerned gaze.

"I-I knew he had to be here somewhere, but then when I didn't see him inside, I hoped he'd escaped. What happened?"

"He was shot. The deputy said he'd likely been dead for several days. Maybe he did try to run away or rebel. They had to unshackle him some of the time." Jo cleared her throat, laid a hand on Gemma's arm. "There's more. Your brother-in-law is dead too, also a gunshot."

"Oh no. It's bad enough he betrayed the family, stole from us. But this... poor Tina." More tears burned, and her heart hammered. *Enough.* She'd have to go to Tina right away. "Nazaroff?"

"Probably. But the cops will have to eliminate Boyd first because he tied him up and left him behind the building."

"Boyd didn't do it."

"No. And his weapons will prove that." Jo stepped aside and spoke with a deputy.

Gemma stood and swept her hands over her blouse and capris, not that brushing would slough off the dried blood.

Boyd and a taller man wearing a Devlin Security ID exited the building. Boyd carried his body armor in his right hand. He held his left arm at an angle around a bulky white bandage on his side.

Was he more injured than he'd implied? She started forward as the other man turned his back to her and faced Boyd.

"...find Gemma Bellini's connection to the forgery ring?" the other man was saying. "The tracker buttons in her clothing would've pinpointed the location of any meeting with Nazaroff or one of his goons."

Boyd's eyes locked with hers as the man was speaking.

For the roaring in her ears, she couldn't hear Boyd's lower-voiced reply. A chill grew inside her, expanding so she could barely breathe. He'd deceived her after all. And she'd thought...

When the tall man walked away, Boyd took two steps toward her. She couldn't read his face, but clearly he knew she'd heard every damning word. She squared her shoulders and lifted her chin.

"I thought I could trust you. What a fool I am. You were just doing your job, spying on me, and having some fun on the side."

Boyd said nothing, stared at her as if his whole being was set in granite.

"Well, it's all over now, isn't it? I don't need a bodyguard any more. I don't need *you* for anything. Send someone to pick up your stuff." She bit her lower lip. "Thank you for saving my life. I'm sorry you were injured."

She turned and walked back to Jo, concentrating on each step. Numb, she let Jo hand her off to the deputy who was driving her back to Linley Harbor.

****

Boyd remained there, his feet nailed to the ground, and watched her walk away. Watched her hair brush her shoulders with each stiff step she took in that pair of ridiculous pink sandals. Watched her get into a sheriff's department cruiser. Her eyes, green ice, were burned into his retinas. He clenched a fist at his side as the vehicle drove away. Thickness spread from his chest up to his throat, and he swallowed it down. Sucked in a breath. The wound in his side announced its presence. That pain he could handle.

"You let her go away mad?" Cassidy got in his face.

"Better to make a clean break." He didn't deserve Gemma. He'd failed to keep her safe. His fault Leo and Nazaroff's creeps kidnaped her. And hurt her.

"Getting shot made you stupid."

When he didn't reply, she huffed. "Here's some good news. The van's license number paid off. Traffic helicopter spotted it going north on the interstate toward

Baltimore."

"They better not let the bastard get away." He kept his breathing shallow, any movement stabbed him with carving knives.

She wrapped an arm around his waist, marched him under the awning, made him sit. Hell, otherwise he might've fallen over. "You're wounded."

"Asshole shot me in the one vulnerable place, under my arm. A graze. Just bled like hell." Marshak had fired as Boyd knocked him to the ground.

"Maybe. You'll need antibiotics and possibly stitches."

"The EMT who worked on the goon Gemma took down bandaged me. He said the same thing."

"Has the sheriff's department cleared you about shooting Parisi?"

"Not yet. I should get my weapon back soon. I didn't fire a shot, and they have the 9 mils belonging to Nazaroff's thugs. I had 'em stashed in my body armor."

Cassidy's phone played bluesy notes. She listened, scowled. "Shit."

"Jo?"

"The van driver was a homeless man. Nazaroff traded the van for the guy's backpack."

Boyd's heart slammed up into his raw throat.

Nazaroff was still out there.

****

Gemma squirted a drop of lotion in her palm and rubbed her hands together. Lifted one and inhaled Boyd's scent, the tang usually layered over the deeper essence of him. She closed her eyes, saw him standing in the middle of that old factory, so tall, so strong, her warrior in armor come to rescue her. But not hers. He was never hers, would never be hers. She should've known not to trust, her mantra for years.

She lifted her gaze upward. "Silvio, thank you for trusting me. You were the only one."

She tossed the bottle in Boyd's kit with the rest of his toiletries, zipped it shut. Exactly the way she should seal away the memories. Zip them up and banish them.

She fitted the kit inside the duffel with his clothes and zipped that. She lugged it down the stairs and dumped it in the foyer.

Banishing his belongings didn't mean she could dump the memories.

Every room in the house made her think of him. Was it all a lie? Not the sex. He'd wanted her as much as she wanted him. Still wanted him. And more. His tenderness, his understanding and caring, his humor. No act. Hot tingles crept up her neck, and her throat grew thick. The operative's words came back to her. *"... find Gemma Bellini's connection to the forgery ring?"*

What had Boyd replied? Nothing came to her. All she'd heard was the fear blaring inside her head.

What have I done?

Sinking to her knees beside the duffel, she hugged herself and let the tears fall. For the past few days, she'd been too busy, too stressed to allow herself to focus on anything but the aftermath of the kidnapping and Leo's death. Now there would be no forgetting, of Boyd or all the rest.

National and local TV news, the *Washington Post*, the *Linley Harbor Gazette*. Headline "Bellini heiress kidnapped" or "Bellini heiress stops art forgery ring." Stories covered the bare bones of the murders and the attempts on her and the art forgery ring. Shudder worthy were the ones about the ringleader on the run. Nazaroff's photo leered at her from all the media.

Reporters phoned her all day and night the first couple days after the story broke, wanting an exclusive. When they hassled her outside Tina's house, her dad sent them away. She refused everyone with "The authorities won't allow me to talk to the press." Not totally the truth, although the FBI had stressed discretion. She referred all callers to Detective Santiago and Special Agent Irwin.

And here she stood still staring at Boyd's duffel.

The doorbell chimed.

She peered out. Jo Cassidy. She'd phoned earlier, setting a time to come pick up Boyd's belongings. Gemma then dithered too long with the packing and remembering. She'd still be in that fog if Jo hadn't been on time.

She unlocked and opened the door.

She looked up at the taller woman, wearing her usual polo shirt and slim black jeans. "Hi, Jo, come in. I was just going to make more coffee. Join me?" The invitation wasn't mere southern manners. Jo had been unfailingly kind and helpful.

Raking unpolished nails through her short blonde do, Jo entered and sent her a warm smile that crinkled lines around her eyes. "I'd love some coffee. Strong and black."

"Just the way I make it." Gemma led the way to the kitchen. "I need a shot of caffeine too."

Jo sat on one of the stools. "This last week has been tough on you."

The matter-of-fact statement, rather than the *poor thing* she'd heard too many times, relaxed the tightness in her shoulders. Her lips curved in a half smile. This older woman's empathetic manner invited confidence. Not that old, fortyish, but Jo seemed much more mature and confident. Service in war as an Army medic might have something to do with that.

"The last few days especially. I'm exhausted." Some of that was lack of sleep, but she wouldn't admit that. "I've been staying at my sister's house, trying to help her deal with—" she waved a hand "—everything. The whole family has been great, very supportive about Leo's betrayal and awful death. An incredible shock. I'm sad and angry at the same time, you know?"

The only upside of the whole mess was that being part of stopping Nazaroff relieved her of feeling like a forger. Something she'd happily put behind her.

She passed a steaming mug to Jo and poured one for herself before sitting on the other stool.

Jo sipped her coffee, lifted it in a toast salute. "Tastes perfect. Out of the blue like that, it must be hard to fathom."

Gemma nodded. "Difficult, for sure. When they release his body, we'll arrange a small family funeral, mostly for his and Tina's two kids, teenagers. He wasn't a bad father, just an unreliable man."

"Here's something you might want to tell Tina. Your brother-in-law's odd partnership with Nazaroff was no accident. Nazaroff knew what Parisi's job was and his relationship to the Bellini family. He targeted him and drew him in little by little. Greed did the rest."

"That doesn't excuse Leo." After a pause to think, Gemma said, "How do you know this?"

"All I can say is we have it from a witness." When Gemma nodded without pressing her further, Jo said, "I'm really sorry about your friend Troy. He too was targeted."

"If only he'd talked to me early on, I'd have tried to stop him from getting involved."

"You could've tried. This may sound harsh, but he made his choice and dived in too deep. He may not have realized how dangerous Nazaroff and his crew were."

"And then it was too late to escape. He paid the price of that choice." Hearing herself say that, Gemma released some of her guilt burden. Jo's words were almost what Boyd had said.

Boyd. She pictured him standing by the awning, pale, with exhaustion dragging at his eyes. He might've even swayed on his feet. She'd been so horrified at his duplicity, she all but ignored his injury. She needed to know, but the words stuck in her throat, neither swallowed nor spit out.

They sat in silence drinking their coffee. Jo was probably waiting for her to ask.

Another sip of coffee. She gripped the mug with both hands. "How serious was Boyd's wound? Is he okay?"

"Wound's a little more than a graze, not deep, but he needed stitches. He's healing, but it'll take a while." Jo placed a hand on Gemma's arm and gave her a stern look. "Boyd really cares for you, you know. You were damned hard on him."

She swallowed. "Did he spy on me? Did he suspect me of being part of the forgery plot?"

"*Never*. Rivera suggested the possibility at the beginning, but it made no sense. If you were part of the scheme, why would Nazaroff and crew try to kill you? Then Quinton picked up the thread, but Boyd repeatedly insisted any suspicions were misplaced. When Quinton asked him Tuesday, he defended you, that you'd never had any part. Which you didn't hear."

Shame clogging her throat, she hugged herself. "What about the tracker things?"

"Tracker buttons. He tucked them into your clothing because he was afraid if you were out of his sight, they'd snatch you." Her brows lowered in a scowl. "Which they did. He didn't tell you because he thought you'd be paranoid about it and refuse. He had a one-track focus, to keep you safe."

Gemma pressed her knuckles to her mouth.

"I have no solution to this," Jo said, "but Boyd needs time to heal. Without drama."

And Gemma needed time to think. Without drama.

Chapter Twenty-Eight

BOYD STOOD WHEN the meeting in Devlin's office adjourned. The boss had included Cassidy, Trask, and him around his conference table in hearing updates from Detective Santiago and Special Agent Irwin, a trim dark-haired woman with a no-nonsense demeanor and fierce brown eyes. The first words out of Irwin's mouth had dashed his hopes that they'd caught Nazaroff. No sign of the bastard anywhere.

Without thinking, he twisted around to pick up his phone and notepad. He sucked in a breath at the bayonet in his side. Five days out from being raked by that asshole's bullet, he was healing but the bastard wound announced itself when he twisted.

"A minute, Kirby." Back at his desk, Thomas Devlin shrugged out of his suit coat and draped it over the back of his chair.

"Sir?"

"You went above and beyond saving the client. Damned risky but it worked. Devlin Security Force has never lost a client. You maintained our perfect record." He snapped a salute. "Well done, First Sergeant."

Boyd stood at attention. Returned the salute. "Thank you, Captain."

One side of his boss's mouth twitched upward. "Wish I'd seen you crash that party. You've earned a bonus. But don't expect to be issued any more company vehicles."

"Understood, sir."

Devlin nodded and gestured toward the door. Both walked that way. "How's the wound? You need anything?"

"Healing. Lets me know when I move wrong." He swallowed. "I expect I'll need light duty for a while. And a few days off." Devlin's eagle gaze pierced through Boyd's effort at a blank expression. Perspiration beaded on the back of Boyd's neck.

"I see. Let my admin know if you need backup."

Backup? His brain froze for a beat. "I... will, Mr. Devlin."

"Dismissed, Boyd. And make it Thomas." He opened the door, closed it behind Boyd.

Boyd waved to Francine, who held the phone to her ear, as he left. What just happened? Did he get a green light?

"You want to get lunch in the staff café before I drive you home?" Trask said, catching up to him.

"You're on. I haven't been out in days, and I can't take much more sitting around here on desk duty and sitting at home playing video games."

A while later, they took their burgers and fries outside. The early July heat hit Boyd, but breathing air not filtered through an air conditioner suited him. The only view was of the adjacent office building. Street noises barely penetrated.

"A bitch they didn't catch him," Trask said. Although they chose a table beneath the awning, he slapped a ball cap on his bald head. Took a huge bite of burger.

"Too much to hope for. He probably had a contingency plan all set." Boyd chewed and swallowed for a minute. Took a drink of iced tea, not as sweet as Devlin's. Better, in his opinion. "What do you think about all the stuff Lucia aka Letty told the Feebs?"

Letty Boggess had apparently insisted her interrogators address her as Lucia. Irwin hadn't said, but it seemed she'd cut a deal for more lenient charges. Marshak and Hubik had lawyered up, were being held in the county jail, pending charges.

"Looked like the evidence bore out what she claimed. She and Nazaroff were camping out in a couple of the offices up front, using the shower in the staff restroom."

Boyd slipped his notebook from his breast pocket. Checked his notes. Special Agent Irwin had forbidden electronics in the meeting, pen and paper only. Hell, leaks could happen either way. At least he had a hard copy.

"Nazaroff's lair contained computer printout with details of several Bellini works, ones they had yet to create or sell."

"Lucia knew the third copier's name, so they traced the woman by fingerprints on one of the easels. County deputies picked her up at an art fair, where she hawks her own paintings." Trask grinned. "Or used to."

They compared notes while they ate. Most of the information came initially from Lucia/Letty.

She met Leo Parisi at a gallery opening, and then Nazaroff targeted him as the weak link in the Bellini family. He lured Parisi into the scheme with promises of sharing the riches. As rental agent, Parisi covered up their squatting in the old factory. Nazaroff feared

Gemma would find out about the forging and connect it to him, and there was the revenge motive. Parisi wanted her out of the way so when his wife took over, he could convince her to sell more paintings faster.

He was key in the attempts to kill Gemma. A device he bought on the internet could pause the security system, but couldn't open the door locks. So then Hubik and Marshak sabotaged the balcony from outside, as Boyd had assumed. Parisi planned the last attempt, but Marshak and Hubik stole the dump truck and rammed Boyd's vehicle off the road.

Trask downed his tea and snorted his disgust. "Parisi was a coward. He let Marshak and Hubik do the dirty work of eliminating Gemma with those manufactured accidents."

Heat ran up Boyd's back to his nape as the information shuffled into a picture. "The other copier said Nazaroff sent her away that Tuesday morning. He also had Lucia make the gallery appointment in Annapolis for that day. Premeditated, getting witnesses out of the way. He planned to kill Gemma once he had what he needed. What's one more murder?"

The FBI had *graciously* thrown the sheriff's department a bone, allowing it to be in charge of investigating the murders and attempts on Gemma's life. Santiago said the bullet that killed Leo Parisi matched neither Marshak's nor Hubik's weapon. The 9mm must belong to Nazaroff.

Troy Dupree bought into the art forgery scheme to begin with, but then got cold feet and disappeared. When he made that call to Gemma, the bug planted by Marshak in his phone located him. After he was dragged back, Nazaroff kept him shackled to the floor or to a cot in one of the offices. During a bathroom break, Dupree managed to get out the back door, but the two thugs took off after him. Lucia never saw him after that. The bullet in him matched Marshak's weapon.

About the money, Lucia said Nazaroff doled out cash from the sales to them all. He stashed the rest in a bank account. She glimpsed his bank login once, CMBC.

"That's the Cleatia & Moldova Bank Corporation. They have a branch in Arlington." Boyd pushed away from the table and carried his plate and glass inside.

"Immigrants use that and a Mexican bank to send money to their families," Trask said as they left the café. "The Feebs will need a stack of warrants to get into that account."

In the parking garage, Boyd said, "Instead of home, Linc, how about dropping me off at the Jeep dealer in Alexandria? I need new wheels."

****

Gemma rolled up her sleep tee and laid it in the open suitcase next to her swimsuit. Maybe a sweatshirt for cool nights. She wouldn't need much beyond capris and shorts. More and she wouldn't be able to close the small bag.

She sipped her wine and poured more for Pia. They'd just finished the takeout sushi Pia brought. Mostly Pia finished it. Gemma didn't have much appetite.

"Girlfriend, I wish you wouldn't do this." Pia gestured with her glass from where she lounged on the slipper chair beside the bed, one shorts-clad leg hooked over the chair arm. Her sandal dangled back and forth. When a tendril of red hair drifted onto her forehead, she tucked it back into the messy knot on top her head. "It's not safe. That monster is still out there."

"It's fine. No one knows where I'm going. Not even you. He won't find me." She folded her favorite pair of distressed jeans with careful motions and laid them in the bag.

"Why not stick around? You can even bunk with me for a few days. Tomorrow's the Fourth. We can go into the city and watch the fireworks over the Mall."

Gemma shuddered. "I've had enough fireworks to last me until the next century."

"Sorry. Poor choice of entertainment." Pia planted both sandaled feet on the carpet and pursed her lips. Serious Pia face. "You said Nazaroff wanted revenge. Revenge can be a powerful motivator. He could've stuck around waiting for a chance at you again."

Gemma's stomach clenched, but Pia's idea made no sense. "His description, his photo are on every screen. He's long gone. Plus he couldn't possibly know about—I mean, know this place I'm going."

"Okay. I won't nag." Pia leaned back in the chair and sipped her wine. "So go ahead. Play the part of that old time movie star who said, 'I vant to be alone.'"

"I'll do exactly that. I've been surrounded by mobs of people for the last week. Asking questions, comforting and needing comforting, spewing saccharine sympathy card sentiments. Now that Leo's in the ground, Tina feels the same need for quiet. I want to be alone to think, to paint, to decide on a few things."

"Like the fashion designer offer?" Pia tilted her head, clearly fishing for an exclusive.

"One of them." Everything she'd been through swirled through her entire being, causing her to examine her life, what she wanted, who she was or wanted to be, what Silvio would think—and Boyd.

"And what about Boyd?" Pia's brown eyes gleamed with mischief. "You're not sleeping. That's why your eyes have bags as big as that one you're packing."

"Mind reader. It's complicated. Something I have to work out." Her throat tightened, and she gripped the hard edge of the suitcase until her knuckles protested. She lowered her chin and stared at her best friend.

Pia shook her head, tumbling an avalanche of hair from the knot. She swiped it out of the way. "Oookay. I know that fiery green look. Pia backing off here."

Boyd had encouraged her and shared with her, even confided in her, as she had with him. He was honorable and kind, protective, beyond it being just his job. They meshed, they complemented each other. She'd made that horrible impulsive mistake of letting one misheard conversation destroy everything. Her first shot at a real relationship and she'd blown it. And he'd let her because of that honorable thing he had going. And his misplaced guilt.

She needed to figure out what to do about all that.

"I'm getting away from everything." Gemma tucked in a cotton sweater and zipped the bag. "In the morning I'm outta here."

"And taking your baggage with you."

Chapter Twenty-Nine

HUNKERED DOWN AMID the pines, Boyd
thumbed up his night-vision goggles and checked his
watch. A few minutes past midnight. He'd just finished
a perimeter check of Silvio's beach house. He settled the
goggles in place. The lenses converted darkness into
identifiable green shapes. All quiet except for crickets
and an occasional sleepy tweet. The only light in the
house emanated from kitchen appliances. Cloud cover
obscured the half moon.

He picked up movement outside the sunroom just
beneath the balcony. That was no deer. His heart kicked
up and the muscles in his legs tensed. He flicked off the
hook on his holster, released the safety.

A tall figure separated from the shadowed building.
Human. Clutching an object.

Nazaroff. It had to be. While Boyd had scouted the
other side of the property, he'd slipped in through the
pines.

Keeping low, Boyd crept closer, 9mm in his grip.
He had to get closer without being seen, or the asshole
could disappear into the trees.

What was he doing? Not a gun in his hands.
Something bigger. A means to get Gemma out of the
house. The hairs on Boyd's arms flared. He was too far
away…

Flames erupted from the object. The man reared back and lobbed. Glass shattered in an upstairs window. The bedroom across from the master suite. Fire exploded in a barrage of deadly light. He backed into the shrubbery, out of sight.

Not gone, he was waiting for Gemma to run out of the house. Boyd ducked behind the hedge and tapped his phone.

Rings on the other end. More ringing.

Smoke billowed from the empty window. He pictured the fire crawling across the wallpaper and carpet, down the hall, into other rooms. Small explosions of lightbulbs measured its pace.

Still the ringing. Where the hell was she?

"Boyd?"

Her tentative, plaintive tone punched him in the chest. "Gemma, Nazaroff is here. He set the upstairs on fire. I called 911."

"Wh-what? Oh, God, no! Wait, where are you?"

"Outside. You gotta get out. But he's watching the doors. Listen to me."

****

Fire? Nazaroff?

Gemma's breath stalled in her throat as she struggled to focus on Boyd's words. Her hands shook. She bobbled the phone while setting it to Speaker, then fumbled in her tote for her Bluetooth headset. A million questions buzzed through her head. Later. For now it had to be enough that Boyd was here. Concentrating on his instructions steadied her.

"Yes, yes," she said, once the headset was operative. "Be right out." She'd chosen to sleep on the living room sofa because she couldn't bear lying in the bed they'd shared. And the empty rooms echoed with her solitary footsteps.

She pulled on her jeans and the cotton sweater, yanked her navy windbreaker on over her head. Dark colors, as Boyd instructed. The phone went into the front pouch. The zipper wouldn't work, or was it her fingers? She stepped into her slip-on beach shoes and crossed to the window. It pained her to leave her tote and laptop, but Boyd said carry nothing.

Returning to the window, she eased up the glass and then the screen. Silently. Thank you for quality windows that didn't protest. She swung one leg over the sill until her foot found purchase, then the other, in the soft loam. The coleus bed, came the inane thought as she closed the window.

Bent over, she scuttled across the lawn to behind the hedge. She knelt, panting harder than in spinning class.

Her phone dinged with a text. Boyd.

U behind the hedge?

She fumbled the phone from the zippered pouch and texted back a yes.

Stay down til I give u an all clear

He was gone.

Crackling sounds, crashes, and heat penetrated her foggy brain. The fire.

She peered above the foliage and on upward. Red and yellow dragon-tongue flames licked the night sky, and black smoke swelled from every bedroom window. The acrid smell stung her nose and throat.

Sirens screamed in the distance.

Hurry, please hurry.

Tears welled. The beach house could be lost before any fire trucks could make it here.

Where was Boyd? And Nazaroff?

She had to know. She had to see what was happening. She crawled across the grass to the boxwood's edge. The cool dew chilled her knees through the jeans. Wavering flames illuminated a man in dark clothing emerging from the bushes. *Nazaroff.*

Her stomach clenched and her mouth went dry.

****

Boyd tensed when he saw the dark figure separate from the tall shrubbery. He crept from his cover by the garden shed. Asshole was probably wondering why his prey hadn't run screaming from the house.

Nazaroff ignited a second Molotov cocktail. The bigger bottle meant more kerosene.

Adrenaline jolted through Boyd. If that fire bomb got lobbed through another window, an even bigger fire could engulf the whole house in minutes. He tore off the night-vision goggles and raced forward.

Creep raised his arm and reared back.

Boyd jumped him. A downward blow knocked the flaming bottle from his hand. It rolled away.

But the other man didn't go down. He turned and countered with a jab.

Boyd ducked the blow. Pain stung his side.

Nazaroff reached toward a pocket. Going for his weapon.

Boyd blocked that move with his left arm, punched his chin with his right.

Nazaroff staggered but didn't go down. Came back at Boyd.

From there, they exchanged blows and wrestled. Each twist and thrust wedged pain like a spike. Sweat droplets flew.

Though much older, Nazaroff fought with strength. And desperation. Their guttural grunts and the thuds of solid blows barely registered beneath the roar of the raging fire.

The pain distracted him, drained his energy. Boyd had to take him down. Now.

He dug deep for strength. Hooked a leg around one of Nazaroff's and slammed him face down to the ground. Knelt on him. The downed asshole twisted around onto his back, but Boyd drove a punch into his throat, stilling him. Sitting on the man's belly, he secured his wrists with a zip tie.

Blood dripped onto them.

Fire and smoke engulfed the whole upstairs of that wing. The wood in the balcony door smoldered and flames licked upward. Heat seared Boyd's cheeks. Smoke choked coughs from him.

Horn blasts and screams of sirens, the intermittent *woop woop* of police sirens grew louder, coming closer.

An investigation of Nazaroff's jumpsuit pockets came up with a semi-auto pistol and a car key fob. The man struggled again, kicking and twisting. Boyd wouldn't risk leaving his legs free a second more. He flung the pistol away into the darkness. It clattered on the bricks by the grill. The older man's legs flailed again but with less strength. Boyd held his ankles together and bound them with a zip tie. He pocketed the key fob.

Finally Nazaroff subsided. Laid his head back on the grass, panting.

A movement in Boyd's peripheral vision shot him to his feet, weapon in his hand. At a pang in his side, he clenched his jaw.

Gemma.

He holstered the 9 mil.

Eyes as big as the moon, she stared at him, then at the man on the ground. She closed her eyes briefly and pressed her palms to her chest.

A dark watch cap slid off, and the fire spotlighted a different Nazaroff. Shaved head and a good start on a beard. No more thick eyebrows. Barely any at all. The changes altered his appearance dramatically. But the eyes, black and deep set, burning with fury, belonged to no one else but him. Like in the prison image.

Boyd edged toward Gemma. She might push him away, but he couldn't help wrapping an arm around her quaking shoulders. His gaze scoured the ground. No sign of the burning bottle.

"If you're looking for the Molotov cocktail," she said, "I threw it in the pond. It's a floating candle now."

Sure enough, behind them, a small fire bobbed on the water. A grin tugged at his mouth. "Didn't I text you to stay down?"

"You were busy." She lifted one shoulder in dismissal. But didn't reject his embrace. Thank God, because he needed her as a crutch. Or was that a metaphor?

"Bitch! You ruined everything," Nazaroff spat in a croaking voice.

"You're the one responsible." Gemma propped her fists on her hips and glared. "You'll go back to prison. Forgery, kidnapping, murder. Troy's death is on you. And my brother-in-law's. A life sentence by the time it's all added up."

"Maybe." He propped himself up on an elbow and cast a sly look at Boyd. "But not before I tell everyone what this whore and I did together. She couldn't keep her hands off me. Begged me for it."

Gemma lifted that stubborn little chin Boyd loved. "Go ahead. Who would believe anything you say now? And so what if they do? I. Do. Not. Care. Not anymore."

Nazaroff sank down, saying nothing.

Boyd's vision blurred. His head swam. The smoke? Probably not. He let go of Gemma and sank cross-legged to the ground. He hugged his left arm against his side.

"What is it?" Gemma knelt beside him.

"Bastard whacked me in my wound. Tore the stitches. Bleeding again."

"Let's get something on that." She tugged off her windbreaker, then the sweater beneath it.

He unzipped the black Ninja as far as his waist and opened it wide.

"Lift your arm if you can."

He closed his eyes and complied, forcing himself to breathe evenly.

She sucked in a breath. "Definitely bleeding." She folded the sweater and eased it inside the garment until it covered the wound. "There. Hold your arm against it. Tight."

After a moment, Boyd opened his eyes. His head had cleared. But Nazaroff… Where was he? He drew his Glock and searched the area.

Still bound, the damn forger was crawling toward the grill beneath the balcony.

"He's going for his pistol. Keep down."

Gemma dropped to her stomach beside him. "He *can't* get away. Dear God, not again. He has the gun. No, no."

The man's other hand gripped the grill. He was pulling himself up.

On one knee, Boyd aimed at the darkness by the grill, but again thick, black smoke obscured the view. Where the fuck was Nazaroff? Did he run off?

The blaze now fully engulfed the wooden balcony overhead. The smoke swirled aside.

Nazaroff leaned on the grill, his bound ankles hampering his movements.

Boyd aimed and fired. Once. Twice.

Nazaroff stumbled against one of the angled struts bracing the balcony.

The strut tilted sideways. Gave way. The balcony crashed down in a whoosh of flames and smoke.

A gunshot rang out, then a man's scream—cut short.

Flashing lights and sirens blared as trucks and police cars streamed up the driveway.

Chapter Thirty

GEMMA CROSSED HER legs, recrossed them. Drummed fingers on her tote. Strangled the strap. Hoped the mingled odors of antiseptic and floral room freshener would clear the smoke from her system. Emergency Room chairs didn't invite relaxing. Or maybe it was just being here at three-thirty in the morning. And rehearsing what to say to Boyd. She had to apologize, even if it didn't bring them back together.

She checked the time. Again. The receptionist assured her he'd be out in a few minutes, but that was a half hour ago.

A deputy sheriff had questioned them while an EMT tended to Boyd. The ambulance had driven away with him before the fire was declared out. Nothing remained of that wing. She'd really miss the sunroom. But the main house was spared except for smoke and water damage. A firefighter brought her belongings from the living room to her at her car. He assured her some of the crew would remain to ensure no embers still smoldered.

The ambulance had delivered Boyd to the small Rimini Beach Hospital. A gunshot wound, the receptionist had told Gemma, was a rarity. They dealt more with sunburns, domestic violence, and boating accidents.

Three other people occupied the waiting room—a

sleeping toddler, its weeping mom in a bathrobe, and a teenager on his phone. An overhead television flickered with a local news station, no sound but jerky captions like the ones in bars that race to keep up with the speakers.

The double doors at the other end of the room whooshed open.

Boyd dwarfed the wheelchair pushed by the nurse. He wore the bloodstained black jumpsuit. A Ninja, he called it.

Gemma had nearly come apart seeing his pallor before the emergency crew loaded him in the ambulance. But now his complexion looked closer to normal color. Seeing his mouth tight with pain and his head sagging with exhaustion squeezed her heart.

His gaze searched the room. When it landed on Gemma, his eyes widened. The nurse wheeled him to the desk, where he signed papers, and then over to her.

"We've topped off his tank," the woman drawled, "and stitched him back together for y'all. I'll wheel him out to the car."

A scowl lowering his brows, Boyd kicked aside the foot supports and pushed to his feet. White-knuckle grip on a clear plastic bag, he squared his shoulders. "I'm good. I can walk. Thanks anyway."

The nurse remained there, lips pursed, head tilted as if she expected him to fall back into the wheelchair.

He wouldn't. Gemma sent the woman a knowing grin and followed his plodding and deliberate steps through the automatic door.

"Car's just over here, not far." She trotted ahead and opened the passenger door. She'd slid the seat way back and cleared her usual junk from the floor.

Once she'd climbed in, Boyd cleared his throat. "I expected Cassidy."

"You got me." A double entendre if there ever was one, but he didn't react. She started the engine, but left the gear in Park.

"I called Jo like you asked and collected your stuff from your new SUV. Very snazzy, BTW. It's in the back. Your stuff, not the vehicle. Jo will drive that to your place. She'll drop off the keys in a day or two."

At Gemma's taking charge, Jo had said nothing on the phone for a beat. Then she breathed a slow okay. She would explain everything to Devlin in the morning.

Gemma eyed Boyd. His head lay back against the head rest. "How are you feeling?"

Rumbles from his throat. "Not too bad. Doc slathered the wound with antiseptic stuff and closed it. Sent me off with more antibiotics." He held up the plastic bag. "Your sweater's a goner, but I'll recover."

"That's the important thing."

"Car's not moving."

"We need to talk. Rather, *I* need to talk."

She scooted around to face him. She had to touch him, to feel his heat, to know he was whole, but where? She settled for curving a hand on his knee.

"First, thank you isn't nearly enough but here goes. Thank you for saving my life. Not just once, but multiple times. This last was a doozy. You can tell me later how you *happened* to be there tonight. You shouldn't have been there with that injury, but I'm thankful. He might've finally succeeded." She shuddered before banishing the fiery images in her head.

"Second, I want to apologize." She crossed her hands over her chest. "I was wrong, terribly, impulsively wrong to believe even for a minute you spied on me to find out if I was involved with the forgery. I bought it because, well, you know…" Her throat closed, but she managed to suck in a breath. "I felt I couldn't trust anyone, especially a man. It was a… burr stuck in my brain, a knot inside my chest. I couldn't pry it loose even when my heart said I could trust *you*. So when that… that—" she stabbed fingers at an invisible enemy "—Devlin Security guy asked you about my involvement, my head whirled and my ears roared. I never even heard your reply. I reacted on gut instinct. Once I got home and had time to think, I knew I was wrong. I'm so sorry."

Boyd opened his mouth, but she pressed a finger to his lips.

"Hush up. You're exhausted and in pain. We can talk tomorrow after we both get some sleep." She grimaced. "Shoot, it *is* tomorrow." She dabbed her eyes with a tissue before fastening her seatbelt. Little to no traffic at this time of night, so she'd make it back to Linley Harbor in an hour.

A few minutes later, her sideways glance found him with eyes closed. His chest rose and fell with even breaths.

****

In the afternoon, after both Boyd and Gemma had slept, Special Agent Irwin arrived to interview them. Irwin struck Gemma as earnest and businesslike in a pleasant sort of way. Except for her brown eyes. They could've belonged to a bird of prey, maybe an owl.

Gemma ushered her into the great room, where Boyd lounged in an armchair, pillows plumped—by her—behind him. He rose to his feet, a maneuver that she could tell pained him. He shook hands with the agent before sinking back down. Irwin sat soldier-erect and stern-faced on the edge of the couch, and Gemma took the other armchair.

After he and Gemma went over everything from the previous night, the agent said, "It's only because the Bureau worked with Devlin Security on this that I can tell you some of what our investigation has turned up, but keep it to yourselves. None of this is public yet."

When they agreed, she continued. She turned her gaze to Boyd. "Your bullet hit Nazaroff in the shoulder and made him lurch against the balcony strut. When he fell, his body covered the pistol, so it was mostly undamaged. Techs should be able to determine if it was used to kill Leo Parisi."

Gemma glanced at Boyd to see if he had questions. When he said nothing, she leaned forward. "It's widely known that my grandfather had a house in Rimini Beach, but the locals never reveal the address. How did he find me?"

Irwin nodded, and checked her phone. Maybe for her notes. "The Rimini Beach police found an old Ford coupe in the pines. Inside it was a blank order slip from a local diner with directions to the house. He told the cashier he was a prospective buyer but the realtor didn't give him the info. The cashier obliged. Also inside the car were his laptop and a U.S. passport in the name Martin Flint. In the photo, he's bald and bearded, like his appearance now. Dated before he came to Virginia, so he planned ahead."

"I guessed as much. He was methodical." Boyd splayed his fingers on his knees. "What can you tell us about the money he got from the forging?"

"He paid for internet and rented furniture with

checks, not cash from the painting sales, so he looked legit. The account at the CMBC branch is in his alias, but contains only fifty dollars."

"So the money's vanished?" Gemma slumped. Those people who bought forged art were out lots of money. People might say they deserved it, but at least some of the buyers were just naïve.

Agent Irwin's mouth remained set in a straight line, but humor glittered in her eyes. "Oddly, the bank has never reported to the IRS what must be huge amounts, first deposited and then transferred abroad. The Cleatia and Moldova Bank Corporation can expect a thorough investigation. And techs should be able to find his investment information in his computer."

"Nobody has profited except the investment fund," Boyd said. "Clawing back money from overseas accounts could take years, even for the IRS."

Irwin finally smiled. "The government is both patient and persistent."

Chapter Thirty-One

BOYD SAT ON the couch, computer on his lap. Gemma had shooed him from the kitchen. She refused his help with the dishes. Insisted he go rest. Trask said the same thing when he left. Thomas Devlin too. Take a week to recuperate but send his report A-sap.

Boyd couldn't concentrate on writing anything. He kept seeing Gemma, cheek bruised and puffy, holding that damn high heeled shoe like a weapon. Then last night, fussing over him and apologizing.

She'd brought him home and settled him in the guest room bed like an invalid. Which he guessed he was. She cooked for him. She hovered like his mom when he'd had his tonsils out. If it wasn't summer, she'd tuck an afghan around his legs. She kept feeling his forehead. To see if he had a fever, she claimed. She could hold that cool, smooth palm on him anytime.

He laid his head back against the sofa. The ache in his side was nothing compared to the pain raging in his soul since he watched her walk away from him a week ago. She was present in his every thought, in the fiber of his being. She fascinated him and made him laugh. He was drunk on her. She was everything he'd never had the sense to know he wanted. Needed. But he was no good for her. The longer he stayed with her, the harder leaving would be.

He'd promised Cassidy to drive her back to her wheels if she brought him his SUV. She'd laughed and ended the call. So until he felt stronger, here he stayed. A day or two, at most.

"I made fresh iced tea," Gemma announced in her diamond bright, cheery voice as she joined him. Ice clinked in the glass she handed him. She sank onto the cushion to his right with a glass of white wine for herself.

He thanked her. Closed the lid and set the laptop on the other side. The twisting motion fired a reminder shot of his injury. He could walk and climb stairs without pain, but side-to-side motions, nope. Not yet. He took a fast swallow of the tea.

"Feeling better?"

"As my uncle in Maine would say, finest kind. Rested. Restored after your delicious pot roast. Red meat to help a man heal."

"You're grimacing." Her free hand cupped his shoulder. A week ago, he would've lifted it to his lips, and then... Damn. "More pain? You want something?"

"No, I'm good for now." A good time to bring up what he couldn't earlier. "When we left the hospital, you didn't let me answer your apology. There's nothing to forgive. I understand why you jumped to conclusions. Your past set you up."

"Thanks for that. I reckon you're right."

"Why were you staying in that isolated house alone?" A target, vulnerable, but she wouldn't appreciate his saying so.

"I thought I was safe, that Nazaroff had gone somewhere else to spend his ill-gotten gains." Her hand fluttered, maybe at the absurdity of that notion, before she replaced it on his shoulder. "I needed to sort out things—you, my life, my work, my family. The official interviews and my family kept me busy for a week. But at Silvio's house by myself, I had days and nights in solitude, without distractions."

"So?"

She curled up her fine legs, showcased in shorts, and regarded him with solemn eyes. "I came to the conclusion that my art is just that—*my* art, my path, not Silvio's. You helped me see that I can do more than one kind of art. I have a meeting next week at Sibyl Simone Fashions to discuss my painting designs that would go on a new line of clothing."

A burst of warmth bloomed in his chest. He held up his hand and they slapped a high five. "Best news I've heard in weeks. Your designs will be a sensation."

"Thanks for the vote of confidence. That remains to be seen. But there's more I worked out. I realized why you didn't defend yourself when I accused you of spying on me."

"How? No—"

"Hush up. You asked, so listen. You thought you failed to protect me because Nazaroff had me kidnapped and hurt me." She held the cool wine glass to where the bruise had marred her cheek. "So you accepted my rejection in stoic silence. But you couldn't have possibly guessed my own brother-in-law would be part of it."

"Perceptive on the first, not on the next. Parisi was the family member I suspected." No reason to mention Uncle James and his affair. "Our operatives followed him for a few days, but saw nothing suspicious, except as a rental agent he su— was a slacker. That old factory was one of three of his unrented buildings that were likely hideouts for Nazaroff. He targeted Leo as the weak link. But I'd have wasted crucial time without the tracker buttons. They led me directly to the right building."

Her laugh rang like a bell. "Is that how you found me at the beach house?"

"No, you didn't pack any of the clothes I stashed them in. I kept watch over you since I bought my new ride. First at the condo, cleared with security. Then I followed you. At the beach house, I did recon outside at night and slept in the back of the SUV during the day." Hell, part of the day. It was too hot.

"Summer heat and a hard bed. Mosquitos too. No wonder you weren't healing."

"Dammit, I was patrolling around the other side of the property, or I'd have seen Nazaroff, headed him off before he got to the house." His gut clenched.

"You couldn't be everywhere at once. Give yourself a break." She sent him a sad smile. "You were certain he would show up? To try to… kill me."

"His fury built over time. Prison will do that. And denial of anything being his fault. His hatred was cold, like dry ice that burns at the touch. Once he got out, it flared into a hot coal. He plotted, stoking it into a need for revenge. The forgery of Silvio's works was for big money, but linked to his plot against you."

"Deep, Mr. Kirby. Philosophical."

"I've had time to analyze things." He shifted position. He'd shrug except it would rouse the demons with spears. He might need one of the doc's pain pills later so he could sleep. "Nazaroff's obsession with revenge fit with stuff I learned in my psych classes."

Tears glistened in her beautiful eyes. She took a long drink of wine before setting the goblet on the cocktail table.

"One of his men killed Troy. It doesn't matter which one. The blame is really on their boss. I'm heartsick about Troy's death, will be for a long time. But I accept that he made his own choices. I spoke to his mom. It's all so hard on her, and on the family. I told her he tried to escape to warn me."

"Could be the truth. He warned you once, so why not? And Nazaroff is dead."

"In the fire he set. No trial, no testimony. It's over."

"For you and me, yes. Law enforcement will be working on this for years. Multiple crimes, multiple jurisdictions. Haven County Sheriff's Department, Alexandria PD, Rimini Beach PD, and FBI Art Crime."

"Don't forget the IRS."

Chapter Thirty-Two

LATER THAT NIGHT, Gemma followed Boyd upstairs. In the guest bedroom, the rumpled sheets and blanket testified to a restless sleep. Was it the pain or a nightmare or knowing she slept across the hall?

She set out antibiotic ointment and a new roll of adhesive tape on the bathroom sink. "The hospital instructions say to change the dressing tonight and twice tomorrow." If there was still bleeding, he was to call a local doctor.

He slid down his left sleeve, and she helped peel off the safari shirt. He'd taken to wearing button-up shirts because he couldn't raise the left arm much without pulling the stitches. Mostly due to nerves, she chattered about her next project as she removed the bandages and examined him.

He was easing away from her, holding her at more than arm's length. Actually, not holding her at all. He avoided contact. No return caresses when she touched him. Few smiles. He still bore that heavy burden of guilt.

He stood planted, still, in stoic silence, watching her with unreadable eyes. Maybe this time due to the pain from holding out his arm.

"No bleeding. You'll be on injured reserve only a while longer. Not deep, but a nasty wound for sure, and nicely stitched. My mom, who does all kinds of needlework—" She glanced upward and chuckled. "I mean knitting, sewing, not skin, although she might've sewed up a couple cuts on us kids. Anyway, she would be impressed." Shoot, she was babbling nonsense.

He said nothing, so she hushed herself and cut gauze and strips of adhesive tape. She held gauze layers gently over the stitches and started taping.

Unless she was terribly wrong about his feelings for her, she had to make her move. If she couldn't convince him they belonged together, she'd survive. But with a black hollow inside her surrounded by pain.

"Gemma, what else did you sort out when you were holed up at the beach house?"

Her hand stilled against his warm skin. Had he read her mind? Or had the omission been bugging him? Whatever, she'd take it. Her clumsy fingers made a wrinkle in the tape. She focused on smoothing the next, last piece of tape in place.

Finished, she flattened her hands on his chest. She forced herself not to stroke his lovely firm muscles. Beneath her palms, his heart seemed to thump a little faster than normal. Glory, glory, he didn't back away from her. She met his wary gaze, bracketed by deeper lines beside his mouth and eyes.

"What else? Only the most important thing. I want to look ahead, to move ahead. And I want you—*us*—to be a huge part of that. I miss what we had before I ruined things between us. The closeness, the sharing, the companionship, and yes, the sex, spectacular sex."

His gaze softened a barely perceptible fraction before he slammed the door again.

She rushed on with all the insight she'd gained in her solitary musings. "We've been together only a month, but I want us to have a chance for a future. I've fallen for you for many reasons, reasons that go beyond you saving or protecting me. You understand me better than I do. You get who I am inside. Although that protective, white knight strand in your DNA is super sexy."

"Look, honey, I don't deserve you. You're rich and successful." On a shrug of his right shoulder, he added, "Semi famous. And funny and brave and generous. I'm nobody, a security operative."

Honey. He called me honey!

Her pulse pinged. He did care. "Not a nobody. You're a hero, honorable and kind and smart. No genuine fake like... well, you know. You're the genuine deal. And working on a degree. Do you need that pigskin to prove you're somebody?"

"Funny. My mom would agree with you about the diploma. But I'm too screwed up to make a relationship work."

"What, you think you're unworthy because of the nightmares and your ghosts? You carry too much on those wide shoulders. The lives of your teammates. Fear you couldn't protect anyone— especially me—because you blame yourself for their deaths. I'll bet you applied to Devlin Security because their jobs usually require protecting objects, not people."

A garnet wash daubed his cheeks. "How do you know all that?"

"I sorted through everything you'd revealed and put it together. But I'm missing a piece about that last mission in Afghanistan. Did intelligence warn of possible rocket attacks? Did others away from your patrol area warn you? Any indications something might happen?"

"We were always ready in case any bad actors returned to a village. But rocket attacks? No intel on that." After a blip of a pause, he added, "None."

She placed a palm on his jaw. "The deaths of those men aren't your fault. The war killed them. It was a fluke *you* weren't killed." The images her words evoked made her swallow hard.

"Cassidy has said the same thing more than once. Didn't put a dent in my dreams and visions. That burr in your brain and heart, it's the same with me. I can't seem to peel it away."

"Not by yourself. Maybe you could try counseling again. The VA must have services like that."

"Yeah, they do, so if…" Blinking hard, he looked up at the light, or maybe just away from her appeal.

Her throat clogged, but she swallowed and pushed on. It was now or never.

"If you believe in a higher power, maybe you were saved so you could save *me*. And now you have. You've overcome your worst fear. Make the best of it. Not the worst."

His focus returned to her, a soft but decisive look in his eyes. His hands pressed hers against his chest. Celebrating, she rose on her toes.

"I've found my best. It's you, Gemma. All the time we've been together, I kept telling myself I would have to walk away. But when that jerk Quinton asked if you were involved in the forgery, I let you believe the worst. I told him you'd never been involved and if he brought it up again, I'd deck him."

She started to speak, to tell him Jo had explained, but he pressed a finger to her lips.

"It wasn't you who ruined things, honey. My chickenshit cowardice did. I made you walk away. The look on your face, like I'd kicked you in the teeth, jammed my chest. It hurt worse than any bullet wound. Maybe counseling will make a difference. God help me, I can't lose you again."

Her lips quivered, but she sent him a soggy smile. "You want to keep debating who was at fault, or do you want to kiss me?"

His eyes went to smoke. He curled his right arm around her and yanked her against his hard body. His mouth came down on hers, hot and hungry, in drugging kisses that flowed heat through her. She wrapped her arms around his waist. Her blood simmered in the power of his embrace, the lush strokes of his tongue, the joy of feeling so alive again.

When he finally lifted his head, they were both breathing hard. He brushed a finger across her cheek and then tugged on her hair. "No colorful braid?"

"I haven't felt much like wearing them. But now I might?" She raised an eyebrow.

He twisted, reaching for her again, but winced at the pain. His expression then was more of a rueful grimace than a smile.

"Honey, if you want to take a chance on me, I'd be a fool to turn you down. We'll have to wait a while for more than kisses. But do I have to do that waiting across the hall from you?"

Her smile beamed him the answer. "How about we wait together in *our* bed?"

Epilog

December, a year and a half later

BOYD CARRIED THE last load of empty containers to the garage. The caterer would pick up everything tomorrow. He returned to the kitchen, where Gemma was stowing the leftover food. Not much remained of the shrimp, individual quiches, and antipasto. He'd hoped for at least a week's worth of snacks.

"Super party." Gemma hip-bumped the fridge door. "People seemed to have a good time." She sipped from her goblet and set it down. "This Super Tuscan blend is good. Even you, the beer drinker, like this one."

"I do, and I had a good time." He hoped for an even better one in a little while. To reassure himself, he patted the small bulge in his pocket. His pulse pinged, but he forced himself to calmness. Finished his wine and set it in the sink.

They'd invited a crowd bigger than their first holiday gathering last year. People from the art world, most of her family, their friends, her friends, his colleagues and buddies. Thomas Devlin even stopped by for a few minutes.

He wrapped his arms around her, letting the tangy scent of her hair, the hint of musk that was the natural scent of her skin soothe his senses. He didn't want to rush this, so he said, "You spent a long time huddled with your sister."

"She had ideas for publishing a new book with images of some of Silvio's preliminary sketches along with the finished paintings, even snippets of his notes. I suggested she write up something formal we can take to the publisher."

Defeating Nazaroff had lifted a burden from Gemma. She and her sister shared the duties of shepherding their grandfather's works. Tina had left behind bridezillas and their mothers and turned to family and pet portraits. Gemma painted canvases when she felt like it, no longer following Silvio's dream for her, but her own. She received a cut of the proceeds for the "Gemma" line by Sibyl Simone Fashions. The proceeds from Gemma's original painted shirt or dress, sold to the highest bidder on the company website, went to a charity of her choice.

He flipped the little braid clipped to the back of her hair. Tonight's was red and green. "Good idea for the book, sharing more of how Silvio worked."

She murmured assent, smoothed her hands down his chest. "Too bad your mom couldn't make it, but grandkids rule."

"Little Lucas is a terror. My brother and his wife needed her help." Today was Boyd's nephew's fourth birthday. The party required all hands on deck.

"I missed her though," Gemma said. "We always have a good gab. I'll have to mail her Christmas pres—" Her eyes popped wide open. "Ooh, I forgot to tell you. I finished painting the design on her tunic. An evergreen branch with a cluster of pine cones."

"She'll love it."

He bent and kissed her. She opened to him, and their tongues parried in a warm, wild taste of red wine and desire. A shot of heat radiated through him as she hummed her pleasure against his mouth. He picked her up and crossed to the bar, set her on it, so they were at eye level. Her small hands gripped his butt, urging him closer, to more. He palmed one breast, then brushed the pad of his thumb across the nipple until she moaned. Heat rose in him, filled his belly and licked at his groin.

He pulled back, panting. Touched his forehead to hers. Watched her eyes open, confusion clouding them. "Déjà vu, honey? I'm stopping, but not because kissing you is a bad idea like I said first time we did this."

"What?"

"I need to talk to you."

At her worried look, he helped her down. Hustled her into the living room and onto the couch. The Christmas tree lights glowed in the corner. More lights—elf lights she called them—twinkled from the mantel and every table.

Counseling helped him lift the last remnants of his guilt burden and anger. And with her support and love, he was able to reconnect with the teammates who'd survived. And finally he faced his fallen comrades' families. They talked—and hugged—at Arlington amid the rows of white crosses. None of them blamed him. It was war, a war that wasn't even theirs, Ritter's dad said. He and Gemma had laid wreaths on the graves of Ritter and Hawkins. And now, no nightmares or ghostly visages in six months.

He was ready. More than ready. After the wrap-up of the Nazaroff case, he'd received a raise. Devlin had told him he could expect another and more responsibilities when he graduated in the spring.

"Boyd, what is this?" She curled up her feet beneath her long skirt.

He took her hands and kissed her knuckles. "I thought maybe a candlelight dinner on Christmas Eve or Christmas morning. But I can't wait. Because of you, I feel whole again, alive again. I've never been happier than with you. I want to make it permanent. Gemma, honey, I love you so much. I want us to be married. Will you have me?"

She stilled, wide-eyed, for a beat, before she launched herself at him. Tangled in her skirt, she nearly fell, but he caught her. Hell, they caught each other.

"Yes, yes, yes, I'll marry you! You big lug, I love you, I love you, I love you." White tree lights twinkled in the tears shining in her eyes.

Boyd handed her a napkin from his shirt pocket. He disentangled himself long enough to extract the tiny box. Opened it and held up the diamond. "This was my great-grandmother's. Mom mailed it to me."

She dabbed at her eyes before slipping on the gold ring. "Ooh, look, it fits." She held it up, still snuggled in his arms. The holiday lights dancing on the facets created tiny spotlights on the ceiling.

His misgivings came back to bite him. "It's an old mine-cut diamond, not fancy like they are today. An old setting too. You might—"

"No, it's perfect. The design engraved in the gold is lovely. Just hush up. I love it and I love you. Stifle yourself." She snuggled closer.

His heart so full it might burst out of his chest, he grinned like a fool. Gazed around at the remnants of the party. A goblet forgotten on the mantel, crumpled napkins under the cocktail table, stumps of candles here and there.

He nuzzled her hair. "You know a lot of people and so do I. We might need a bigger house, one we buy together."

"With a two-car garage, room for my studio and all your workout gear." She cast him an uncertain glance. "And even a family?"

"Perfect. All of that."

Her dimples winked at him. "What would also be perfect is finishing upstairs what we started in the kitchen."

A word about the author…

Occasional bouts of insomnia led to Susan Vaughan's writing career. When she couldn't sleep, she made up stories to fill the long, dark nights. Her stories throw the hero and heroine together under extraordinary circumstances and pit them against a clever villain. Besides curling up with a good mystery or romance, Susan enjoys walking her dog, boating, traveling, and volunteering. A former teacher, she is a West Virginia native, but she and her husband have lived in Maine for many years. Susan is the author of 16 novels and one children's book. Find her at www.susanvaughan.com, where you can sign up for her newsletter or contact her, or at https://www.facebook.com/susanvaughanbooks.

A word about the author...

Having been born and raised on Long Island, New York, my husband and I were both eager to leave the urban lifestyle behind us and explore our futures. With his encouragement, I'm living my dream of writing romance novels full time. Our new rural setting allows us time to enjoy each other and leaves me guiltless hours in my imagination indulging my other passions. www.cornellromance.com

Thank you for purchasing
this publication of The Wild Rose Press, Inc.

For questions or more information
contact us at
info@thewildrosepress.com.

The Wild Rose Press, Inc.
www.thewildrosepress.com